the blue bath

the
blue bath

Mary Waters-Sayer

St. Martin's Press ☙ New York

THE BLUE BATH. Copyright © 2016 by Mary Waters-Sayer. All rights reserved. Printed in the United States of America. For information, address St. Martin's Press, 175 Fifth Avenue, New York, N.Y. 10010.

www.stmartins.com

The Library of Congress Cataloging-in-Publication Data is available is upon request.

ISBN 978-1-250-08821-5 (hardcover)
ISBN 978-1-250-08823-9 (e-book)

Our books may be purchased in bulk for promotional, educational, or business use. Please contact your local bookseller or the Macmillan Corporate and Premium Sales Department at 1-800-221-7945, extension 5442, or by e-mail at MacmillanSpecialMarkets@ macmillan.com.

First Edition: May 2016

10 9 8 7 6 5 4 3 2 1

For Jacob

the blue bath

prologue

Entering the front hall, Kat saw it coming, but could not stop it. The swift and silent arc of the sledgehammer came to its own abrupt end as it smashed through the smooth plaster wall. She squeezed her eyes shut, momentarily stunned by the force and the sound of the impact. In the loud silence that followed, Kat peered through the dust swirling in the sunlight and stepped closer, her shoes crunching on bits of atomized plaster. She saw the adjoining room clearly through the sudden hole and noted with surprise that the wall was hollow. Between the thin layer of cream-colored plaster in each room was only narrow wooden lath, visible just inside the rough edges of the hole, and nothing. This was an old house. The wiring and plumbing had been reconfigured so many times that a bit of—what had the builder called it?—exploratory surgery was necessary to determine what was where inside the walls. Somehow she had expected it would be carried out more delicately. The word "surgery" had not conjured up a sledgehammer.

Shouldering his hammer easily, the builder regarded her, eyes twinkling behind his safety goggles.

"Takes you by surprise, doesn't it, love? Something so solid as a wall."

She nodded, her heart beating quickly. She felt as if she had absorbed the force of the blow. Dust was in her eyes, making them itch. As the builder made his way up the stairs, Kat turned away, back into the large drawing room that spanned half the width and the entire depth of the building, and drifted to the large window facing the creamy white stucco-fronted houses that lined the wide street.

It seemed she was seeing it all for the first time. Was it possible that she had never stood in this exact spot before? They had only just moved into the house when she had left for New York. Here, everything looked different. Standing in the darkness of the large room, far on the right side of the window with her shoulder pressed against the wall, Kat looked out at the pale silhouettes of the houses across the street, mirror images of her own. The trees were bare now, their gnarled fingers frozen in winter rigor. She shifted her gaze to the Greek embassy. Even in the murky early-morning darkness, its utilitarian brick face was a sharp contrast to the pallid confections lining the rest of the street. To its left was the back entrance to Holland Park. A small wooden door set in a whitewashed wall. Such an improbable gateway to what lay beyond it. So different from the main gates on Kensington High Street, twisted iron hung from twin brick pillars that offered visitors a greeting more befitting a royal park.

She remembered when she had first entered the house, earlier that year. She had felt like a child walking through the large double doors, up the sweeping staircase and through the echoing rooms. And like a child, she had fallen in love with it. The bare cream walls, with their intricate moldings clinging fearlessly to the edges of the ceiling, fourteen feet in the air. The perfect weathered wood and smooth marble floors. It had seemed to her to be very romantic, all spirit and possibility, as are all things lying fallow. Coming home at night, Jonathan had taken to phoning her from the front door to find out where she was in the house. Not that either of them had been home much lately. Jonathan had left for Hong Kong the day before she had returned. It was his third trip in as many months to visit a large corporation, a sometime competitor, that had expressed interest in buying the company. It would have been a significant development except for the fact that it was almost an annual occurrence and had yet to come to any fruition.

Since her return earlier this week, she had found a certain solace, a kind of symmetry between the bleak, frozen season and the events of the past few weeks. She knew that it would not last. That spring would come and breathe life back into the city, and back into her. Even now there were sometimes whole hours when she did not think about her mother. Not often, but there had been a few.

Kat strained to hear something that might indicate where the builder was, this stranger in her house. She could hear muffled noises coming from the upper floors, but with more than a hundred years of history, the house had its own noises and she was only beginning to learn its language. Its sounds and its stillness. Its sighs and creaks. And anyway, it still echoed from lack of furniture and carpets.

In truth, Will had quickly commandeered most of the house. He had taken to riding his scooter around the dining room, which held only their table and chairs, suddenly elfin in scale. More toys and scooters were stacked and parked in most corners, and the couch cushions spent more time arranged as a fort than as a couch. With no concerns about scratched paint or damaged upholstery, he had the run of the house.

The sudden sound of the phone reverberated in the stillness, startling her. She answered it more to silence it than for any other reason.

"Hello, beautiful." Jonathan's voice sounded almost as far away as he was.

"What time is it there?" she wondered out loud.

"It's late. Or early. Can't tell. How's our boy? Off to Hampshire already?"

"You know your parents. Crack of dawn."

"How are you holding up? Shall I come home?"

It was a real offer, she knew, but she was already shaking

her head. "That would be lovely. Not sure what good it would do, though. You need to be where you are now."

"You may be right. Kowloon gave us a letter of intent this morning. It looks like they're serious this time."

"Now? With the stock price where it is?"

As she said the words, she realized that she did not know where the stock price was. She had not looked at it for days.

She barely recognized the company as it was today. One bright October morning two years ago, she and Jonathan had sat in the bankers' offices in the City, watching numbers on the screen tracking, rising and then rising again, and she had understood that something was happening that would change them. Gone was the fast, action-driven, nimble band of colleagues. In its place was a large, proper public company. With each uptick, she had seen him move further away from what he was doing and closer to what he had done. She watched as the bankers' deference increased in time with the upticks of the stock price. Thousands of employees in many countries worldwide, regulations, structure, politics, and lawyers, lawyers, lawyers. It is always easier to love something that you can hold in your hands, and the company had become too big and too complex to allow any one person that depth of understanding anymore, although Jonathan came close.

"It's the momentum. They're afraid the deal with the Chinese is going to ramp sales more quickly than even we anticipated. They're realizing that they need to move before we update guidance for the first quarter. And they are right."

She recognized the sharp, quick cadence. This was a

language she knew, a world she understood. "I don't know. An LOI is pretty meaningless. And the Chinese deal is hardly news. Why would they move now?"

"Doesn't matter why. So long as they're willing to pay us what it's worth."

"So what's it worth?"

"A thing is only ever worth what someone is willing to pay for it."

"So then you can make something more valuable simply by paying more for it than what it's worth?"

"Sure. Happens all the time."

She sighed, too tired to engage. "Okay. So what are they offering? Are they still pushing a stock swap?"

He cut her off. "Kat . . . I'm not looking for your thoughts on valuation. We have a whole team of analysts working on that." She heard the subtle emphasis on the word "analysts." "I'm just looking for a little perspective."

The phone line crackled. Silence was hard to maintain over such a great distance. As if without the words, the connection would collapse under the weight of all that was between them.

"What would I do if we sold it?" he asked.

"Something else."

He laughed, the sound rough with lack of sleep. "It is that simple, isn't it? But it's quitting. I would be giving up my seat at the table. For what? Money?"

She leaned against the icy glass and closed her eyes, letting him talk, listening to his voice in the darkness. This was what he wanted. What he needed. Somewhere in the waning blackness, the day stretched out before her. She had been up early to see Will off with Jonathan's parents for a fortnight in the country. She had awakened suddenly well before dawn, and gone into his room, curling around his warm, still-sleeping body. Breathing in his powdery smell and feeling the rise and fall of his back against her chest, she had thought that maybe this was all there was.

Unable to fall back to sleep, Kat had used this time to come up with several very creative and semiplausible reasons why Will could not go to the country. None of them had been quite plausible enough, though. She fought against her desire to keep him home with her. He was so looking forward to his trip to his grandparents' house, an annual visit with his much-revered older cousins. She didn't want to be selfish. And maybe she did need some time to deal with her grief. She didn't want Will to be burdened with her pain. Although the possibility of her bundled up in a blanket, weeping, seemed equal parts unlikely and pointless.

She had a photograph of Will taken moments after he was born. In it she was lying propped up in the hospital bed, holding him in her arms, and Jonathan was leaning in over her shoulder. In the weeks after they brought him home from the hospital, she would sometimes stare at the photo, waiting for emotion to overtake her the way everyone said it would. She knew that one day that photo would mean the world to her.

Opening her eyes, she saw her mother's face in the smooth pane of glass before her.

"What is it like?" she asked.

"Hong Kong?"

"Tomorrow."

He laughed softly and she heard the static on the line, reminding her of the distance between them.

As Kat hung up the phone, she saw the builder move in the doorway. She was unsure how long he had been there. He looked smaller under the high ceilings. Seeing her look up, he pointed a thick finger at four large rectangles of fresh emulsion on the otherwise bare walls of the drawing room. The varying shades of delicate eggshell were difficult to distinguish in the wan early-morning light.

"To give you a better idea of the colors. Should dry quick. Sorry for the smell."

Kat tipped her head back and breathed in deeply.

"Don't be. I love that smell."

chapter one

Sometime after the arrival of the second builder and the ensuing chorus of intermittent hammering, Kat left the house and made her way through Holland Park, glad for the relative peace of its wooded paths. The tops of the trees strained to catch the low, rose-colored sun. It was well into January, with less than eight hours of daylight a day. It seemed impossible to believe that in just a few weeks the daffodils would bloom, nodding their hope-colored heads along the wide paths. It was all there underground, waiting to happen. She pulled her scarf more closely around her neck. In the winter, when it was too cold or wet to run outside, she ran at the gym just on the other side of the park.

Years of distance running had taken its toll on her knees. These days she limited herself to four or five miles several times a week. She kept her time up, running about an eight-minute-mile pace, which meant that it was always over before she wanted it to be. On the days that she ran, she would pass the Greek embassy on her way home. Seated on a folding chair inside his small hut, the security guard would look up from his newspaper and smile at her, out of breath and covered in a combination of sweat and morning moisture, and unfailingly greet her with the same word. "Why?"

Kat found solace in running. In the beginning of her mother's illness, she had made deals with herself. If she ran for an extra mile in the morning, her mother's white-cell count would increase. If she could cut two minutes off her usual time, this week's tests would be negative. The thoughts had come to her unbidden, and she had recognized them as both pointless and childish, but once they had presented themselves, she could not bring herself to dismiss them. It had become a kind of active form of prayer.

She set a challenging pace for herself on the treadmill and was about halfway through her run when she saw his face. He reentered her world just above the drinking fountain and to the left of the Pilates studio. She recognized him immediately. She might have gasped, she could not be certain, but the noise was lost in the din of the gym. His hair was darker and seemed somehow closer to his head, making his face appear larger. He seemed so near—or maybe that was just a result of seeing him on television. He was speaking, but she could not hear him. Stepping unsteadily onto the side of the treadmill, its belt still spinning, she plugged in her headphones and switched the audio channel to the BBC. She missed the question, asked by the reporter, but she caught the pause, always the pause for thought before the answer, which followed, delivered in a steady, unbroken stream.

"I believe in the immediate, visceral reaction to art. Or to anything. I think it's dangerous to subvert that."

His voice was surprisingly clear. Amid the newly unfamiliar surroundings of her daily life, the effect was the opposite of disorienting. She half heard the reporter again, her eyes remaining on his image now frozen in the upper left-hand corner of the screen.

"Before this beautiful, haunting collection of work came to light, the name Daniel Blake was little known outside a small corner of the art world. That looks set to change as an exhibition of his works opens to the public this Saturday at London's Penfield Gallery. Blake is also in the running to do a series of paintings for Sir Richard Hawthorne's new Tate Restaurant, a commission widely regarded as among the most prestigious in contemporary art today. The artist is here in London for this, his first solo show."

And then he was gone. Replaced on the screen by the latest sports scores. Looking around, Kat was surprised to find all that remained. Registering her absence, the treadmill had come to a halt.

The artist was here in London.

꧁꧂

EVEN IN THIS house where she had spent so little time, Kat knew just where to look. On the top shelf in the corner of the second-floor library—lined with three walls of books, and furnished entirely with brown boxes of more books, stacked in various configurations in the room and in the hallway outside. Baudelaire's *Les fleurs du mal*. It was a French-edition paperback. There was a newer English translation here somewhere as well, but this was the one she was after. Still in her running clothes, she sank down against the wall by the window, letting the book fall open on her lap. She was oddly proud to see that it did not open automatically to the page she was seeking. She did not visit it often.

Flipping to the back pages, she found what she was after. As her eyes fell on the endpaper, she savored the feeling in her chest—at once familiar and surprising—grateful as it took her breath once again. The sketch had been done quickly in pencil. Nothing more than a few lines and curves and some gentle shading defined the face—eyes closed and mouth relaxed, but with the unmistakable hint of a smile. Feeling the ache in the pit of her stomach, she closed her eyes. Not to block out the memories, but to conjure them. It was only in darkness that she could properly call up that time.

Unwilling to postpone the inevitable, she had arrived early for her program in French literature at the Sorbonne. Four months early. There were blossoms on the trees and tourists in the streets. Her first impression of the city had been that it must always have been old. It seemed to have been born in that sweet state of decay. She found it so beautiful, so beguiling, that she had no initial desire to enter its museums, restaurants, galleries, shops. She was content to know it from the outside, to gaze on its face in all its pale pink perfection.

Waking up one April morning in her small flat overlooking the rue Saint-Honoré, she gathered a blanket around herself and opened the shutters on the tall double windows to watch the changing light color the wet rooftops. This morning was uncharacteristically dark. After a moment, she dressed quickly, grabbing her new hat and her camera and leaving the flat quietly, careful not to wake her roommate. She loved walking in the very early mornings before the tourists were out. So quiet and still that it was easy to imagine that there were no other people in the city. She had been in Paris for three weeks.

The Tuileries were mostly empty. The sand crunched under her footsteps. The air was thick with moisture and the wind felt cold on her skin. Impossibly, dawn appeared to be losing ground, as the sky darkened. Unhurried by the weather, she walked slowly through the garden before choosing her spot on the grass beside a pathway. Standing very still, she brought the camera to her eye and scanned the softened landscape. She stood there for a long time, watching the light change within the frame of her lens, feeling the cold air brush her skin and hearing the sound of the traffic increase.

She liked the protection of the camera, which immediately defined her as observer rather than participant. People seldom approached her when she was taking photographs. She was invisible. She relished the ability to examine things up close without being detected. Alone, she savored the cool, smooth feel of the machinery in her hands and the deliberate, metallic blink of the camera.

She had been taking a lot of photographs since arriving in Paris. It was an indulgent, solitary activity that suited her. She found it to be almost a philosophical exercise, allowing her to think about how she looked at the world, to play with light and space and time. This city of sand and stone and water was so beautiful that it was very nearly overwhelming. Photography allowed her to isolate the smallest details. The intricate forms of the gilt-bronze statues on the Pont Alexandre III. The changing palette of light that laid itself across the Seine. The different textures of the sand in the Tuileries.

Passing over the more obvious beauty of the gardens on this damp, dark morning, she rested her lens on a small, hunched man who sat on a bench, his head listing toward his right shoulder. He might have been sleeping, he was so still. Only his arm and hand flickered as he reached into a crumpled paper bag by his side and scattered handfuls of its contents on the ground. She watched him through her lens, examining the creases on the paper bag and the creases on his weathered face. He seemed to take no notice of the increasing number of nervous, gray birds bubbling at his feet. When the bag was empty, he stood immediately to leave, stuffing it into his coat pocket before shuffling through the pigeons, eyes downcast.

Such was his familiarity with the garden that he had become blind to it, navigating his way out solely by memory.

Camera still at her eye, she scanned farther into the park, watching the trees change color as the wind blew the leaves upward, exposing their pale undersides. Following the low line of linden trees that led to the river, her lens caught on a tall figure with wide shoulders, standing very still in the middle of a path, hands in his pockets. What little light remained was behind him, having the effect of making him appear in her lens as a dark angular tear in the fabric of the Tuileries. As she brought his face into focus, she was surprised to find that he was looking directly at her. Startled, she quickly removed the camera from her eye. At this distance, without it she could no longer see him clearly, but she could see that he continued to look in her direction. He was about her age, she guessed. The only other thing she had noticed was his black eye.

Her self-consciousness was cut short by the arrival of the rain. As she ran for cover, instinctively tucking her camera under her jacket, she noticed that the raindrops filling the air seemed to be coming not only down, but up. Big drops, like marbles, bouncing off the ground. It was only a short distance to the nearest tree, but she was wet through well before she got there.

Safely under the tree, Kat wiped the water from her face and looked out through the wall of rain at the barely visible figures clustered under the neighboring trees. Rainwater swam and pooled around her feet. The garden was transformed.

What had been near was now far, as the trees became individual islands of refuge in the storm. She brought the camera to her eye to capture the curtain of rain hissing at the edge of the tree, then opened the aperture and set a faster shutter speed to freeze the different shapes of the raindrops. Falling fast, they hit the ground hard, the force of the impact sending them back up, and then, unbelievably, at the apex of their trajectory, they seemed almost to hesitate—caught between gravity and flight, between inevitability and will—before succumbing to their fate. With each click of the shutter she imagined what the image might look like. The drops, elongated as they fell to the ground and then flatter, rounder as they bounced up.

"You're missing it."

The voice made no apologies for interrupting her. Startled, she turned around, dropping the camera from her eye. Standing five feet behind her under her tree, slick and dark from the rain, he stared directly at her, his face matching the rough tone of his voice. In the silence that marked the absence of her reply, he continued.

"The moment. You're missing it. If all we remember is what we feel, then all that you'll remember is what it felt like to take a picture."

She was so surprised to be addressed in English that it took her a moment to notice the British accent. This time he waited until she found her voice.

"I'm not missing it. I'm saving it."

"What for?"

"To save it. Because it's beautiful, I guess."

"What are you going to do with it?"

"What? I don't know. Look at it. See what the camera captured. Sometimes you can't see everything in the moment."

The rain danced in the brief pause before his response. Under any other circumstances it would have been rude to stare at his injury, but the fact that it was at his eye made it necessary. The dark purple bruising surrounding it made his eye look even paler than it was. His face was wet with rain, which made the colors seem liquid, as if she could have wiped them away with the corner of her sleeve.

"If you look at anything long enough, you'll see all sorts of things that you didn't notice at first. That doesn't make them real."

Kat frowned and shook her head. "No, but, just because you don't see something in the moment doesn't mean it isn't real. There's always more to things than what we see."

They were still standing about five feet apart, isolated in silence under the tree. He made no move to approach her. He wasn't as scruffy as he had seemed from a distance. Another student, she guessed. She had a strong urge to put the camera to her eye at that moment and photograph him, but she couldn't seem to break eye contact with him long enough to do so. His hands hung at his sides. It seemed a conscious effort for him to keep them there. His stillness was a contrast to the urgency of the rain. The silence stretched out between them.

After what must have been a long moment, he spoke again. "You're a photographer?"

She glanced down, momentarily surprised by the camera in her hand. "Maybe. I don't know yet."

A flicker of amusement crossed his face.

"Is there a problem with that?"

"If you don't know, then I doubt that you are."

She looked down at the wet ground.

"You're offended."

"I'm not."

"You are."

"What are you doing here?" She wasn't sure if she meant under her tree or in Paris.

"Just looking."

The silence that followed seemed louder than it had before, and she realized that the rain had stopped as suddenly as it had begun. Looking out from under the tree, she found that the garden had become two gardens with the reflection in the water puddled on the ground.

She turned back to him.

"I guess the moment is gone."

He held her gaze and then shrugged.

"If you say so."

He turned away from her and walked out from under the tree, hands tucked back into his pockets. His steps left faint traces in the thin layer of rainwater that hadn't yet drained into the ground. Suddenly feeling the weight of her camera in her hand, she brought it to her eye, found his receding shape through the lens, and snapped one photo before lowering the camera and watching him until he was out of the garden and lost to the city streets.

And then she was alone under the tree. Rain had soaked through her clothes and found its way onto her skin and the air was cold. Her hand holding the camera was shaking. She walked home quickly, treading lightly on the new world beneath her feet.

chapter two

The party had started late, but was definitely still going when Kat had arrived. The face in front of her leaned in close. Too close. The room was very loud, but she wasn't entirely sure that was the reason. It was becoming increasingly obvious to her that the French had different ideas about personal space than Americans had. The double cheek kissing was unnerving enough, but was it possible that three inches between faces was the norm for polite social conversation?

The flat belonged to Jean-Paul, a popular Parisian in the program who had quickly established himself as the epicenter of the social scene. With its tall shuttered windows and smooth herringbone floors, it was almost a caricature of classic Paris chic. The furniture was certainly not what would be expected in a student flat. An elegant, eclectic mix of contemporary and antique. Kat remembered her roommate, Elizabeth, telling her that Jean-Paul's mother was an interior designer.

The face belonged to another student. It was particularly angular in that specific European way. All jutting cheekbones and chin and an aquiline nose that shone with a faint sheen clearly visible at such close proximity. Since hearing her American accent, it had regarded her with an oddly impatient hostility, as if merely waiting for her to demonstrate all that it already knew to be true about her.

A clutch of young women stood on the threshold of the dining room. Their backs to her, they seemed to be waiting for something as well. Peering between them, she could make out Jean-Paul and Christopher Hastings in conversation within the room. Christopher was tall and handsome with manners that could charm snakes. A Fulbright scholar from a prominent East Coast family, he was in Paris studying international relations. His political ambitions were already widely known.

Her companion turned and followed her gaze. Catching sight of Christopher, he pulled back from her for the first time since they had begun talking, and regarded her triumphantly.

"I think I know him," she explained. "He's . . ."

Her companion made a small dismissive noise. "A puppet," he said dryly.

"Excuse me?"

"He is a puppet. He has no thoughts of his own."

"You know him?"

"There is nothing to know. What can it mean? To have your life placed in your hands? To do something simply because you have the capacity to do it. Because it is expected." He sniffed loudly, accusingly. "Do you do everything you have the capacity to do? I think you do not."

As her companion leaned in closer, she felt a hand on her shoulder. Turning, she saw Christopher, smiling at her warmly from a suitable distance. He must have overheard the conversation, but he gave no indication.

"Katherine? I thought that was you. Chris Hastings. We met at the Brewsters' Fourth of July party last summer."

"Chris. Of course, I remember."

She did not have to struggle to recall the occasion. She had a very clear image of that particular evening. It had been one of those incandescent summer nights that seemed to go on forever, when the sun itself seemed to hesitate at the edge of the horizon, waiting to see what would happen next. She could hear the crickets and taste the sea air on her lips as she moved across the lawn, feeling the heels of her shoes sinking into the soft, damp grass. She had been wearing a long backless dress with ropes of pearls down her back that brushed against her skin as she moved. She remembered the way the men had looked at her as she crossed the lawn that night. She could feel their gazes on her skin just as surely as she had felt the pearls.

As he inclined his face imperceptibly toward her, the other face melted back into the crowd. "I had no idea you were in Paris."

As they talked, she became aware of a decidedly different

type of gaze. Several of the women at the party were stealing glances at them. Kat guessed that this time it had little to do with her. Chris was witty and charming and had the singular ability to make her believe this even more when he listened to her than when he spoke. He never once mentioned his uncle who was a senator. He never once mentioned his grandfather who had been secretary of state. And it was only when she looked away that he discreetly scanned the room.

Kat listened to him talk, alternating between his English and the French that surrounded them, amused by the patchwork of conversation that her efforts yielded. She was bored. The ease with which they had slipped into conversation. The solicitous way he asked all the right questions. They discussed all the things they had in common. Life back home, life in Paris, college, acquaintances. Shared history and perspective. It was all so easy and so familiar that here in this most Parisian of Parisian places, within stone walls that had felt the breath of history for centuries, she felt Paris begin to fade. Leaving her sitting at a party, one foot halfway out of her shoe, talking about home with a companion who was half listening.

"I head back to Boston in a few months. I have a position lined up with Poole and Poole in their corporate practice. I start in September." He took a small sip of what she had first assumed to be white wine, but now realized was water; and smiled in a way that was warm and yet clearly signaled the end of the conversation.

"But you are going to run for office?"

"That's the plan." He stood up.

Kat was suddenly curious and followed him up from the couch.

"Why?"

He laughed. He seemed amused and slightly surprised by the question. For the first time that evening, she felt she had his full attention.

"I mean, is it because of your family? Or is it something you want to do?"

Christopher didn't need time to consider this. He answered immediately. "I believe in free will, so I don't think the decision was beyond my control, but it is based on some things that are—the feeling that I can make a difference, the sense of responsibility to do so. I know that there are sacrifices." Here his face clouded momentarily. "But it's about having the courage of your convictions. Once you decide what it is you believe in, everything becomes very clear."

He fell into it without thinking, she thought. The reverent tone. The rhythm of persuasion. She considered this beautiful, fully formed explanation that had sprung so effortlessly and so immediately from him.

"Is that true?"

"Mostly."

He smiled at her. He was shaking her hand now. The final gesture in the separation pantomime. He paused momentarily and leaned forward, looking out at her from under earnest eyebrows. When he spoke his voice was softer than it had been.

"Sometimes I worry that it will never mean as much to me

as it did to the people who came before me, simply because I won't have had to sacrifice what they had to sacrifice for it."

Here he stopped speaking suddenly and shook his head.

"I don't know why I am telling you all this."

"I have that kind of face."

"You absolutely do not have that kind of face."

KAT FINISHED THE wine in her glass. The noise level at the party was reaching dangerous heights. She had already stopped trying to translate the speed-of-light French being spoken at increasingly higher volumes around her. The wine seemed to speed up the rate of speech while simultaneously slowing down her rate of translation. Following Christopher's departure, a dour young man had positioned himself in front of her and was currently lecturing her about French politics. She nodded at regular intervals.

To their immediate left a heated argument was unfolding between a tall, lanky expat and a shorter French student with wild corkscrew curls. She was not sure what the quarrel was about, but it seemed to involve a gaunt blond girl who stood smoking nearby, apparently utterly unaffected by the disagreement. They were almost shouting by now, which might otherwise have alarmed her, but, again, she was still not clear what passed for normal in terms of social interaction in this country. None of the other guests appeared to be concerned.

Looking around the crowded room, she located Elizabeth, her blond hair swirled into a loose chignon, standing by the front door along with Jean-Paul. She didn't know her new roommate well. They had been put in touch by mutual friends. A pretty girl from South Carolina, she possessed just the right amount of plump so as not to be perceived as threatening by other females. This was her first time out of the country and she seemed fiercely determined to get it right. In the brief time Kat had known her, Elizabeth seemed to be in a constant state of self-examination and grooming. Her hands always in motion in what looked like a singular, precisely choreographed dance of touching, smoothing, and rearranging herself.

Before Kat could make her way over to them, she was startled to see a familiar figure come through the door. He entered the flat purposefully and was immediately intercepted by their stylish French host and Elizabeth, who directed him down the hallway leading away from the main rooms. Kat leaned forward, craning her neck to watch them as Elizabeth pushed at the edges of her upswept hair with nervous fingertips. They entered a room off the hall and shut the door abruptly behind them. Luckily, her companion was now on about the Parti Socialiste, while his eyes periodically ran up and down her body, and her active participation did not seem to be essential to the conversation. She kept one eye on the door.

After only several minutes filled by a less than concise condemnation of the provincial nature of American politicians, the door in the hallway reopened and he emerged alone, pulling the door shut carefully behind him before making his way back down the hall. He looked different in the posh flat. Less at ease than he had appeared in the Tuileries, his shoulders rigidly hunched, as if in anticipation of a blow. Reaching the main room, he stopped dead when he saw her and smiled slowly, his cheeks crenellating into something new and un-expected. She smiled back—not entirely sure if it was because she was happy to see him again or if she was simply reacting to seeing him smile for the first time.

It was at that exact moment that the first punch was thrown in the dispute over the hungry blonde. Fortunately, it was slowed by the amount of wine that had been consumed and the intended target was able to duck and avoid being hit. Unfortunately, in doing so he bumped into the Socialist, who in turn fell forward into Kat, who found herself suddenly on the floor.

A hand reached down through the crowd to her and she took it reluctantly, presuming it to belong to the Socialist—as much as anything can belong to a Socialist. She was up off the floor before she saw that it did not. They stood toe-to-toe. He wasn't smiling anymore. Instead he looked at her intently, as if trying to memorize her face. It might have been a long moment, but the party was disintegrating around them as the combatants wrestled on the floor and their host protested loudly, while attempting to gather the more breakable objects from their path.

He was saying something, but it was hard to hear over the noise. He leaned in closer, bringing his face to hers, his eyes fixed on her mouth. She caught her breath, but did not move as he came closer. In the last moment before his lips touched hers, he turned, and brought his mouth to her ear.

"Come with me." She felt his warm breath in her ear.

Kat exhaled against his neck before he withdrew. She saw surprise manifest itself in the form of a raised eyebrow on the face of her Socialist comrade, who was now pressed up against the wall in a defensive posture, as he watched her moving with him across the room to the door.

Outside, the night air was warm and still. They walked in silence through the small, close streets of Saint-Germain, allowing the noise of the party to fall away from them. She could see small, oddly shaped patches of sky, like puzzle pieces, in the gaps between buildings. Eventually they emerged onto the Quai de Conti. They crossed the four lanes easily only to be halted by the Seine. It was only then that he let go of her hand, depositing it safely on the stone wall. She had not realized that he was still holding it. As they leaned on the low wall just next to the bridge, only the silence and two feet of stone separated them. She felt the cool breath of the river on the side of her face.

Looking out over the water, he spoke.

"I once saw a couple arguing on this bridge. Really going at it. I was fairly sure one of them was going to end up in the water. At the time I thought, how can you fight here? But now I understand. It's so beautiful that it reminds you of all that is possible, and all that you may have settled for."

His voice was low and moved through the words as though he was realizing them that very moment. She felt his gaze on her as she looked out into the darkness that pressed down on the river. Silence returned around them and her hand felt cold where he had left it on the smooth stone. They stood for a long time until he spoke again, pulling her gaze away from the black water.

"No camera tonight?"

"No camera tonight."

"Why do you hide behind it?"

"I'm not hiding." She examined his face in the dim light, trying to focus on his eyes and not on the bruising, which had turned a shadowy purple in the reflected glow of the street-lights. "What exactly is your problem with photography?"

"It's lazy. There's no art to it, just a finger on a button. But that's not the worst of it." He seemed to shudder, but moved quickly to cover it, shifting his weight from one foot to the other. "All those things that the camera captures. Things that move too fast or too slow to be seen by the naked eye. That isn't truth."

He fell silent. It seemed to have been too many words for him. Perhaps he had run out.

"Is that all?"

He thought for a moment, his silhouette defined by the soft glow of the first light on the bridge behind him. That was not all.

"Nothing great is created that suddenly."

Perhaps it was the volume of wine. Or maybe the volume of words. Suddenly she felt that this mattered. That she could not let it pass unrefuted.

"What does time have to do with greatness or beauty? So much beauty is fleeting—it's practically a defining characteristic of it. And what makes you think photographs are created suddenly? It is not just the click of a button. I think the best photographers create the picture in their minds before they ever see it. But then it can take a lifetime to find the precise moment, the right light, the exact perspective. Sometimes they never find it, but they know it is real because they can see it."

She hesitated. He remained silent. She watched the cold night air playing with his hair. Lifting and then dropping it around his face.

"And really, what is beauty if it is not recognized? All joy comes from that. What could be more worthwhile? What is there except to recognize beauty?"

She looked up at him, watching her though his wounded eye. Then he smiled. Like fire from flint.

The darkness was draining out of the sky by the time she found herself across the wide boulevard in front of her flat. Just as she was about to start across the street, she turned back to him.

"How did you know I wasn't French?"

He cocked his head at her and she wasn't sure he had heard her. She took a step toward him and gestured in what she thought was the direction of the Tuileries.

"Under the tree. You spoke to me in English. How did you know I wasn't French?"

After a moment he pointed to her head.

"Beret."

Traffic was light at that time of morning and she crossed the wide avenue quickly. As she entered the doorway, she turned back and saw him leaning against the building across the street, watching her. Not in the protective, proprietary way that the boys at home did, waiting to see that she got in safely. In more of a saturnine, almost predatory way, as if the small distance across the street had changed him back into a stranger. Inside, she took the steps two at a time and, reaching the landing in front of her flat, breathless, peered out the window to the street below. He was gone.

SHE SLEPT IN the next morning, awaking just before ten o'clock. Something she hadn't done since arriving in Paris. Emerging from her room, she nearly tripped over Elizabeth, who lay sprawled on her back on the floor of the drawing room, arms resting limply at her sides, head propped up on a pillow. Hearing Kat, she opened her eyes, focused briefly on her, and then closed them again.

"Well, hello, sunshine. And how was your evening?" Kat savored the extra syllables that the girl's accent squeezed out of the words.

"How was yours?" Kat countered, stepping carefully over her supine form on the way to the kitchen.

"Let's just say it was the epitome of a great party." The girl pronounced the word "epitome" incorrectly. As someone who had only read it and never heard it spoken aloud might do.

Elizabeth waited to continue until Kat reentered the room a few minutes later to perch on the chair across from her, teacup balanced on her knee.

"And I couldn't help noticing that you did, in fact, miss much of it . . . ."

Elizabeth turned onto her stomach slowly and propped herself up on her elbows, smiling mischievously at Kat, her round face oddly childlike with its smudged makeup and wine-dark lips. Thick tendrils of her hair had worked themselves loose from the bonds of their arrangement and, exhausted from the effort, hung limply down her back. "Last I saw you, you were engaged in conversation with the next senator from the great state of Massachusetts. Lucky girl. Did he get your phone number?"

"I'm sure Christopher Hastings has better things to do in Paris than spend time catching up with people from home."

Elizabeth looked up at Kat with a mixture of disdain and disbelief. "My God. You have no idea what he is up to, do you?"

"He's a Fulbright scholar."

"Not that." Kat could clearly see that she was trying her patience. "He is interviewing prospective wives."

"What?"

"Oh, come on." Elizabeth rolled her eyes, a rash act that proved unwise and seemed to throw her momentarily off balance. Once recovered, she continued. "Even you must know this. He needs a wife or, at the very least, a fiancée before he runs for office. Time is ticking. He identifies suitable candidates and takes them out and sees who he likes."

"Well, I guess that is what everyone does, to some extent." Kat blew gently on her tea, still too hot to drink. "Anyway, I don't really know him. I only met him the once."

"Well, apparently you made an impression." Elizabeth rolled over, repositioning the pillow under her head, and addressed the ceiling. "He was getting serious with a Danish girl last summer. She was very, very pretty." She uttered the last word reverentially. "But then he came to his senses. I hear she took it very hard."

"You certainly know a lot about Chris Hastings."

"It's common knowledge. Anyway, since then he has limited himself to Americans, which is probably wise. Of course, there are only so many American girls of a certain age and family background in Paris." She twisted her neck sideways and looked pointedly at Kat. "You, my dear, are fresh meat. I bet his family will do a background check on you. You know, your family, who you associate with, all that . . ."

Elizabeth's voice trailed off and her hands moved distractedly to her neck, where they came upon a long strand of pearls left over from the previous night. The girl followed the trail of smooth spheres to the clasp, which she squeezed open deftly between practiced fingers. The beads slipped immediately from her and she caught them easily. Pausing, she seemed to consider the necklace idly for a moment, letting it flow from one hand to the other. When she continued her voice had a deliberately blasé tone.

"I wonder if they'll contact me."

After a moment, she turned back to Kat.

"When did you leave the party?"

"About two. After that fight broke out. Over a girl, I think."

"I heard about that." Elizabeth frowned. "So if you weren't

with Christopher and you weren't here when I got in . . . where were you?"

"There was this guy I had met in the Tuileries—who was at the party—and we just ended up walking around the city."

Elizabeth raised an eyebrow—half curious, half accusing. "What guy?"

"His name is Daniel. I think he knows Jean-Paul." She hesitated, her cup warm on her knee. "Do you know him?"

Kat looked at Elizabeth intently, but the girl's face was blank, except for the diaspora of eye makeup fleeing her lids. "I don't think so. Is he in the program?"

"I don't think so." Kat frowned, realizing that she had never asked him.

"I don't understand. What about Christopher?"

"What about Christopher?"

"You tossed him over for some guy who you met in the park?"

"I don't think he was ever mine to toss. And anyway, we're in Paris. Why come here and date boys from home?"

Elizabeth struggled to rearrange her robe, which had become twisted around her legs. Another lock of hair freed itself, landing soundlessly on her shoulder.

"Why? Because that is the world we live in. That is the world we are going back to."

chapter three

When Kat finally left the flat that morning, the sun was up and the tourists filled the streets. She very nearly walked past him, leaning up against the wall in the exact spot where she had left him earlier that morning. How long had he been there, she wondered. Would he have let her walk by if she hadn't noticed him?

They spent every day together that week. Daniel would meet her outside her flat in the mornings and they would walk. Along the banks of the Seine, pulled along by the gray-green water. Among the stalls at Les Puces, crowded with furniture and objects of forgotten beauty—mirrors, porcelain, silver, ancient maps of erstwhile places. Through the dark, silent catacombs below the streets, among walls of bone and incoherent graffiti—lamentations of the living or prayers for the dead. Although it seemed they talked about everything, never once did he ask her what she was doing in Paris or how long she would be there or where she was from or even her last name. He made no overtures toward her. To the contrary, he seemed to actively avoid any physical contact with her.

Facing into the sunset on the Pont Neuf at the end of that week, she saw that the Seine was on fire. Orange flames jumped from the waves to ignite the windows of the buildings facing the embankment. The melting blue sky dripped into the river, punctuated by the dots of the boats and the dashes of the bridges. She felt the warmth of the light on her skin and tasted the city in her mouth.

The light was changing so quickly. Feeling the urgency of the setting sun coloring the passing seconds, each different, Kat reflexively brought her camera to her eye. Standing behind her, Daniel moved his hands up on either side of her, pushing the camera down gently, away from her face. She felt his arms surrounding her, his hands on her hands, his breath in her ear. The sudden physical contact shocked her.

"If you really see it, then it becomes part of you." His whisper made her shiver and he pulled her closer to him. "You can never lose it."

She had half turned in to him by then. In the moment before she closed her eyes, she saw that the color around his right eye was now a sallow yellow, the last traces of it nearly gone from his skin. She thought that she would miss it—the daily newness of it.

She had never understood how people could kiss that way in public. She saw it all over Paris. Couples in the middle of the pavement, in crowds, pushed up against buildings, coiled around each other. The kind of kiss that could mean only one thing, that led to only one place. The kind of kiss that embarrassed you just to look at. Indecent, insistent, undeniable.

She didn't think. About the people around them, about whether an appropriate amount of time had passed, or about the importance of making him understand that this was not something that she did regularly. She didn't think about the larger questions or consequences. She had no idea how long the kiss lasted, but was slightly surprised to find that it was still light out when they broke apart—briefly, necessarily—to cross the wide boulevard in front of her building. The sun had sunk lower and the light seemed somehow to be emanating from under the pavements.

Inside they began the climb up the narrow staircase as his hands moved up her body. They were about five feet from her door. His shirt was open and the buttons on her dress were undone when one of them tripped and they both fell, landing hard and breathless on the tile floor. Her keys flew out of her hand and skittered across the floor. She listened to them bouncing off the railings on their way down the stairwell. And so then, on that particular evening, on the small landing outside her door, with the dust swirling in the waning light that shone through the small round window, the only sound was their breath.

In the weeks that followed they showed each other what they loved. Kat waited for a particularly bright morning and led Daniel over the little bridge that leapt the Seine in a single bound. The chestnut trees along the banks of the Île de la Cité were newly dressed and the wind sent their full skirts waving. They climbed the spiral stone staircase to the vaulted upper chapel of Sainte-Chapelle and stood under the soaring windows, the web of intricate, slender tracery all but obliterated by the sheer volume of radiance, any narrative shattered into pieces of pure color. Daniel stood silently, watching shafts of light illuminate faithful and unfaithful alike in otherworldly hues of rich red and blue. Kat watched his face.

Daniel took her to the Musée Rodin, sacred temple of flesh and stone. They stood together at the edge of a lofty room of bronze figures enlivened by various shades of patination. Sunlight from the unshuttered windows fell in long yellow stripes across the floor. She made a move toward the next room, but he took her hand to stop her.

"Watch."

They waited, their backs to the window, as still and silent as the permanent residents, as the crowd filtered by. After a few moments, a wary-looking teenage girl entered the room and approached a felled bronze figure. Daniel shifted his weight from one foot to the other, nudging Kat softly with his shoulder. Kat watched the girl's hand find the edge of the plinth and slide along the rough stone base, a somnambulist fog rising in her eyes as her fingers found the dark ankle before her and moved along the leg to the knee, tracing the smooth torsion of the burnished limb.

"It never takes long," Daniel whispered. "They can't help themselves. It's instinct. Or compulsion. Something."

As he spoke, Kat watched the girl's other hand rise from her side and move over the dark metal figure. Alarmed, Kat glanced around the room, but no one seemed to be taking any notice. The girl continued to run her hands over the sculpture for several seconds, before bestowing a final pat on it and moving on. As they followed her out of the room, weaving among the dark figures, Kat understood completely. Who could resist the potent vitreous sensuality of their arched backs and outstretched limbs?

They wandered among the life-size casts in the walled garden behind the *musée*, the square and solemn thinker on his high perch; heavily draped Balzac, disappearing under his vestments; the six barefoot burghers. Daniel pointed out the slight seam lines where segments had been joined together and how some of the figures had identical heads, hands, and feet, modified only slightly by position or expression.

Of course it was only fitting that there be an Eve in this Eden. Head lowered, face hidden in shame after the fall from grace, she appeared rough and unfinished. Daniel explained that the story was that Rodin had been unable to complete the work, as his model had become pregnant and run off to Italy with one of his apprentices.

They tried other museums—the Louvre and the Musée

d'Orsay, even Pompidou—arriving at odd hours in an attempt to avoid the summer tourists, but Daniel never took to them. They seemed to overwhelm him in a way that Rodin and his gardens did not. And so they spent much of their time in the garden behind the *musée*, a fine film of chalk accumulating on their shoes from the gravel paths. It was there that Daniel made his first drawing of her on the end pages of Baudelaire. She had fallen asleep under the warm sun, the book prone on the grass between them, and had found the drawing later that week.

BY THE TIME she started school, in August, they were living together in his studio, under a sloping roof on the top floor of an ancient building on the rue Garancière. The studio, reached by a narrow spiral staircase, was smaller than her kitchen was now. It was not what it had been before for her. For perhaps the first time, she had met someone completely disconnected with her world. They had no mutual friends, hadn't gone to the same schools or summered in the same places. He came without shared experiences and without references. And because of this there were no second opinions, no background knowledge, and no expectations. So much of her life was shared. But it was different with him. He was hers alone.

She had brought very little with her to Paris in anticipation of a peripatetic existence, and she took even less to the studio. She packed as if she were going on a short trip, leaving most of her things behind in the rue Saint-Honoré flat. She would maintain her address there. There was no need to worry her mother. Her stripped-down existence included her books, some clothing, the minimal toiletries that would fit in the small cabinet above the sink alongside his toothbrush and razor. As time passed, she found it increasingly difficult to remember exactly what she had left behind.

She had spent her first afternoon alone in the studio going through the kitchen cupboard, searching through the contents of the small wardrobe, and even looking carefully among his paints and canvases. Tentatively at first, stopping to listen for footfalls on the stairs or a key in the door. And then boldly. For what, she was not certain. Evidence of who he was or who he had been? Remnants of prior lovers, maybe? But the studio revealed few clues. Most of the stories it told were enigmatic. Mounds of wax on the windowsills and faint scorch marks on the walls. Crimson crescent moons on the floorboards by the bed, and the beautiful, strange cerulean bath. Evidence of others, now known only by the marks that they had left behind.

Daniel's legacy was already apparent. Dripped and spilled paint was everywhere. The sill of the window was feathered with cast-off brushstrokes—myriad greens and reds and pinks that had fallen outside the canvas. Evidence that an artist had once lived there. But try as she might, she could foresee no legacy of her time there. She would leave no trace.

The bed took up most of the room. Besides it and the small wardrobe, the only other sizable objects were an easel, his canvases, and the paintings themselves, which lived with them in the studio long after they were completed. She grew accustomed to the smell of the paint and the linseed oil. She learned to slip past the canvases as they leaned against the walls and he learned to avoid the stacks of her books on the floor. So many books. Occasionally she wondered how she would ever get them home.

She learned that oil paint dries not by evaporation, but by oxidation. That despite the fact that the paintings might feel dry to the touch just days after they were completed, they could take up to a year to dry fully. She learned that under certain circumstances drying oil paints could generate enough heat to spontaneously combust and so it was important that the studio be properly ventilated. Daniel was careless about this and seemed not to notice when the small room became suffused with the odor of paint. Coming home from classes, she would open the windows, allowing the cool, soft air of evening to permeate the room.

There was much that he seemed not to notice that summer. He had lived rough before and was accustomed to it. For her, it was new. It would have been understandable to think that she took no notice of it either. That she didn't see the dirty paint peeling in large, rounded flakes from the walls and ceiling, or didn't feel the drafts coming through the cracks in the windowpanes. That she was unaware of the erratic nature of the hot water or blind to the dark, persistent stains in the corners of the bathroom. But she did notice. She noticed everything that warm, dusty summer. She read Proust and Baudelaire and Rimbaud in their original tongue and fell asleep tangled up with Daniel in the narrow bed, listening to the sounds of mice scratching in the roof above them. Most mornings she woke to feel his eyes on her.

Daniel's studio was closer to the Sorbonne than the rue Saint-Honoré flat had been. Kat walked to her classes through the Luxembourg Garden, often waiting in the early mornings for the gates to be unlocked. Several times at the start of the term Jean-Paul stopped to offer her a ride on his Vespa, removing his own helmet to proffer it to her, but she declined, preferring the walk.

On her way home in the afternoons, Kat shopped at the street markets, often making her selections solely by color, drawn by heaps of dusty blue plums, punnets of glossy red cherries, and tangerines so bright they seemed to blur at their edges. Each week, she would buy a small loaf of walnut bread from Poilâne, waiting in the queue on the rue du Cherche-Midi with Parisians and tourists alike, feeling the heat from the ancient wood-burning ovens below the street.

Sometimes the food she brought home was all he ate. Other times she would return from class to find it undisturbed—the fruit exactly where she had left it, the bread still wrapped in cellophane. On these evenings, Daniel would surface from his work, famished, and allow himself to be coaxed out for a proper meal. There were only two ways into or out of the rue Garancière, both of which entailed some degree of contortion: around the jutting protrusion of the corbeled chapel of Saint-Sulpice or under the high arch at the rue de Vaugirard. Passing underneath the arch, Daniel never failed to duck as its shadow reached down to brush against him, which never failed to make Kat laugh. They avoided the cafés and restaurants frequented by students. Daniel seemed to know exactly which ones they were.

When she wasn't in class or after the light was gone they would walk, often through Montparnasse or the endless meandering narrow alleys of the Marais. Regardless of where they went, they never came back the same way that they had gone, so that occasionally she was surprised when she spotted the familiar mismatched towers of Saint-Sulpice or came upon the curved iron fence surrounding the Luxembourg Garden.

Returning from Passy Cemetery one afternoon, they found themselves between distinctive rows of pruned and pleached trees of the Champs-Élysées. Kat hadn't been there since her very early days in Paris. She slowed down, taking in the fanciful shopwindows where shoes and handbags were animated and elevated to art in opulent displays. The wide windows also provided brief glimpses of their reflections sliding across the glass. She stopped to admire a quartet of intricately beaded minaudieres hung like sighs above an ocean of scarlet silk tulle. After a moment Daniel's reflection appeared among the waves, arms crossed impatiently where he stood just behind her.

Maybe it was the slight downward slope of the pavement, but Daniel quickened his pace as they moved toward the place de la Concorde. He seemed eager to leave the shops behind, steering them off the broad boulevard, past the Grand Palais and then over the Pont des Invalides just as it swallowed an open-topped tourist boat headed downstream. Daniel eyed the shadows cast by the bridge across the water below.

"Let's go to Rodin. There's time."

The wind had picked up and the rows of chestnut trees in the esplanade in front of the Invalides swayed in languid, exaggerated waves, releasing showers of late petals that clung to her hair and his shoulders.

It was Wednesday, so the *musée* was open late, but they arrived just before closing time, entering under the stern eye of the guard. She thought that he should know them by now. As they settled themselves on a wooden bench, Daniel reached down to retrieve a brown stone from the gravel, placing it in his palm and peering at it curiously before holding it out to her.

"A snail. A live snail," she clarified, the latter being the more surprising reality.

She could see its horns waving just inside the shell. Daniel placed it in the grass beside a bed of tulips. Kat watched the variegated blooms sway forward in the wind in extended arabesques, as if to get a better view of the tiny creature.

"You think he'll be safe there?"

"You want to take him home with us?"

"I feel like we should put him on a plane. Get him out of Paris."

Daniel laughed and she lay back, settling her head in his lap and watching the long shadows spilling across the lawn. Over his shoulder, unseeing Eve stood mute with her barely rounded belly. Daniel's hands moved in her hair.

"They don't rust?"

"Hm?" He glanced down at her briefly, his hair falling into his face.

"The bronzes. They don't ever rust?"

"I don't know."

She squinted up at him. "Really?"

"It's not my medium."

"You seem to know a lot about them."

He shrugged. "I mostly know what I can see."

"And what is it that you can see?"

She could tell he was smiling before he turned his face back down to her.

"You."

Beyond him the gilded dome of Les Invalides and the distant spire of the Eiffel Tower were visible over the top of the wall. She shivered, thinking perhaps winter was crouched just beyond the wall as well. He moved his hands to her bare shoulders and shifted underneath her.

"It's not always going to be like this, you know."

"Like what?"

"I know this isn't the kind of life you're used to."

Before she could respond, he continued. "The paintings I'm making of you are the best work I've ever done. I used to believe it was all craft—all hand and eye. Subject was almost irrelevant. But with you I can see things that I never could." He leaned in closer, blocking out the surrounding garden. "I can see a future for us. I don't know what's going to happen, but I know I don't want to look away."

"I don't want you to look away."

And in that moment she saw that they were like the others. Two frozen figures inside the fluttering whole. Here in this sacred place of ordinary moments around which the world turned, they had become the art. And in that moment she knew that it was true.

The quick, purposeful footsteps of the approaching guard emerged from the silence and she sat up. Closing time. Daniel took her hand, still focused on her.

"If you ever doubt my feelings for you, that's where you should look. The paintings."

"I don't doubt."

"But if you ever do."

They walked back the same way they had come, leaving the guard behind them to make his final sweep of the grounds, checking among the statuary and between the conical hedges before locking the doors and gates for the evening. The pavement was freshly spattered with the spent finery of chestnut trees, creamy petals heaped along curbs and in corners like rice after a wedding. The wind had calmed, but she felt its steady hand pressed against her back, hurrying her along.

ELIZABETH HAD ARRANGED to meet her for an early drink in the bar at the Ritz Hotel. Emerging from the arcaded passage of the rue de Castiglione, Kat found the place Vendôme transformed into an enormous sundial, bisected by the shadow of the bronze column at its center. Age and oxidization had covered the unlikely gnomon in a soft green patina. It struck her that somehow the shadow falling across the cobblestones and up the face of the building seemed more solid than the thing itself.

Spying Elizabeth nestled in a cozy chair against the interior wall of the sparsely populated bar, she made her way past the grand piano and across the expanse of patterned carpet. The weather was warm and the doors to the terrace were open. Elizabeth greeted her with the customary double cheek kiss and pushed a menu across the table at her. As Kat opened it, Elizabeth regarded her coolly, fingers tracing the edge of her collar, feeling for loose threads.

"So, as the spurned roommate I feel I am entitled to ask. What exactly is going on with this one?"

Keeping her eyes on the menu, Kat couldn't help but smile. "Which one is that?"

She could feel Elizabeth's frown.

"How much do you know about him?"

Kat ignored her, continuing to peruse the menu instead. She noticed how quiet it was. People here spoke in the muted voices of those accustomed to being listened to.

"Every artist has a day job. Do you even know what his is?"

Kat thought fleetingly about Elizabeth and Jean-Paul closing the door behind themselves and Daniel in Jean-Paul's flat. She looked up at her roommate, meeting her eyes.

"Do you?"

Elizabeth leaned forward and glanced around the bar in a

way that almost made Kat giggle. "He may not be who you think he is."

Kat leaned in, mock conspiratorially. "Who is he?"

Elizabeth's voice dropped to just above a whisper. "Let's just say, he may run with our crowd, but he is not one of us." The girl raised an eyebrow emphatically and sat back in her chair, casting a brief critical glance at her fingernails. Finding them wanting, she frowned and began to pick delicately at them.

"Maybe I like that."

Elizabeth looked up at her and sighed heavily, overcome by either the state of Kat's situation or by the condition of her nails. "Don't get me wrong, Kat—I can see the attraction." She smirked wickedly before regaining her composure and continuing. "But this is not someone who you have a relationship with. A fling—sure. But don't kid yourself that this is going somewhere. He is collecting you. You are a pretty thing he can put on canvas. There were more before you and there will be many more after you. All I'm saying is don't get hurt. And don't throw away your scholarship."

"I'm not throwing anything away."

"You haven't told your mother about him."

Kat looked up at her sharply.

"She calls. I am just suggesting that you might ask yourself why."

In truth, it was a question she had been asking herself recently. Kat wrote her mother every week. Carefully crafted missives composed during classes as her professors discussed the intricate, nuanced worlds of Baudelaire and Sartre. The letters were filled with detail about her studies and about Paris. Artful renderings of a truth very nearly lived. Carefully skirting around the edges of him, so close as to nearly graze his skin. Almost. But not quite.

So carefully had she excised him from her daily life that she wondered whether her mother could see his outline framed on the page. Bordered by the beauty of the city and the small moments that she glimpsed on her way to and from him.

But her mother's letters to her betrayed no hints of suspicion. No probing questions or veiled innuendo. They were not in contact as often as they always had been before. She could sense her mother giving her space. Holding back and allowing her to enjoy and explore on her own.

It had been the two of them for as long as Kat could remember. As the only child of an only parent, Kat had been spoiled by her attention and her interest. Her father had died before she was born. He was older than her mother. Their wedding had followed a whirlwind courtship of just three months. His family had disapproved of the match and had demonstrated their disapproval by cutting him off financially. They had been married for just over a year when he had been killed in a car accident. Two weeks afterward her mother had found that she was pregnant.

Kat looked up to find Elizabeth regarding her, suddenly still. "Do you know how they say love at first sight in French?"

"*Coup de foudre.* Bolt of lightning."

Elizabeth shook her head sadly, her blond hair, newly

cropped into a tidy bob, swinging forward to touch each cheek in turn. "Some things are just not built to last. That which burns brightest . . ."

That afternoon Kat took the long way back to the studio. Maybe Elizabeth was right about Daniel. They were both strangers in Paris. She knew little about him. She knew that he had left art school in London, and eventually made his way to Paris. He had been studying drawing and painting at the École Nationale, but had left that program as well. Artistic differences being the only explanation he provided. He had told her that his mother had died when he was a child. But other than that, he didn't speak much about his family or his past.

When she turned onto Saint-Germain-des-Prés, the wide, light-filled boulevard ahead of her seemed to go on forever, extending past the horizon. The illusion was beautiful. She stopped at Les Deux Magots, where she sat surrounded by the strained and stilted sounds of the tourists' elementary French. Watching the shadows of tiny birds' feet on the awnings above her head, she thought that she knew the city from the inside. That while she might not know its face, she felt its beating heart every night in her ear.

chapter four

Let me understand this. In all the hours that we've spent discussing my storied love life, you never thought to mention your dalliance with the famous artist?"

Jorie's disgust showed clearly on her face.

"In my defense, he wasn't famous when I knew him. And, until yesterday, I wasn't even aware that he was famous now."

On the word "famous" the waitress glanced down at her momentarily as she deposited their porcelain cups on the small, round marble-topped table. They were sitting by the back window in the small French café on Thackeray Street in Kensington. The air inside smelled like strong coffee and warm butter.

"*Merci,*" Jorie said, dismissing the waitress with a little wave.

Jorie spoke French to anyone who was not immediately identifiable as English. As it turned out, this was a great many people, including anyone who had not yet spoken to her.

Kat had acquired Jorie at a party during her first year in London. At the time, Jorie had been married to one of Jonathan's clients. Jorie had approached her early in the evening, confiding that she had forgotten how dishy her husband was. She had then asked Kat what besides his good looks she found appealing about Jonathan, wondering aloud what was behind his "robot-like exterior." After a few glasses of champagne, they had ended up talking in the kitchen until long after most of the guests, and indeed the caterers, had gone. Jorie perched on the edge of a countertop, whippet thin, her delicate legs like two matchsticks tipped in Louboutin red. When they parted, Jorie had told her that although she liked her, she simply didn't have women friends, as she found little use for them and disliked the competition.

On the cab ride home, Jonathan had inquired about their conversation, expressing surprise that they had found so much to talk about and suggesting, half teasingly, that Jorie was a bad influence. She had asked him what he knew about her, what she was like.

He had frowned, considering for a moment before answering. "Sharp."

"She didn't strike me as the particularly brainy type."

"Not clever sharp. Actual sharp. Pointy. Spiky."

They had continued to run into each other at social events over the next few months and always enjoyed each other's company. And so, despite intentions, they had become friends.

Jorie leaned forward, hands cradling her cup. "I'm picturing it now . . . . Young, provincial American girl. Brooding French artist type. Tell me more."

"Not to mess with what you've got going on there, but actually he's British."

"I can work with that. Did you love him?"

"Yes," she answered immediately. And then, "As much as you can at that age."

"But that's the only age when you can truly love someone. After that is when it gets complicated."

"I don't believe that. I wasn't even sure of who I was then. I wasn't fully formed."

"Ah, first love . . . ." Jorie looked wistful for a moment, an emotion that seemed incongruous on her sharp features. "Doomed by definition to fail. And you haven't seen him since?"

"No. I haven't thought about him in years."

It was a lie, of course. Not that she thought about him often, and it was never really a fully formed thought. But sometimes, maybe twice a year, she was blindsided by a memory. Mostly, it was the silences that reminded her of him. The absences.

There weren't even the usual artifacts of a love affair to trigger her recollection. She had no photos of him. No letters. No gifts or souvenirs. Just his drawing in the back of the book.

Unsigned. Undated. Scant and accidental evidence of a significant passion.

Because of the lack of any real relics—with the exception of
the drawing—she relied solely on memory to take her back to
that time. She indulged in it very sparingly, though, aware
of the delicate nature of memories and of how every time we
take them off the shelf to examine them, we change them.
We take something away with us or we add a little of whatever is on our hands or in our heart at that moment.

Jorie leaned forward again.

"And the sex?"

Kat looked down at the worn floorboards, blushing at the
sudden memories. "We were nineteen."

"I remember nineteen." Jorie hesitated for a moment. "Just
last Friday I was on the Eurostar and this buttoned-up banker
type was seated across from me. The kind you want to unbut-
ton." She licked her lips. "And he looked right through me. No
reaction whatsoever."

She paused to consider this, frowning without the aid of
the muscles in her forehead. "I think that might have been it
for me."

"Might have been what for you?"

"You know." She looked pointedly at Kat, licking the froth
off her spoon before setting it down beside her cup. "Every
woman has that moment. When you suddenly realize that
men no longer look at you with longing or desire."

Kat chose a polite smile, rather than responding to the
deliberate slight.

Jorie's face grew thoughtful. "And then, of course, once you realize what has happened, you desperately try to recall that last time. The tragedy of it is that you never know when it's happening that this will be the last kiss, the last touch, the last whispered indiscretion. You don't have the chance to savor it."

They sat in silence for a moment. The walls glowed pale yellow with reflected light. It was late morning and the café was nearly empty. Just a few Parisian expats in search of the smells and sounds of home. The two women behind the counter maintained a constant, lively conversation in French as they arranged new pastries in the display case. Kat half listened, catching bits of it. Her French was not what it had once been.

Kat considered the possibility that perhaps she had had her moment as well. It had been in her forties that her mother had lost her looks. At least her more obvious looks. She was always beautiful, with her singular, regal grace, not to mention the flame-colored hair that Kat had inherited. But the kind of raw, undeniable beauty that catches the eye of strangers the way a nail catches a thread—that had waned. Kat was coming up on forty herself. She could see it most around her eyes—the beginnings of a vaguely tired look. She wasn't being dramatic. She knew she was still pretty. But for the first time, she truly understood that she wouldn't be pretty forever.

She saw it in her friends as well. And, inevitably, the drastic measures had begun. The peels and the lasers and the injections, the nips and the tucks. Better living through science. But what science could not erase was the knowledge that the process had begun. And once begun, although its progress might be slowed, it could not be arrested.

Jorie sighed. "And so then I suppose the question becomes, what do you do now that no one is looking?"

Leaving Jorie lingering over a second café au lait, Kat stepped outside and dialed Jonathan's parents, hoping to catch Will. She did. Breathless, he told her of the plans to build a dam across the small stream at the bottom of the garden. She listened to his voice, thin and slightly distant due to his tendency to hold the phone far away from his face. The last time she had heard him over the phone was when she had told him of her mother's death. He had cried. Small wet sobs she heard on the other side of the Atlantic.

In the days since her return from New York she had been witness to him disseminating the news of his grandmother's death several times. He had earnestly informed their housekeeper, who already knew; the elderly gentleman who walked his springer spaniels along the path just inside the park, who likely did not know; and most recently, the pretty woman they bought meringues from yesterday at Ottolenghi. After pronouncing the words with deliberate solemnity, eyes grave, he had accepted their condolences.

But even in his careful tellings of it, she saw her mother diminishing for him. He was so young. She wondered what of her he would retain. Kat thought of all her mother's trips to London. All their time spent together. Countless hours feeding the ducks at the Round Pond, riding the double-decker buses, stalking the fat koi in the Kyoto Garden, catching tadpoles in the pond behind Lord Holland's statue. What would he even remember of his first real loss?

Kat headed to High Street Kensington Station to catch the Circle line into the City. She came out of Bank tube station and made her way through the imposing shadow cast by the Bank of England and down Throgmorton Street. The morning commuter rush had ended some time ago and all who remained were decidedly late, although they seemed sharply divided between the concerned majority, who flowed along at a quick pace, and the unconcerned minority, who moved more slowly— small solids within the larger sea.

A rabbit warren of small winding streets, the area northeast of the Bank of England was populated with small brokerage houses, boutique investment banks, barristers' chambers, and smaller law firms. It seemed to her to be an unusual place for an architect's office.

She had worked a few streets away years ago in one of the older buildings, in a small office that seemed to smell perpetually of tea. In those days, she awoke in darkness, commuted in darkness, worked under the glare of overhead fluorescents, and then returned home in darkness. Any sunshine that might have occurred during the day was obscured behind the silhouettes of the taller buildings in the narrow streets.

It was there that she and Jonathan had first met, while working for the European office of an American investment bank. She remembered a particularly lengthy meeting about six months after she had joined the firm. The negotiation had been tense from the beginning. The bankers were clashing on the terms of the deal and the tempers of the management team of the target company were rising and falling in reverse proportion to the purchase price. Despite that, Jonathan maintained a firm hand on the meeting.

As negotiations escalated, he had jotted something down on a sheet of paper and folded it in half. Still addressing the room, he stood and walked around the table to where she was sitting and placed it in front of her. He frequently did this in meetings to consult with others on the finer points—the regulatory or tax ramifications—of something he was considering. She pulled the note into her lap discreetly and opened it. She read it once and then again. She could hear his voice as he continued to negotiate, calmly walking the target company back point by point. Without looking up, she wrote the word "yes" on the paper and refolded it. She stood and walked around the table to return it to his outstretched hand.

The note had been brief. "Have dinner with me tonight."

Looking back, she saw how the long hours, the sleep deprivation and travel had created a kind of anticipatory intimacy between them. That overnight flights spent lying side by side, cocooned in semidarkness, separated by three inches of armrest, meant that she was already familiar with his face slack in sleep and the broken rhythm of his dreaming breath. So that she recognized the man who had said to her that night, "I think I could be happy with you for a long time."

Leaving the wider street, she turned in to the quiet of Angel Court. While the layout of the streets here remained mostly true to their medieval origins, the Blitz had transformed the buildings into a patchwork of old and new. While one side of the curved street belonged undeniably to modern times, on the opposite side, with its low Georgian buildings, fronted by a row of neat black bollards emblazoned with the crest of the City of London, it could easily have been the early 1900s.

Jonathan's idea for the company, a forum that allowed financial institutions to trade securities off the exchanges, was beautiful in its simplicity. She thought sometimes that ideas like that could occur only when people were somehow disconnected. That there must be some sort of alchemy, some sort of altered perspective, that came from intervals of forced stillness on airplanes, moving above the clouds at speeds approaching that of sound. These intervals also fed a fever to do more. To move. To make. Jonathan always walked very quickly after disembarking from airplanes.

It had been a big risk when he had left the bank to start the company. The principals had not been pleased and had declined to make the hoped-for investment in his new venture. Bridges were burned.

There had been many points, especially during the first year, when they had come close to losing it all. She remembered the early board meeting when the directors had advised them to shut the company down. She had listened in silence as the people whom they trusted the most, whom they respected the most, made the case, methodically, rationally, that they should cut their losses. And then she had listened as Jonathan refused, methodically, irrationally.

Although it had been difficult and risky, she had enough perspective to know that it had also been quick. A few years of undeniable struggle, of hard work and no sleep, of blood, sweat, and takeaway food, had resulted in a viable, international company that was now listed on the LSE. So much had changed in such a short time. What hadn't changed was the time commitment. Jonathan still worked constantly.

She had left the company about a year before Will was born. The fertility specialist had suggested it as one of a litany of other measures. It wasn't time to worry yet, he had assured them. They had been trying for less than a year and there was still a good chance that they would be able to conceive naturally. "Conceive" was not the word he had used. "Fall pregnant" was what he had said. As if it were a condition, a malady.

And fall pregnant she had, although it had taken another eight months. And while she had tried to maintain a presence within the company for a time after Will was born, she found that her identity had been compromised. The company had moved to a larger building and the security guard at the front desk insisted on providing her with a visitor badge. The small adhesive rectangle proved prophetic as former coworkers smiled polite, impatient smiles at her and inquired about the baby. She was no longer a colleague, an insider. She was Jonathan's wife. She was a mother. She was a reflection of someone else.

Entering the newer building through its polished red marble facade, she took the small lift up to the twenty-first floor. After a brief journey in silence, the doors split apart like theater curtains, revealing the city, spread out in all directions. Her immediate impression was that there were no walls around her, such was the completeness of the view. It was only after a moment that she noticed the reception desk and the presence of the offices contained inside the view and judged it wise to step off the lift.

She was led through a maze of low partitions and glass walls that dissolved into an immaculate corner office. Protruding into the sky like the prow of a ship, it offered unobstructed views of the city below, punctuated on one side by the pale, cross-topped catenary dome of Saint Paul's. In the distance she could see moments of the Thames as it slunk through the City. It was low tide and the tiny shapes of birds were just visible as they moved over its wide banks. Turning from the windows, she laid her handbag gingerly on the large glass conference table, watching to see if it would cause a ripple in the smooth surface. It floated there, a singular spot of color in the room. After a moment, she removed it and placed it in the lap of a chair.

She stood surveying the large monochromatic canvas that anchored the room. Hearing the door to the room click closed, she turned to find a man standing close behind her, small and tidy in his black polo neck and rimless glasses, arms folded and eyes fixed not on her, but on the artwork in front of her.

"Do you like it?" he asked.

"I do. What is it?"

"What do you think it is?"

"It's a Rorschach, isn't it?"

He nodded. "One of the ten original inkblots. Number seven, in fact. It reminds me that things are as we perceive them to be. That all meaning is subjective."

He turned to her. "So what do you see?"

She turned back to the large symmetrical shape. Almost immediately, a figure emerged within the gray.

"It's a woman."

"Just one?"

"Yes. She is looking at her reflection in a mirror."

Kat looked at the figures. They seemed at first to be identical. Two articulated halves of the same whole, fused at the base. She took in the slight white spot behind the heart where the ink had not adhered to the paper, noting that this small emptiness was echoed in the other figure. As she studied the image more closely, she began to notice small differences between the figures. Imperfections in the jagged edges and the subtle shadows where the ink had bled beyond the margins of each figure. There was something about the opaque clouds gathered just below the surface that seemed at once ominous and vaguely familiar.

She turned away from it. "I thought they were meant to be kept secret, so as not to compromise the general population."

He looked at her sideways and smiled, his eyes bright. "Consider yourself compromised. Mrs. Bowen, I presume . . ."

"Lind," Kat responded automatically. "But please call me Kat."

"Kat. I am Charles." He shook her hand firmly. "Shall we discuss your home?"

As she settled opposite him at the conference table, she tried to focus on him, and not on the view through the glass behind him. Sir Charles Eliasson was one of the most sought-after architects in London. She and Jonathan both loved his work—minimal and eclectic. A native of Sweden, he fused traditional with modern using practicality and beauty as glue. She had missed the first meeting with him. It had been in the diary for months. Before anything had happened. Jonathan had gone alone because she had been in New York.

The glass tabletop prevented her from slipping her feet out of her shoes, as was her habit.

He perched on the edge of his chair across from her and removed his glasses, placing them gently on the table, where they disappeared into the larger glass surface. His facial features immediately receded without their subtle definition.

"Your house presents an interesting challenge. As a Grade II listed building, there is much that we cannot change. But I suspect that is one of the aspects of it that appealed to you. And sometimes the hardest decision is what to keep, so perhaps this is lucky for you."

As he spoke, Sir Charles slid a pile of thick, crisp white paper across the surface of the table until it came to rest between them. Kat glanced momentarily at the drawing on top, a massive, sprawling floor plan—precisely rendered and swaddled in detailed annotation. Replete with swatches of wood, marble, wallpaper, and paint arranged around the edges, it resembled a magpie's nest.

"There's been a mistake. This is not my house," Kat said, pulling back slowly from the drawing in front of her.

Plunging his hand into the table to retrieve his glasses, Sir Charles leaned closer to the drawings, peering at them. After a moment he looked back up at her. "This is your house."

She looked down again at the busy black-on-white drawing. Slowly, a familiar image emerged from the thicket of computer-drawn lines on the page. She hadn't recognized her own house. Embarrassed, she looked up at him, not knowing what to say. He leveled a knowing glance at her and after a moment pushed the materials to the side, clearing the space between them.

"This is why I do not like the man and woman to be separate." He sighed. "It cannot work. All this is based on the meeting with your husband."

He leaned back in his chair. "We start at the beginning, then. Why don't you tell me what you want. "

What did she want? What were they going to fill the house with? They didn't need more things. She didn't want the new textured wallpaper on the walls. She didn't want to replace the old marble or, even worse, to carpet the timeworn wood floors. She didn't want to paint it in the latest colors or to stuff it full of furniture—things that would fill up the beautiful space, curtains that would obscure the views. She wondered when they had started to need so much stuff.

Part of it was the money. They had made such a massive leap in the last few years that she was uncomfortable with the amounts of money that the project demanded. But it wasn't the money alone. She loved the space, the smooth white walls topped with frothy moldings; the enormous windows looking out over the tree-lined street or onto the large, overgrown wisteria-and-rose-filled garden; the vast expanses of distressed wood and worn-smooth marble. The idea of covering it up was anathema to her. She liked it naked. She liked the possibilities.

The feeling was even stronger since she had gone through her mother's possessions. It all ended and what were you left with?

She looked back at him mutely for a moment. "That's rather a broad question."

"It's often helpful to start with something you love," he suggested. "Something beautiful that gives you joy. Something that reminds you of things you don't want to forget. Something of value to you. A piece of art, perhaps?"

Kat thought of her bare walls and smiled.

After a moment, he continued. "I think I may have something you would be interested in seeing. As we have only just found it, I didn't have it to show your husband when he was in previously."

He rose and made his way to an oversize credenza at one end of the room. The more time she spent in the office, the more aware she became of its contents. Things that had been invisible at first. It was as if her eyes were becoming accustomed to the view. Adjusting themselves to its brilliance. The room, which had first appeared spare, gradually became populated. She noticed a collection of African masks that hung on one wall, their smooth, mute faces watching her impassively. On his desk were framed photos of two blond children. In front of the sea. Behind birthday cakes. In public-school uniforms.

"Your children?"

He glanced back at her. "As they used to be. They are older now. Klaus is at university. Liff is engaged to be married." He hesitated. "It is what it is to be a parent. Always looking backwards. You have children, yes? Your husband said."

"One child, yes." She smiled.

Opening a drawer, he carefully lifted out a sheet of over-size yellowed paper and carried it gingerly to the table. As he spread it out in front of her its age was immediately obvious. The delicate parchment was nearly translucent under the bright light.

"The original drawing of your house. Courtesy of the National Archives."

The hand-drawn diagram glowed softly. Its age and imperfections clouded just below the surface. She took in the simplicity and clarity of the lines. With the exception of scale and orientation, there were no annotations on the page. Here was the form, unadorned. This she recognized. She leaned closer, reading the graceful curling lettering within each of the rooms. Drawing room. Dining room. Principal staircase. Servants' hall.

"Drawings from this period contain much less detail," Sir

Charles explained. "There was a common knowledge of standards and techniques at the time, so less instruction was necessary."

Kat pointed decisively to the gleaming drawing in between them. "This is what I want."

She thought he smiled, but it was gone before she could be sure. "It is impossible to raise the dead. Your house will never be exactly as it once was, but it can be beautiful again. Nothing lasts forever, Kat. And you wouldn't want it to."

"Then why spend so much time on it?" It came out before she could stop herself. "So much money? Choosing the perfect marble and wallpaper and paint colors. The best furniture and appliances, the most exquisite art . . . if none of it lasts?"

He frowned. "I think because it's in our nature to do so. And because perfection is possible—but only for a time. And if you know that one secret . . ." He held up a pale forefinger, its slender shape hovering among the skyscrapers of the city beyond it. ". . . that nothing lasts forever. Then it is even sweeter."

He hesitated for a moment. "It's interesting that we often think of a home as being a part of our story, when in fact we are a part of its story."

Leaving the building, Kat crossed back from the present to the past.

Kat had grown up in a New York apartment, its walls covered with artwork. A color-soaked Derain looked down on her from above her bed, its garish hues crowded under the low ceiling. The rest of the collection was tightly arranged in an eclectic mosaic in the drawing room.

The paintings had been lovingly collected by her father's paternal grandmother. Initially viewed as an indulgence, they had proven to be a shrewd investment over the years. Upon her death, she had bequeathed them to him, her favorite grand-child, a choice that had not sat well with other family members.

Kat had grown up alongside the paintings. She thought sometimes that she could recall them all. Certainly the shim-mering Fauvist seascape over her bed, its bright boats floating in a small harbor. The sea and sky separated into vivid parti-cles of pure color. The scene was viewed from above, so that, even as a small child lying below it, she had felt as if she was looking down on it. Suspended somewhere in the dappled sky.

Then there was the sad-eyed woman, placed at the top corner in the drawing room so that she could look upon the other paintings with her downcast eyes, her empty hands clasped together tightly in her lap. And the young soldier, his expression far too grave for his age. Kat had wondered what he knew.

Close to the center of the wall was a quartet of birds, so devoid of detail that she thought that they were already gone. That their silhouettes were all that remained, sculpting the pulsating blue sky around them. The other paintings seemed to orbit around it. Its vivid tones providing an anchor to the surrounding chaos. She imagined what it might look like from the different vantage points of the other paintings. The soldier. The sad-eyed woman. How they saw it.

The collection had been a wedding present from her father to her mother. The beau geste of a besotted groom and the final straw for his disapproving parents, who found beauty without provenance to be suspect. They had disapproved of the marriage, fearing that she was after their money, and the gift of the paintings played into these fears. Worse, she was Catholic, as certain an indication of lower class as they required.

There had been a larger canvas that had hung just to the left of the birds. Although she suspected that it had not been the first to go, it was the first one whose departure she was conscious of. She could not have been more than five years old at the time that the empty space appeared where it had been. She remembered the feeling of it, more than she did the actual painting. There was a girl before an open window—the light casting her flesh in a soft, shellfish pink. She had thought that there must have been an ocean outside the window, not because she remembered seeing an ocean, but because the light that poured into the room was a kind she had only ever seen reflected off the sea in the early evening.

And while she was too young to understand everything about the paintings, she still felt them. She thought that the great ones were like that in any art form—music, painting, dance. While the technical genius might not be easily visible to the naked eye, that which was beautiful and true needed no explanation. Later, she had also come to know them by the artists who had painted them. But despite this later knowledge, they had always remained for her as she had first known them to be. She thought that it was best this way. To first experience something in its pure state—to feel something before fully understanding it.

Over time, their number continued to diminish. After the initial departure, she took more notice of them. Cataloguing them with her callow child's eye. Each its own world. Of color and line and style. Of age and time and reason. Each with its own rules, its own borders, its own palette. She had made a story from the pictures. Her story drew them together. United them and changed the rules of each of their worlds, blurring the boundaries that separated them.

The Matisse had been the last to go. For a while it hung oddly off-center on the wall. And then for a while it was only the ghosts, but then they went as well, there being no one there to remember them.

The empty spaces where the paintings had hung were never filled. Instead, the walls held only their shadows. Their varying degrees of darkness on the moss-colored wall, a testament to how long each painting had been there. The last ones to be removed were memorialized by squares of deepest green—deeper even than the surrounding wallpaper.

Sometimes long periods passed between departures, as had been the case following the exodus of the girl before the window and the seascape. When she grew up, she understood that they were more than pretty pictures. That they were important. That they had value. And that her mother had sold them off one by one, as needed. The paintings had sustained them. Perhaps not in the way that her father had intended, but in the way that had been necessary. She saw all that they had given her and she felt that maybe she owed them something in return.

She had seen the Matisse once, years after its departure. Through the window of a small gallery in SoHo. It had seemed to her that they had recognized each other at the same time. Old friends passing on a crowded street. After her initial excitement, an odd sense of shyness and propriety had caused her to keep walking, preventing her from stopping and running her eyes over its familiar curves, allowing her gaze to linger in its expanse of blue, as if she did not have the right. Not anymore. When she had found herself on the same street several weeks later, it was gone from the window.

She wondered about the order in which they had been sold and those that had been the last to go. What did they represent? Were they her mother's favorites? Each possessing its own special significance? Or were they simply the most likely to sell? Would they have fetched the best prices at auction? She thought about her mother and how she would never know the whole of her story. She thought about the possibility that what had shaped her, what had defined her most markedly, was not what was in her life, but what was not. And how she had built her life around those empty spaces.

When her mother had informed her father's family of her pregnancy and of her intention to raise the child in her Catholic faith, her father's family had responded that they had no interest in the child. And so she did not know them.

There had been one time. She could not have been more

than five years old. It had been a weekday, but her mother had instructed her to put on one of her Sunday dresses. As she pulled the smocked garment over her head, Kat had wondered expectantly at the occasion. Coaxing the strap of her shoe into its buckle, she had heard the doorman ring up and, minutes after that, the doorbell. When her mother had called her to the drawing room, she had entered shyly. The good tea set sat on the low table, its small delicate white cups embroidered with flowers and rimmed in gold. An older woman perched behind it on the edge of the couch, the frayed edges of her tweed jacket perfectly matching the fringe of the pillows.

As Kat entered the room, the woman turned and rose slowly. Her lips were shiny red and her face wore an alert, almost surprised expression. After a moment she extended her hand stiffly. Her skin felt soft and dry, like crumpled tissue paper. Kat looked at the blue veins visible just under the surface.

"Katherine, this is your grandmother." Her mother seemed almost as incredulous at the unlikely figure before her as Kat was.

Kat had been amazed. She had a grandmother. She knew of them, of course, from stories and fairy tales. She regarded hers with interest. Her hair rose off her head and was frozen in high waves around her face.

Her mother had excused herself and gone into the kitchen, leaving the two of them alone in the room. Mother and daughter, separated by the one absent person who made each of them so. She was surprisingly tall. For some reason Kat had imagined most older people to be small. She had looked down on Kat, arrayed before her in her Sunday best.

"You are the image of your mother."

Even to her young ears, it had the ring of accusation.

She had answered solemnly. "I have the red hair like my mommy."

"So you do." As she spoke, her gaze slid off Kat, and onto the paintings behind her, where it lingered. Kat had been keen to regain her attention.

"You like Mommy's pretty pictures?"

Her grandmother wrinkled her nose and pressed her lips together. Kat thought that maybe she had smelled something bad.

"Pretty pictures. Is that what they are?"

After a moment, she refocused on Kat, although her face still retained traces of its prior expression. "Well, now, no need to let the tea go cold, I suppose."

Her grandmother had leaned toward the table between them and lifted the teapot. Its bulbous shape threatened to be too much for her thin wrists to bear and her hands shook slightly under its weight. Kat closed her eyes and listened to the distinctive sound of the hot liquid being poured, so different from the sound of something cold being poured. The faintly citrus scent of the tea reached her and she opened her eyes in time to see her mother emerging from the kitchen bearing a tiered platter of small, round cakes in varying subtle hues of such delicacy that they seemed like petals from a flower.

"Look at what your grandmother brought."

In her delight at the sight of the cakes, Kat opened her arms wide to clap. Her right hand made abrupt contact with one of the cups, sending it flying off the table, its contents arcing out behind it like the tail of a comet. The older woman let out a short scream, rising from her chair, a look of abject horror on her face. Kat froze. The back of her hand stung from the momentary contact with the hot porcelain, and tears welled in her eyes. It took her a moment to realize that she was not burned. It took her another moment to realize that her grandmother's concern was not directed at her. That instead she was looking past her to the trail of tea that traced a path across the rug to the wall, where tiny dark liquid drops had fallen in a fan shape, its far edge interrupted by the lower left corner of the painting of the young soldier. The older woman turned on Kat, her face taut with anger.

"Dear God! What have you done?"

"I'm sorry! I'm sorry!" Kat sobbed, looking from the unfamiliar angry face of her grandmother to the familiar concerned face of her mother, who was already kneeling on the floor beside her, reaching for her hand, which she clutched close to her chest.

"Are you okay, darling? Let me see your hand."

Kat nodded meekly, extending her hand to her mother, who rubbed it gently between her own hands, murmuring, "It's all right. It's only an accident."

After examining her hand to make sure she had not been scalded, her mother stood. Plucking a napkin from the table, she moved to the canvas, blotting gently, working quickly to remove the small traces of tea that had fallen on it. Turning the napkin over, she repeated the process, diligently examining it when she was done to make sure there was nothing on it.

"Is it all right?" her grandmother asked anxiously, edging closer to the wall.

Her mother turned away from the painting and addressed Kat. "Go into the kitchen and get me another cloth from the drawer, would you, darling?"

Taking care to angle herself away from the table, Kat retreated hastily to the other room. She reached up to open the drawer, standing on her toes to find what she sought. Pausing to press the cloth to her damp cheeks, she hesitated at the door, listening to her grandmother's deep patrician voice in the next room, shaping and polishing her words so that they shone with admonition.

". . . irresponsible to have a child in an apartment with something of such value . . ."

After a brief pause, her mother's voice.

"You have made no secret of the fact that you find my behavior to be irresponsible. And today you have made it very clear that you value the paintings more than you do your own granddaughter. They are what you really came to see." Her mother's voice was ice. Kat froze where she stood, her hand on the doorknob. "Take a moment. Have a last look at what you love. Then see yourself out."

While the incident had put a stop to any further contact with her father's family, it had not stopped the discussion of her father.

"What was he like?"

It was almost a refrain in her childhood. There had been many responses, of increasing depth and detail as she grew older. A few she remembered better than others. Some she remembered because they had been repeated, becoming answering choruses to her refrain. "I sometimes think we must have known on some level that we didn't have much time." Others she remembered because they had not been repeated. "Maybe I was lucky. It never had a chance to fade."

chapter five

Kat changed her clothes twice. Stopping before the mirror in the front hallway, she braided her hair in one long, loose plait, wrapping a bit of the ends around it to hold it fast. She liked having it out of her face. She should just cut it short, but it seemed somehow to be an admission of age.

Passing the arched window on the landing, she realized she was not alone. She wondered how long he had been there, body cloaked by lingering night, just beyond the garden doors. She had first seen the bright yellow eyes watching her the week that they moved into the house. She had seen the small red foxes on the paths in Holland Park in the early morning. In the springtime, reckless with desire, they came into the gardens behind the houses to mate, their sharp, keening cries waking her at night. Something both urgent and mournful about them. It surprised her to see such an untamed thing in the city. Somehow, just knowing that they were there gave her hope. As if she needed that wildness—even if she never did more than lock eyes with it. She needed to know that it was out there.

She had dismissed their driver early in the day. She seldom used him when Jonathan was out of town. Instead, she caught the number 9 bus to Mayfair. It was nearly full and she took a spot standing by the back door. She kept her long coat pulled tightly around her, hiding her dressy clothes. She very rarely bumped into anyone she knew on the bus in London. She felt that it was her own little secret world of public anonymity.

Two young women got on at Palace Gate, tottering on spindly heels, talking animatedly about a party. Kat wondered briefly what she was doing, thinking that Jorie must have talked her into it and reasoning that she was just curious about his work. And maybe he wouldn't be there at all. Daniel had never liked openings.

An older woman in a bright red coat boarded at Exhibition Road and took a spot by the door, her long neck hidden under the folds of an expertly arranged Hermès scarf. Kat watched her as she swayed gracefully in sync with her fellow passengers as the bus stopped and started its way through traffic on Kensington Gore, her fluid movements elevating them to a corps de ballet.

Her mother had loved spending time with them in London,

visiting so frequently over the years that Kat would tease her that she knew the city better than Kat did. On the mornings that Will was at school and Kat had something in the diary, her mother would set out alone to the museums. She had fallen on the last visit. Misjudging the distance from the bottom step of the bus to the pavement, she had fallen. Kat had gotten the phone call from the National Gallery and had raced over to find her resting on a couch in the staff break room, a cup of Earl Grey by her side. If she was shaken by the incident, she had not shown it, insisting on viewing the Vermeers that she had come to see, and then maintaining that it would be rude not to pay her respects to the Turners, as if they were old family friends. And so Kat had followed along beside her as she moved from Canaletto to Rubens to Ingres to Goya. Watching the changing shapes of joy in her face as the paintings passed her from one to the next. Looking like a schoolgirl with plasters on her knees.

Kat tightened her grip on the slick metal pole as the bus slid around Hyde Park corner, eliciting surprised giggles from the young women as it stacked them neatly against a stout man in a well-worn mac.

Walking the few blocks from Green Park, she arrived at the gallery, immediately identifiable by the news trucks parked outside. She was surprised by the amount of media there was. Someone was doing their job well. She paused briefly outside the gallery to check her phone. There was a message from Will. As sad as she was to have missed his call, she was glad to have the message, a little piece of him that he had left behind.

Making her way through the crowd on the pavement, she entered the handsome Georgian stone building and gave her name to the woman at the door, who found it on the list and waved her inside. There had been no hesitation, no resistance, when she had telephoned the gallery asking to be added to the guest list for tonight. She had used her married name.

She was well aware of the effect that Jonathan's surname had begun to have on people in London. She had become inured to the immediate, subtle change in attitude that it engendered. A strange mixture of curiosity and resentment. When she married Jonathan, she had opted to keep her maiden name, a decision she had stuck with even after the success of the company had imbued his surname with new prestige. Jorie, who collected her husbands' names and wore them about her neck like so many trinkets, continued to be puzzled by this decision.

Once inside, she declined to check her coat. The gallery was packed. She spotted Jorie waving to her from the less crowded side of the lobby and she made her way over, intercepting a flute of champagne on her way.

Jorie took her arm in the way that only European women can.

"Darling, it's a madhouse. I swear that I just saw Richard Hawthorne."

As with many of the names Jorie dropped, Kat recognized it in a vague way, feeling that perhaps she had read it somewhere recently.

It was sometimes difficult to tell predator from prey in the art world, but this crowd was all predator. Dressed to the nines in the type of vintage clothing whose value was detectable only to the trained eye—watches that cost more than most cars, handbags with two-year waiting lists. Nostrils flared, heads thrown back the better to look down their noses, they prowled the openings, sniffing out the latest prize. Daniel was nowhere to be seen.

Observing the crowd as it funneled in through the door into the room on the right, Jorie guided Kat purposefully to the left. "It's less crowded this way. Why follow the herd?"

The canvases in the first room they entered were massive. Much larger than anything she had known him to paint. They certainly would not have fit into the rue Garancière studio. The first one confronted her immediately—a milk-white hand seen from above. Long, slender fingers clutching a fistful of cloth, tendons taut and straining, knuckles showing white through pale skin. The painting itself had to be eight feet tall—allowing even the detail of the thin, fair hairs and tiny creases between the thumb and forefinger to be seen clearly.

It took her a moment to identify the next one. Her eye was drawn immediately to a sharp pink shape punctuating the lower edge of the expanse of pale canvas. Only when she recognized it as the corner of a mouth, barely open, did she see the rest of the canvas as cheek. The discoveries of the first two made the rest of the paintings in the room easier to decipher. Looking around, she saw that the room also contained a throat, stretched out in a way that suggested a head flung back just out of view; and a shoulder streaked by several loose

strands of hair and the unmistakable curve of a female waist
pushed back against a tangle of wrinkled fabric. There were
others that she could not see, as they were obscured by the
crowds.

"Like pieces of a broken statue," Jorie whispered, squeezing
her arm.

Kat nodded. Jorie was right. Taken alone, the individual
pieces were like fragments of an unseen whole, strangely un-
satisfying for all their detail. But together they had a distinctive narrative quality, coalescing into an undeniable portrait
of a woman in the throes of passion. The individual paintings
seemed to be glimpses of what a lover might see in the moments when he opened his eyes. The size of the paintings tested
the limits of the space, filling it with what amounted to a frac-
tured, flickering confession.

And yet there remained a persistent sense of something that
was absolutely broken. There was a strong incongruity between
the heat of the subject and the cold, almost bloodless approach
to it. Given the intimate nature of the subject, she found the
scale and detail disturbing. She rubbed her fingertips up and
down the cold glass in her hand, tracing paths in the conden-
sation.

Spotting a face she recognized at the far end of the room,
Jorie gave Kat's arm a quick squeeze before she dropped it with
a murmured apology and pushed through the crowds, leaving Kat to navigate the gallery alone.

Coming to the end of the room too quickly, Kat stopped
to examine the canvas by the door. The long curving edge of

a female form clung to one side of it, barely distinguishable from the pale sheet that occupied the rest of the canvas. The last glimpse of the figure before she moved off the canvas and out of view. Its vertical shape seemed to serve as punctuation at the end of the room.

In an attempt to escape the current of the crowd around her, Kat stepped closer to it. From a few feet away she could clearly see the thin layers of paint, pulled taut across the canvas. As she followed the shape up the side of the canvas, a sharp jolt of cold made her aware that she had involuntarily brought her fingers, chilled from the glass, up to her neck. Suddenly alert, on the banks of the moving crowd, she became aware of distinct voices within the crowd directly behind her.

"This is the one." The male speaker was authoritative, demanding.

After a moment, the same voice again, louder and more insistent. "Did you hear me, Martin? I want your word on it."

Before any reply could be made, a woman's voice broke in, seemingly unaffected by her companion's bluster. "How did you find him?"

After a moment, a second male voice—Martin, she presumed—responded to the woman in a soothing, indulgent tone. "He has been in the stable for years. Found him in Paris and then took him to New York with me. Had great success doing commissions—portraits of the glitterati. Women mostly . . . . Very technically adept, but missing that elusive something that separates the good from the great—that essential spark. Then about a year ago he calls and tells me he has something to show me. Tells me to meet him at this warehouse—in the middle of nowhere. Hands me a key to one of those awful rented storerooms."

Here the voice wavered and the speaker paused to collect himself before going on. When he began speaking again, his voice was lower. Kat took a step back toward the group.

"I've never seen anything like it. There were paintings everywhere—leaning against the walls, stacked on crates. I knew the moment I saw them that this was something special. That he had found his passion. I knew instantly that this was going to be the first line of my obituary."

The woman's voice again, as soft as it had been, but with a hint of edge in it that had not been there before. "And his obituary."

There was a brief pause before the man replied. "Of course." After a moment he went on. "I actually bought a painting from this series when he first came to see me about twenty years ago. One of the earliest ones he had done. *The Blue Bath*—the one I pointed out in the last room. It was the first one he sold to me. It was the piece that first made me take notice of him."

His voice grew quieter, and Kat took another step backward, straining to hear him. "I kept it, which is rather unusual for me. I had absolutely no idea there were more like it. At the time, he needed money, so I set him up to do a commissioned portrait. An ambassador's daughter. Not very lucrative, I grant, but good money and a good entrée into that world, as the portrait would be seen by the right people. The art world is all about exposure to the right people. Began representing him shortly thereafter, but never saw any more like that first one until that day at the warehouse."

There was a pause, as the speaker and his audience considered his story, before the woman spoke again.

"She is beautiful."

There was another pause before Martin responded, his voice slightly cold.

"Perhaps. But the paintings are more beautiful."

The first voice again, impatient and a bit too loud. "How much did you pay for it? The blue one."

The second man chuckled softly, as if he felt the situation required it.

"Now, Nicholas, do you think me cruel enough to tell you that? Suffice it to say that he was unknown at the time and as I said, he needed the money. But that painting was what got my attention, which is what ultimately led us to this." Kat imagined the speaker gesturing to the crowd around him in a proprietary way as he continued. "So I would say it all worked out in the end."

Succumbing to her curiosity, Kat glanced furtively over her shoulder at the threesome. A tall man stood with his back to her and the painting, while a well-groomed brunette woman stood opposite him, squinting at it. Between them another man stood facing her, short and preemptively bald. In addition to setting him apart from the crowd, the particular shade of his dark green suit served to underscore the fact that he was shaped remarkably like an avocado.

The tall man spoke again, still impatient. "How much is it worth? What's its value today?"

Kat watched the pale face atop the green suit and saw its features relax as its small eyes swept across the expansive canvas behind her.

"Did you know, in painting, the term 'value' refers to the lightness or darkness of a color or a canvas? I have always thought that to be a marvelous way to regard the concept of value—the inherent darkness or lightness of a thing." Kat thought that his voice sounded suddenly tired.

"Are you interested in selling?" the tall man persisted.

Kat saw the curve of his lips return as he replied. "You know me, Nicholas. For the right price . . ."

Before she could look away, the small man caught her eye, shooting her a quick, sharp glance before turning back to the group.

Scanning the crowd, Kat spied Jorie on the far side of the room, hand on hip, head tossed back in laughter, standing only slightly too close to someone else's husband. The crowd was pushing Kat backward and she had to keep moving to avoid being forced back the way she came. So she left the room, the conversation dying behind her.

THE NEXT ROOM was populated with smaller canvases. At first she could see only bits of the paintings among the heads of the crowd. As she focused on the first one she could see whole, on the wall to her right, green eyes stared back at her from a pale face, appearing at once far away and very close. At once, her stomach lurched and the sounds of the room receded, replaced by a low buzzing in her head.

She blinked, opening her eyes to find that the face before her remained. It looked different in the bright light of the gallery, over the bobbing heads of the crowd, but she recognized it immediately. It had lain on its side against the wall under the windows for months after he had finished it, looking up at the stained ceiling. Against the smooth expanse of immaculate white wall it seemed larger. More bold. Less warm. But she was certain it was the same one. The figure on the canvas looked sleepy and sensual, completely at ease lying across the unmade bed.

Panicked, she cast her eyes over the surrounding crowd, and struggled to control her breathing. As her eyes panned around the room, she recognized another painting—a smaller study of the bath. An almost irresistible urge to run filled her, mitigated only by an equally strong impulse to move closer to it. A previous occupant of the studio had painted the inside of the bathtub a deep shade of blue. Although meant to be permanent, the paint still imparted a slight blue tint to the water when the tub was filled. For all its intimacy, the painting was quite discreet, as the water obscured most of her body. From where she was standing, she could see a finger smudge on the upper left side of the unframed canvas. Often, when finishing a detail, Daniel would grasp the upper left corner of the canvas, leaving smudged fingerprints on its edge, which he never bothered to remove.

She met her own eyes—wide and wet—in the next canvas. She looked as if she had just finished laughing. And the next one—a close-up of her sleeping, the corner of the sheet brushing her cheek. And the next one—her eyes downcast as she sat curled in the fading pink sunshine of late afternoon, bent over a book, her hair held up by both of her hands, stray strands seeping out between her fingers.

The painting in front of her was so close that she could reach out and touch it. Trace the lines of the body. There was something about it that seemed so real. Much more real than the crowded gallery that surrounded her now. It seemed that if she stood and looked long enough, the girl's hand would move through the length of her hair, fingers disappearing among the soft strands. That the hint of smile in her eyes would spread slowly, inevitably, to the rest of her face. Kat felt a tightening in her chest. An ache.

Backing away from the paintings, into the center of the room, she realized she was surrounded. She scanned the paintings that ringed the room. Her face. Her body. Made young again and laid bare around her. She wondered briefly if it was voyeurism if you were looking at yourself.

Each of the paintings triggered a barrage of memories. They crashed into her, immediately more real to her than the crush of people brushing past her. She remembered the circumstances of each painting. The tepid water of the bath and the strange sensation of disconnection with her body while it was submerged unseen in the murky water. The warmth of the morning sun on her face, and the feel of the smooth cover of the book in her hands. She remembered how she felt when he was painting her. So safe. So understood. It was almost an abdication of herself. As if he held her and she was free to wander. Although she had not strayed far from the studio that summer.

She remembered the smell of the paint and the slight damp of the studio in the mornings. The feel of the cool wooden floorboards under her bare feet. Being woken by the sunlight coming through the thin glass panes in the windows.

She remembered Daniel stretching the blank canvases, mixing the colors and then washing them off his brushes. Their traces on the edges of the drain—mingling briefly to become something other than what they had been separately and then fading, faded, into the worn porcelain basin. She remembered the clumps of paint, like dried leaves, on the rough wooden palette and all the colors that she had not known were in her—black, green, burnt and raw umber, ocher, white, and then more green or blue for shading.

She remembered the strange silence of the studio. The paintings seemed out of place in this loud, crowded, windowless room. A man pushed by her roughly, mumbling a perfunctory apology through thick lips as he passed by, reminding Kat of where she was in the center of the room, her feet anchoring her to the floor as the crowd moved around her.

She kept her head down, pulling nervously on the end of her long plait, taking small breaths. The air in the room felt too warm, heated to a viscous syrup by the movement of the crowd. Looking around, she realized that most of the people had their backs to the paintings, talking among themselves, while her face looked on from different vantage points on the walls. The current of people swelled against her, urging her back the way she had come. She had obviously come the wrong way, viewing the exhibit backward.

There was something else in the air at the gallery. A different kind of excitement. Brash, eager, slightly tarnished, she recognized it in the excited laughter and conversation of the crowd. Money. The paintings had passed beyond what they had been in the studio on the rue Garancière, beyond even what the early critics had recognized in them, and were being regarded with a new kind of lust. They had become commodities. Looking more closely at the crowd, she was surprised to see so many familiar faces. These were the men and women who bought and sold things in London. Companies, property, buildings, art. He was in her world now.

A thought gripped her. Just how close was the resemblance between her and the girl in the paintings? How easy would it be to link her face to the face in the portraits?

Hearing a heavy sigh, she turned to find a tall brunette woman standing beside her. Kat recognized her as one-third of the trio she had overheard in the other room. The woman smiled at Kat and scanned the crowd distractedly as it moved past them. Turning her gaze back to the painting in front of her, she sighed again. Kat froze. Was it too late? Had she been recognized?

"Does great art inspire you or just depress you? I mean,

there is no way I could ever create anything like this. Frankly, it would be embarrassing for me to even try. Don't get me wrong, I appreciate the aspirational aspect of it, but I think that if we're honest, part of it's also about teaching us our limitations. After all, if everyone could create something like that, would we value it the way we do?"

"Maybe not," Kat managed, but doubted that she had been heard over the noise. The woman's gaze remained on the painting in front of them. She frowned, addressing her words directly to it.

"Although, I don't suppose the alternative is any better. Even if you have the talent, by turning what you love into something that pays the rent, you destroy it in a thousand daily cuts. Familiarity, complacency, compromise . . . Although, at least you have your arms around it as you do it. At least it dies by your own hand. I don't know—maybe there's some solace in that."

The brunette cocked her head at Kat, smiling widely. "I just think having something like that in my drawing room would suck the life right out of me."

Kat felt a tidal swell in the crowd. The woman nodded toward the far side of the gallery. "Here comes the talent now."

Kat turned in the direction she indicated. And there he was. A head above the crowd, looking too big and too volatile for the spare, white room. The same craggy face—more lived-in and more weathered than she remembered. Hair slicked back from his forehead. Clean-shaven. More solid. Older. She had anticipated these possibilities. What surprised her was not all that had changed, but all that had not changed. Somehow she hadn't expected him to still be Daniel.

Staying very still as the crowd moved around her, she studied him in the brief glimpses through the changing kaleidoscope of bobbing heads, watching as, outnumbered, he met his admirers, greeting and kissing and shaking hands.

In that one moment, watching him across the room, she saw the arc of his potential condensed, realized. She saw him as he had been and she saw him as he appeared now through the eyes of the crowd. The artist. As if in that moment he became all that he could have been so many years ago. It was like witnessing a birth.

It took her a minute to see the girl. She was beautiful. Delicate and small against him, she seemed more at home in this place than he was, although she was clearly here for him. He clutched her tightly, his arm wrapped around her waist, hand resting on her hip.

Her reflection was all too brief. Interrupted, as she clung to the wall on the far side of the room, when his eyes met hers. There was no double take. No lag between him seeing her and recognizing her. Apart from a brief flicker, his expression did not change. Excusing himself from his conversation and unwrapping himself from the girl, he began to make his way toward her through the crowd—eyes locked on her—pinning her to her spot like a moth. She could not read his expression, but she felt a familiar intensity in it.

But the gallery was too crowded with pilgrims, paying

homage, seeking his attention in return for theirs. As he momentarily lost eye contact with her, she pulled away from his gaze and made for the door. Reaching it, she turned back, but he was gone, obscured by his admirers. Sliding between the bodies entering the gallery, she felt the rough pavement beneath her shoes and the cold wind on her face.

Kat made her way quickly down the street, her breath escaping back toward the gallery. When she was a safe distance away, she moved to the edge of the pavement and waited for the traffic to clear so she could cross the street. Hearing voices behind her, she turned. Was she being followed? Had someone in the gallery noticed the resemblance between her and the girl in the paintings? Holding her breath, she turned to find two men standing beside a black cab idling at the curb.

"And the schedule? He can complete it on time?" It was the older gentleman whom Jorie had pointed out at Daniel's show. Kat tried to remember his name, but she had not glanced down at it after it had been dropped.

"Of course." The answer came even before the question had been completed. The voice sounded immediately familiar and she recognized the short man in the green suit from the gallery. Martin. "I've been looking after Daniel for years. I know what he is going to do even before he does."

The other man considered him gravely for a long moment, allowing him to squirm like a fat worm on a hook.

"Because, you know, we hear things. Addictions, perhaps . . ." He shook his head sadly. "There are, after all, visible scars."

"We all have our addictions, Richard." It was spoken in a low tone, with real menace in it. "Some are more productive than others. Without them, I doubt we would be having this conversation today."

Crossing the street, Kat did not hear the reply, if there was one.

After a few blocks she slowed down and walked for a while through Mayfair, drinking in the cold air. Above the constellations of Christmas lights on Oxford Street, the sky was leaden and still. The streets were slick. It must have rained earlier. The reflected light off the pavement seemed somehow brighter than the streetlamps themselves. She was flooded with an overwhelming sense of nostalgia and regret for a delicate and vanished time. For the brief, fragile peace of simply being seen.

She recalled her astonishment standing in front of the first completed painting of herself in Paris. It was evening and the studio was wrapped in blue darkness. After a moment, she had turned to Daniel.

"Is that who you see when you look at me?"

He had looked around the room briefly, searching for something. Then, laying his hands on her shoulders, he had steered her to the window and indicated her reflection in the glass pane.

"That is not what you look like. At least not to others. We are not what we see in the mirror—our images are, in fact, reversed. We are not what we appear to be, even to ourselves."

It was true. While immediately familiar, the face in the painting was not quite the same face she saw in the mirror or in photographs. Nor somehow did she believe that it was the face that others saw. Yet the feeling of recognition was overwhelming. The only way she could think to describe it was that girl he captured on canvas looked the way that she felt. And that sense of shared truth was more seductive than being admired or even being loved. And unlike love, which often engendered a broader affinity for others, its sharp edge severed all other connections, leaving only the two of them.

He had painted her whenever the urge struck him. She would suddenly hear the pages on the sketch pad being flipped over or the crisp sighs of the charcoal on paper. Sometimes she wouldn't notice at all, discovering it only when she moved and heard his urgent whisper for her to stay where she was. Half prayer, half command. He often drew her while she was sleeping.

And slowly, she had begun to become more aware of herself. Of the pleasing shape her neck made as she bent forward over a book. Of the way the shadows fell beside her as she sat or reclined on the bed, and the varying effects of sunlight in her hair at different times of the day. She became conscious of the way different textures of clothing or blankets looked against her bare skin and she began to pay more attention when buying books at the markets, selecting the ones with the most interesting covers, soft, mottled linens and rich, distressed leathers.

Daniel would sometimes begin to sketch her in the early morning, drawing her outline swiftly, without taking his eyes off her. Often turned away, she could not see him, but she could feel his eyes just beyond her view, moving over her, holding her to her spot. And when he had enough, when she was free to go, she would feel him release her. Daniel hardly acknowledged her departure when she left. When she returned to the studio in the early evening she would find herself taking form on the canvas. It was as if time obeyed different rules in the little room under the eaves of the ancient building on the rue Garancière. He didn't need her to be physically present to paint her. When he was painting her, she remained with him.

As she made her way past the shuttered shops, Kat thought about Daniel at the gallery in his immaculate dark gray suit, its carefully cut lines betraying it as bespoke, a perfect complement to the confident smiles and brief greetings, the earnest eye contact, the seemingly effortless charm. Playing the artist. And he was good at it.

She supposed it wasn't really surprising. After all, she had gotten better at it, too. She could sit through the endless dinners and cocktail parties. She could make conversation with the nervous first wives and the defensive trophies. She could smile and nod and not have to excuse herself from the table too often to sneak out the back door to the dark garden and fill herself full of night air, enough to get her through the rest of the evening.

It might all have seemed real if she weren't watching so

closely and if she hadn't known what had come before. She noticed the telltale way he shifted his weight and how stillness seemed to elude him. He was acting. Pretending. And although he was better at it now than he used to be, there remained a lingering suggestion of volatility about him. He seemed to be actively restraining himself.

She was embarrassed for leaving the gallery the way that she had. Seeing him in a crowd like that had been so unfamiliar. In all her memories of him, it was always just the two of them. As if there hadn't been anyone else in Paris.

And the paintings. She remembered living with them while they were drying. How they had surrounded them. And she realized at once just how rare that intimacy was. How it was almost impossible to achieve, in a museum or even in the smallest of galleries. How even the most hallowed of spaces were haunted by the footsteps and whispered incantations of others.

She caught a cab on Park Lane. As it cut through Hyde Park, her mobile rang. Jonathan.

"Darling—where are you?" His voice was muffled.

"Hello. Just in Mayfair."

"Right—the Cancer Foundation ball, it's tonight?"

"No—not yet. Just a gallery opening. With Jorie."

"Ah, Ms. Thibaud-Paxton-Bowles . . ." Jonathan always included all of Jorie's surnames. "Any eligible bachelors there then?"

Kat winced. "Not for long . . . . How are you? How's everything?"

"Moving forward. Omega starts diligence tomorrow."

Her confusion lasted for just a beat. "Oh. Are we at the code-name stage?"

"We are. Especially on phones."

"I hadn't realized."

"You haven't said anything to Jorie, have you?" His voice rose suddenly in panic.

"Jonathan. Of course not."

She knew better and he knew that she did. She knew how information moved in their circles, functioning as currency, as entertainment, as proof of status. Even more literally in this case, as any information about the impending sale was insider information. There could be no confidences.

"Sorry. It's just that the press is all over this. I'm pretty sure that someone has been following me since I got here."

"Really?" She could not help the incredulous tone in her voice and immediately regretted it.

"Yes. Really."

She heard the thin thread of his voice pull taut across the miles and she spoke quickly. "Don't be cross with me. I know this is serious. It just seems so absurd."

"Do you remember that bastard, Warre, the one who wrote that hatchet piece in the *Mail*? Apparently, he has started calling our analysts and some major shareholders, inquiring as to their opinions on the impending sale of the company to a foreign firm."

The article, which had appeared more than a year ago, prompted by a photograph of Jonathan having dinner with

executives from the Chinese company, had been a vitriolic na-
tionalistic tirade. Citing the usual long list of venerable British
institutions that had been recently sold off to foreign interests—
the Savoy Hotel, Fortnum & Mason, Harrods, Cadbury—
the reporter had cast Jonathan as the latest in a long line of
money-hungry CEOs, cashing out after bleeding Britain dry
of talent and resources. The piece had served as a nasty surprise
to Jonathan, who was accustomed to a rather different sort of
coverage.

A photo of the columnist, Alistair Warre, had appeared beside the article. A small black-and-white rendering of a hirsute,
slack-jawed man peering through large horn-rimmed glasses.
Since then, Kat had seen him at events occasionally and even
on the street once or twice. He had a distinctive, scurrying gait
that suited a person much younger. A kind of eager, halting
pace that gave the impression he was about to break into a run.
Come to think of it, she might have seen him just a few days
ago on Holland Park Avenue.

There was silence on the line.

"So, I met with Sir Charles . . ." she began brightly.

"I don't know why. If this deal goes through, we may never
even live in the house."

She stopped short, holding the phone to her ear in the darkness of the cab. "What? Why?"

"Turns out they want me to stay on as CEO."

"Right. In London. The company is in London."

"But management would be in Hong Kong."

She was silent.

"I assumed you knew this was a possibility . . ."

"You never said anything about moving to China."

"Look, this gives me a chance to take care of our people. Make sure they're integrated into the new organization. They've been loyal to us. They helped build the company. It's the right thing to do."

AFTER THE CALL, she sat stunned in the back of the cab. Hong Kong? Had that possibility been lost in the shuffle that had been their lives over the past several months? Mistakenly packed away? Mislabeled? Or had she simply not been paying attention? What other possibilities had been misplaced or over-looked?

For years, they had lived an unsettled life. And she had learned to enjoy it. She had come to find that uncertainty had a certain charm. But since buying the house, she had believed that had changed. The size of the house, the financial commitment, the scope of the renovation—all of these things had led her to allow herself to believe that they were putting down roots. After all, wasn't this what they had worked toward? Wasn't this the dream?

She became aware of the regular thump of the speed bumps as they moved onto the residential streets off the High Street. She switched on the overhead light to find her house keys in her bag. In the dim glare she caught sight of her reflection in the smooth black window of the cab. The deepening wrinkles around the edges of her eyes and mouth, the softening jawline. A far different face from the one that had looked back at her from the walls of the gallery. Kat let out a sudden laugh, startling the cabdriver, who turned round to look at her. Perhaps she needn't have worried that anyone would recognize her.

chapter six

What the Artist Kept to Himself

Thomas Lowry

A bright new light in figurative painting is shining from a wholly unexpected place. In an unprecedented move, Mayfair's stalwartly modern Penfield Gallery has thrown the full weight of its considerable influence behind a fairly unknown realist and his series of portraits.

Although this show is the first major exhibition for the artist, his work already hangs in the homes of many of New York's finest collectors, disguised in that most easily dismissed of forms— portraiture. Daniel Blake has long been the portraitist of choice amongst New York's elite. And I must admit that while I have been exposed to his work in this capacity on several occasions, this is the first time I have been aware of his talent.

Over a span of twenty years, unbeknownst to his many patrons and purportedly even to his own agent, Blake has created a series of works that serve as an intensive study of one unidentified model. This series, in addition to representing a notable augmentation of his catalogue raisonné—both in terms of breadth and depth—provides a rare view of the stylistic and emotional evolution of the artist.

The works in this show are, first and foremost, compelling portraits of a young woman, gracefully realized and technically adroit. Indeed, one could devote an entire article solely to the artist's renditions of red hair. Not since Titian has there been an artist more enamoured of the redhead.

But, there is more to his story. The obvious mystery here is that the young woman herself neither ages nor changes during the course of the series. This anomaly has captured the imagination of the art world, sparking a debate over whether his model is real or is simply a product of the artist's imagination.

The exhibition is divided in two distinct parts. In the initial stage Blake's talent is on full display in his mastery of the subtle textures of flesh and plaster and cloth. It is these early works that belie the depth of the artist's connection to the subject and it is this emotional intensity that distinguishes his work. The delicate, varied brushstrokes, the intimate scale—these are moments stolen out of time. In the later works, the paintings themselves are the moments—attempts to recall time past.

The early works have a voyeuristic quality. In "September

Morning" the subject, seen in profile before an open window, is both observed and observer. While the artist's vision extends only as far as the borders of the canvas, the girl's vision knows no such boundaries. It is her expression much more than the artist's smudged, ruddy brushstrokes that convinces us of the world beyond the confines of the small room. And yet, there is a sense of timelessness in these portraits. It seems his subject could have just as easily existed a century ago as today.

While the washed-out palette is familiar, the later work sees a sharp departure from the earlier portraits. Here Blake moves closer to his subject. His paintings from this period, numbered rather than titled, are broken down into highly detailed elements. What we see is a freckled shoulder, the detail of the corner of a pink mouth, the curve of a waist, the myriad colours within a single plait of hair.

The irony is that the closer Blake moves to the girl, the more distant she becomes. In recalling the detail, the whole is lost. The extraordinary tenderness of the earlier works is also missing, replaced with an almost scientific approach. What starts as an exploration of the whole person becomes an obsessive exhumation of pieces of the whole.

This change in approach is reflected in a change in technique and tools. Blake abandons the nuanced brushstrokes of the earlier paintings for a flat, stripped-down look. His use of palette knives on the dead spaces of the canvas serves to actively separate the girl from what surrounds her. In many of these later works, it is the dead spaces themselves that seem most alive. In "Fourteen," the bed—stripped of covers and alive in cold light—seems *to serve as a canvas within the canvas. The artist seems to be painting absence itself.*

The later works are much larger and possess a deliberately talismanic quality. Their scale seems a desperate attempt to magnify their memory, to fix them in time. Unlike the earlier pieces, which seem effortless, here is where you see the effort. They are constructed with resolute, painstaking discipline. You feel each scrape of the blade across the canvas.

This part of the series seems compulsive—a conscious turning away from truth to beauty. It is the fast moment, slowed down, halted and stretched across the canvas to be examined close-up. These efforts to render the moment so clearly convey the power and the sadness of his yearning to hold on to it. These canvases haunt you. The artist provides just enough pieces to suggest the whole and you cannot stop yourself from trying to fit them together.

Blake came by his skills through a combination of classic training and osmosis. He studied at the Slade in London and then briefly at the École Nationale in Paris. His mother, Mary Blake was a popular landscape painter until her death two years ago.

Kat read the last sentence over again.

Some critics have called the show provincial. And indeed, there is nothing in the subject matter that particularly distinguishes Blake's work from countless others. It is about a girl, as it so often is. And so why Blake? Why not Castillo with his resin spheres or Xiaolin with his lurid murals? Why not any number of other artists? Greater talent? Not necessarily. Better craft—perhaps. Timing? Ah, warmer . . . . Story? Warmer still.

There are those who say that the true masterpiece here is in the story. After all, Blake has been around for a while. Within a short space of time, the mystery surrounding his choice to paint this one subject over the course of so many years has done more for his fame than his considerable talent was able to achieve in his career to date. Indeed, it threatens to eclipse even the work itself.

And so what of the girl? Who is she and what is she to the artist? Blake himself has thus far refused to comment and his agent, Martin Whittaker, is cagey, saying only that whatever else their relationship was, it was certainly productive.

This writer, for one, hopes that she is not real. Because if Blake invented her, he can invent another. But if she is real, he will have to wait for lightning to strike again, something that may never happen. But while that is my hope, it is not my belief. The level of detail and the consistency with which she is rendered would be unlikely without a real subject from which to draw. But even more than this, there is a sense of purity or even piety about these portraits. A sense of urgency, a compulsion, to make us see his truth. And inherent in this is the acknowledgement of the ephemeral nature of the subject. Why bother to capture on canvas that which is going to last forever?

Sadly, what I believe most likely is that the girl in the portraits is dead. This would explain both the lack of aging, and the fact that in later works she becomes hardened, more defined; and his approach to her becomes almost clinical.

It is telling that much of this article and much of what is being discussed about this show is about the story, not about the paintings themselves. We are so susceptible to context. To provenance, to criticism, to popular opinion and packaging—all that surrounds and attends. A truth that the artist, or at the very least, his agent, seems to understand well. The viewers will do well to remind themselves that it is the pictures themselves that matter. Look into the face of the young woman in the Penfield Gallery and decide for yourself what is true.

KAT'S EYES MOVED down to the reproductions of the paintings at the bottom of the page. She breathed a sigh of gratitude that the ones the *Time*s had selected did not show her face, or indeed any of her, full on. In one she was sitting on the edge of the bed, her face half turned away. The thin spine of a book visible in her hand. She felt a rush as she recognized the faded red cover. It was Rimbaud, but she could not remember which one. She bent closer to the photo. She had found it in a shop on the rue Mayet in Montparnasse. The margins had been filled with small, scrawled notes from a previous owner. Messages from a stranger. She had read them as she read the book, so that the stranger's voice and opinions had become intertwined with those of the author. To this day, she could not be certain how much of what she knew of Rimbaud was really his thoughts and how much was the opinions of her fellow reader. She examined her face in profile. Although she was entirely familiar to herself, she doubted that anyone would be likely to identify her from this particular image.

Her eyes moved down to another, unfamiliar image reprinted at the end of the article. One of the later paintings, it was a close-up of the back of her head. Her hair was gathered loosely from the nape of her neck, held fast between the teeth of a large jade-green comb in the shape of a serpent. She looked at it closely. Although she could not remember ever having owned a comb like it, a faint sense of familiarity dogged her as she examined its intricate curves. Had she forgotten?

The review was also accompanied by a photo of Daniel, leaning forward and gazing impatiently at the camera. His hands, resting on his knees in the foreground of the photo, appeared unnaturally large. Kat examined his face, its hard planes more prominent rendered in the stark grays of the newsprint.

She was still studying it when the phone rang, startling her. Even with the volume turned all the way down, the sound reverberated off the bare walls. While her eyes lingered on the newspaper in front of her, Kat reached behind her and felt along the counter for the handset.

"Hello?"

There was a brief pause. When it came, the voice on the other end of the line was flat.

"Did you think you could run away from me again?"

She recognized the voice before the sentence was completed. Staring into his eyes in the newspaper before her, she caught her breath.

And then he laughed. Suddenly, graciously, convincingly.

After a moment she laughed, too. Eagerly, gratefully, not entirely convinced.

"Daniel."

"Hello, Kat."

Again there was silence. It was her turn to speak. "I'm sorry . . . I shouldn't have just come to the gallery last night."

"Yes, maybe not the best time or place for a reunion." His voice was smooth, betraying no trace of emotion.

"No, I suppose not. I'm sorry . . . we didn't get a chance to talk. Congratulations on the show . . . ." While she spoke, her eyes strayed to the window, following the guard across the street as he approached a dark blue sedan in the diplomatic parking space in front of the embassy. She watched him stop short as it pulled away suddenly from the curb.

"Yeah—it's all a bit mad at the moment. Listen, can we meet up? I'm at the Dorchester." She heard a male voice saying something in the background. "Actually, how is this afternoon, if you're free?"

Kat had stood up and was crossing the drawing room, moving deeper into the house, away from the front windows. How had he found her? Her name was on the guest list, but it was her married name. How had he known it was her?

"So, you'll come, then? This afternoon—say, two o'clock?"

The words were out of her mouth and the phone back in the cradle before she registered what had happened. She looked around the empty room for witnesses, but there were none.

chapter seven

The short, balding man from the gallery answered the door. Upon seeing Kat, he paused only briefly to run his eyes down the length of her body and then back up to her face in that involuntary way some men do. Opening the door wide, he smiled brilliantly at her.

"You must be Katherine. I'm Daniel's agent, Martin Whittaker."

Although he stood very straight, he must have been only five and a half feet tall. He was slightly larger on the bottom than he was on the top, which had the effect of making him seem closer to the ground than he actually was. She took his outstretched hand, which felt small and soft in her own.

"Come in, come in," he said, ushering her into the large sitting room of the suite. "Daniel will be along shortly. Do make yourself comfortable."

Hotel rooms. Kat had always found them such odd, artificial places. She had spent too much time in them while she was working. She looked across the room. Glass doors spanned the far wall, leading to a terrace overlooking Hyde Park. The decor was more modern than she remembered of the Dorchester. Less chintz. When had she stayed here last? Could it have been ten years ago when she had first moved to London? The firm had put her up here while she looked for a flat.

The city had seemed so different to her then than it did now. Everything about her life in London back then had seemed so wonderfully new. As an expat she had not known how long she would actually be here. Daily life had a veneer of the temporary that had made her appreciate it more. At some point in the past ten years, her perspective had shifted and all that had been exotic and fleeting had become comfortable and familiar.

Kat unwound her scarf and took off her coat. Too tense to sit in a cab, she had walked from Holland Park, an alternative that had proven ill-advised, as her newly acquired paranoia had impelled her to hide behind her sunglasses, scanning the faces around her and altering her course every time she thought she saw anyone she knew, anyone who could have been at Penfields, anyone who might make the connection between her face and the face on the walls. This had resulted in a rather circuitous route through the park at a rather frenetic pace.

She was warm. Her face felt flushed. She stood with her coat in her hand for an awkward moment while Martin regarded her impassively, before it occurred to him to offer to take it from her. Once he had done so, he didn't seem to know what to do with it, finally laying it over the back of an armchair. Would she like tea? After ten years in England there was only one answer to that question. This seemed more within Martin's area of familiarity, as he ably picked up the phone to ring room service.

With Martin occupied, Kat moved toward the wall of glass. The park stretched out in the distance, brown and bare in the meager winter sunshine. It was an unusual perspective on a place that she knew so well. She and Will walked through it nearly every day. It seemed so close, a sensation enhanced by the fact that from this height she could neither see nor hear the moat of traffic that separated her from it. The sun was so low that the hotel's shadow stretched nearly to the Serpentine.

Martin put down the phone and walked over to stand beside her at the glass doors, smiling a wide, solicitous smile at her. He was dressed simply, but the carefully curated materials belied what at first glance was modest attire. She took in the soft cashmere sweater, the solid silver cuff links, and, most notably, the watch. A vintage Piaget, it looked in perfect condition. Encircling his wrist loosely, it moved smoothly as he raised his hand to his chin, coming to rest against his shirt cuff, so that she could almost feel the weight of it. Everything about him spoke of wealth, while simultaneously dismissing it in favor of the most discriminating taste and pedigree.

"Did you enjoy the show?" he asked, turning briefly from the windows.

Kat regarded him with mild surprise. He recognized her from the gallery? He had been so absorbed in his own conversation that she was surprised she had even registered on him. Or had Daniel told him she had been there?

"I did."

"Daniel is getting marvelous reviews. We are very pleased. Very pleased, indeed."

He paused and after a moment turned and regarded her with a practiced thoughtful expression.

"Of course, all of this has been a long time coming for him. Wouldn't you agree?"

Kat wasn't sure where he was heading, but was uncomfortable with his sudden familiarity. "Has it?"

"Well, at least the twenty years since I met him in Paris." He paused, letting the reference break over her. "I believe I have you to thank for that, Katherine."

It was at this moment that she heard the door to the bedroom open and she and Martin turned at once to see Daniel emerge, unshaven and more wrinkled than the evening before. Gone was the immaculately tailored suit, replaced with jeans and a shirt that looked as though he might have slept in it.

He strode effortlessly through the room and through the years between them to kiss her lightly on both cheeks, startling her with his presence and his proximity, as his face brushed hers. He smelled like coffee and shampoo, and she laughed out loud despite herself. It seemed such an odd greeting. She wondered whether it was always so strange to greet old lovers. To have had that intimacy and to then to go back to being polite acquaintances seemed so affected. So dishonest. Although she could not think what would have been more honest.

Distracted, she glanced at Martin as he looked on, smiling broadly. Was he still here?

It took her a moment to realize that the voice she heard talking to Daniel was her own.

Was he really asking her about the weather? Was she really replying? She glanced at Martin again. Was he really going to stay?

The knock on the door signaling the arrival of room service brought her back to herself. As Martin excused himself to answer it, Daniel opened the glass doors leading to the terrace, letting in the cold air and the traffic noise from Park Lane below. Looking back at Kat, he inclined his head toward the terrace.

"Come," he said softly. "See the view."

Kat crossed the room and stepped out to join Daniel on the terrace, only too glad to be leaving Martin inside. After waiting in the cold air for a moment to make sure Martin wasn't going to tag along, she turned her attention to Daniel. Alone at last. They stood in silence, the small talk having evaporated in the open air. As he leaned forward gazing over the park, his hands braced on the railing, she had a chance to study his profile.

There had always been something faintly indecent about

his lower lip. A slightly crooked, surprisingly soft, pink interruption of his strong, lined face. She wanted time to examine it. To remember it. She needed to study him. To place him in a context she could make sense of. There were things that she had forgotten. Important things. She needed just another minute to get a grip on him again, to figure it out. Perhaps she didn't know him now, but she knew what the hollow of his throat smelled like and the way his hands felt on her skin. She knew the sounds he made in the dark.

He glanced at her sideways, causing her to blush, before turning back to the park. Again, older. And again, unnervingly, Daniel.

He turned to face her again. She could see him dismissing thoughts and looking for more appropriate things to say. The Daniel she had known didn't know how to do that and had no interest in learning. The fact that he was trying so hard was new. He looked tired, she thought. She wanted to help him, but couldn't think what to say.

"How long have you lived in London?" he asked finally.

Although he was trying his best to appear relaxed, his features seemed to be in constant motion, struggling to avoid settling into a particular expression, although which particular one was not clear.

His manner was so incongruous that for a fleeting moment she questioned whether she could have remembered it wrong. The way it ended. Or the whole of it even. Or maybe time had simply smoothed off the sharp edges.

"About ten years now."

About two feet of flat metal railing separated them. Beneath them seven floors of hotel. Beyond them only the sky and the tops of the bare trees.

"Do you like it?"

It was as if he were reading from a script. Saying the things that people are meant to say if they have not seen each other in many years. Slipping into character, she conjured a response.

"I love it. It's a wonderful, vibrant city and it is great to be so close to the rest of Europe. Only two hours and you're in Paris . . . ."

She blushed and let her voice trail off. Paris. The scene of the crime. The repository of memory. Maybe she couldn't handle small talk with him after all.

It was true, Paris was only two hours away. Not that she went there often. They had bought a French company a few years ago and she had been there for a fortnight handling the negotiations. It had been an intense deal and she'd had little free time. She had sneaked out of the closing dinner early and gone for a walk along the Right Bank, telling herself she needed to clear her head. As she walked along the river, seeing things that were not there, she felt the city watching her back with familiar eyes. In the glow of the yellow bulbs it all seemed unchanged. It was harder to forget in a city that wears its past so conspicuously.

She had thought of the studio on the rue Garancière. She traced the path there in her memory. Across the Pont Royal and through Saint-Germain-des-Prés. She could be there in ten minutes. She started over the bridge, its cobblestones lit up by garlands of lights. Her shadow moved ahead of her, splintered and broken on the uneven stones. Lifting her gaze, she was surprised to see the bridge disappear before her. The arch meant that she could no longer see the other side. Instead, it seemed to end at its apex. She imagined the cars and people dropping off the high curve into the dark river below and strained to hear the splashes as they entered the water.

She stopped. It was too late. She turned back.

On her way back to her hotel she walked past the Tuileries—trying to identify one tree from the many through the bars of the fence. It seemed that she should be able to do so. Whatever else was gone, Paris remained.

She swam through the eddies of cars on the place de la Concorde, emerging on the other side in front of her hotel both more alert and more tired than she had been when she started out. Back in her room she felt the kind of loneliness that comes of full days and empty hotel rooms. But it was brief. There were calls to return and work to be done.

There had been only one other visit to Paris. She and Jonathan had gone there for a weekend just before Will was born. It had been his idea—a surprise for her. She had cried in the taxi from Gare du Nord to their hotel as the city unfolded around them, her feet not even touching the ground. The kind of hysterical, uncontrollable sobs that you cry as a child. She could not stop the tears. Could not catch her breath. Jonathan had been alarmed. He had never seen her cry like that. She had attributed it to hormones and he had accepted the explanation. Later she had felt bad about the lie. Up to that point, her history with Daniel had been a lie of omission. She had never told anyone about Daniel. He remained hers alone. Sacred and apart.

A sudden awareness of the prolonged silence put a stop to her ruminations. She looked up to find that Daniel was studying her. He made no attempt to fill the gap in conversation. Even when she broke away from his gaze, she could feel his eyes still on her. She laced her fingers together nervously on the railing. Did it used to feel like this when he looked at her? She remembered it differently. Turning back to face him, it was her turn to grasp at conversational straws.

"Congratulations on your show."

He turned away from her to gaze out over the park. His voice, when it came, competed with the wind coming off the park and the traffic noise rising from the street below.

"Did you see it all?"

"Yes."

He smiled. An abbreviated smile—pressing his lips together, and took in a deep breath, exhaling his words into the air above the park.

"I suppose I should have . . ." He paused, still gazing out over the trees. It seemed to her that her presence was unnecessary for the conversation. That it wasn't really she whom he was addressing. "Look, no one knows who the girl in the paintings is. Even Martin didn't know until last night."

She could not think what to say and so remained silent.

He paused again and glanced over his shoulder at her. "I suppose I should have asked you." At this, he turned away again and laughed.

She shivered, suddenly chilled, and waited to see if he would continue. The wind coming off the park was beginning to pick up. Daniel turned back toward her, but looked past her. She had forgotten how pale his eyes were. They seemed to be the exact same color as the cloudless winter sky, as if she were looking through him to the sky beyond. She thought about how much else she might have forgotten.

"Listen, Kat," Daniel continued, once again addressing the congregation of tall plane trees on the edge of the park. "I know some of the paintings were probably a surprise to you. Martin thought we should talk to you to assure you that we will keep you a secret. And to make sure you were okay with all this."

He glanced back at her briefly, as if to make sure that she was still there. "I told him that you would be. At the same time, we recognize that you were a part of this and we are prepared to compensate you for that." He recited the words flatly, automatically. She imagined him discussing this with Martin. She heard the words he had just spoken coming out of Martin's mouth.

Her face felt suddenly hot against the cold breeze. The naked trees beyond him, stripped bare of their leaves by the wind, seemed to beseech her with their sharp, twisted appendages.

"A bit late to be asking this, don't you think, Daniel?" Her voice, when it came, was small and sharp.

A moment passed and she thought maybe he had not heard her over the wind. Then he turned slowly to face her, his features finally stopping at an expression, although one that she did not recal. She returned his gaze, suddenly remembering that she was stronger than she knew. That she was capable of much more than she realized.

"Yes. I suppose it is." This time his voice was heavy with sarcasm. "But it's not as if you left a forwarding address. And it is not as if you weren't willing at the time. You remember Paris, don't you, Kat? I admit that I have wondered since then what it was for you. The hope of immortality? Or just plain vanity? Either way, it looks like you got what you were after."

"That was twenty years ago, Daniel. I don't remember giving you permission to keep painting me forever."

It was the word "permission." His features hardened into a mask of barely controlled rage and he stepped closer to her, so close that she could feel his breath on her face. There was so much fury in his eyes that she wondered for a moment if he was going to hit her.

"And I don't remember giving you permission to . . ."

"Stop!" Her shouted word had the desired effect of preventing him from finishing his sentence, but she knew that it was powerless against the long-pent-up memory gathering inside of her, savage from neglect.

She could hear him breathing. When he spoke again, his

voice was just above a whisper. "I need to know why. You owe me that."

"What exactly did you think we were going to do? Raise a baby in a tiny, filthy studio?" She shot the words into the wind.

Before he could reply, Martin appeared in the doorway, clearing his throat and making little attempt to hide the fact that he had been listening in. The wind pulled at some papers he held in his right hand. Daniel stepped back as the smaller man moved to position himself between them. Daniel turned away but she could see his shoulders rising and falling under the thin fabric of his shirt and knew that he was breathing hard.

"Listen, Katherine." Martin's voice was even and low, making her realize how loud theirs had become. She forced herself to look away from Daniel and to focus on him. "Daniel has a real chance here—his work is finally getting the kind of exposure and attention that it deserves. You know at least part of what he has been through to get here. We are just trying to do the right thing here. We want to make sure that his work can continue to be seen. If you take a look at what we are proposing, I think you will find that we are fully prepared to give you a reasonable slice of the pie."

She reached out and took the papers from Martin's extended hand without glancing at them. Martin watched her expectantly, a willfully sympathetic expression fixed firmly to his poached face.

She glanced at Daniel's back. The breeze grabbed at the papers in her hand and she was tempted to open her fingers and allow the wind to take them.

"I don't want any pie."

It was the kind of sudden and dramatic exit that she had never quite been able to pull off. She turned on her heel and stalked off the terrace. Pausing to grab her coat off the chair, she passed the open door to the bedroom and glimpsed an empty champagne bottle, upside down in a silver bucket on the floor beside the bed. A glass, or maybe two glasses, lay beside it, half hidden under folds of discarded bedding. Heart racing, she made her way down the long hallway without looking back and jabbed at the call button for the lift. It arrived mercifully swiftly. As she stepped inside, her face hot, she heard the hurried footsteps as the doors began to close. Instinctively, she retreated farther into the lift, pressing her back against the dark wood paneling. Despite all her entreaties to a higher power, a hand interrupted the closing doors. It was not the hand that she expected.

Martin stepped into the lift and let the doors slide closed after him. They stood facing the closed doors. She could feel her heart beating erratically inside her chest. She wondered if Martin could hear it as well. He turned toward her. She focused on the indicator panel above his head, as it counted down the floors.

"Look, Katherine. I know all this must be quite a shock to you. Not just the paintings, but seeing Daniel again."

"You don't know anything about me." She kept her eyes fixed on the indicator as they descended.

Seven.

Six.

"You may not believe this, but Daniel is trying to do the right thing. The truth is that he doesn't have to give you anything."

"Good. I don't want anything from him."

Five.

Four.

Kat glanced down briefly at Martin's blurred reflection in the brass doors in front of them, his smart outfit reduced to wide smudges of color. What had Daniel told him about her? About them?

Three.

Two.

"I would strongly advise you to take what we're offering and go back to your life. This is Daniel's time, let him have it."

"Who decided that this is his time? You?"

One.

Ground.

The doors to the lift slipped open soundlessly and stealing a glance to her left Kat saw Martin's soft face tilted earnestly toward her, his neck overflowing the confines of his heavily starched collar. Exiting the lift, she paused to get her bearings, and felt something alight gently on her arm. Looking down, she saw his short, pale fingers, like caterpillars, on her sleeve.

"Just think about it. You owe him as much." His voice sounded kind. "It would be a shame if we had to do this publicly."

He paused and took his hand off her arm. She thought maybe he was done and she began to move away from him.

"You're married now, aren't you, Katherine?"

She stopped instantly and turned back to him. He smiled, his eyes receding into the flesh on his face. She felt as if she had been punched. Glancing around the yellow and black marble lobby, at the uniformed staff bustling about on the slick floors and conversing in hushed tones, she felt that someone should have heard the threat. That it didn't belong in a place like this. That it would have stood out from the other muted words being spoken around them.

She turned away from him and, without looking back, walked out of the hotel. Eschewing the black cabs queuing in the curved driveway, she crossed the four lanes of busy traffic on Park Lane, emerging in the peace of Hyde Park. She let her feet carry her through the park, treading on the paths she had looked down on just minutes before. If she looked back, she would have seen the balcony of Daniel's room. Was he still there? Watching her as she walked away? How small he would have seemed from such a distance.

She was already well into the park before she remembered her paranoia, but the temperature had dropped and there were fewer people on the paths than there had been earlier this afternoon. As she crossed from Hyde Park into Kensington Gardens, the lines of trees revealed themselves and the seeming wildness of the landscape gave way to pattern. The sharp point of the spire of Saint Mary Abbots Church was visible above the tops of the trees. He thought she wanted royalties? Money? Was that what this was all about? Was that why he had wanted to see her? As she grew closer the trees gestured wildly at her in the wind, a mute warning.

She closed her eyes, remembering how the sun had come out that afternoon. She had sat in her eighteenth-century-poetry class and let the instructor's words float past her and out the open window where the city shone under a slick layer of rain. All but one that had laid itself at her feet. One that needed no translation. "Sacrifice." A word that she had heard all her life and yet it was only now, hearing it in this foreign tongue, that she felt she truly understood it.

She thought that it was terrifying to realize what you were capable of. She had heard her voice on the phone to the clinic, saying words that she could not remember learning in any language class. She could see herself waiting outside the bank to withdraw the money and then taking the short journey on the crowded Métro. Breathing the thick, sooty underground air.

And then she is there, in the waiting room, alternately examining the severe metal edges of the receptionist's desk and counting the crooked floor tiles. Actively avoiding the faces around her, just as they are avoiding hers. She hears her name being called—both familiar and not in the smooth inflection of the native tongue. She has given her real name, feeling that it is important somehow that it be her name that is called and she who answers it.

She lies back on the table. Knees up, legs apart. The dark-skinned nurse sits beside her, hair smelling of almond oil, long fingers squeezing her hand, as she whispers comforting, French words—Kat's mind suddenly rigid, unwilling to translate. The insipid Monet print on the wall, its colors blending together even more through her tears. She doesn't move when she feels the tightening inside of her, the dull ache in the center of her. She has learned well to stay still for him.

And then it was done. Her incomprehension that the city looked much the same on the way back to the studio. Perhaps the air was a little warmer, the light a little colder. There were fewer people on the Métro and her shadow on the boulevard was shorter. Were it not for the dull ache and the slow, steady dripping between her legs, all might have been as it had been. She was grateful for this. She felt it was only right that she should be cut, damaged. That there should be a wound that she could feel. Real, physical evidence of what she had done.

Walking along the wide straight boulevard, she recognized the sharp buds on the trees. It was spring again. She recognized the smell of the city after the rain, the high-pitched buzz of the scooters, the creaking of the awnings being extended over the cafés. It was all suddenly familiar. She had been here before. Not everything was new anymore and some things never would be.

chapter eight

In Paris, Daniel hadn't seemed to have a job outside of painting, although to be fair she didn't really know what he did while she was in classes during the day. She had thought about asking, but was unsure that she wanted to know. And while he exhibited and sold some of his work, she doubted whether that was enough to support him, modest though his lifestyle was. She told herself that it was possible that he was living off the proceeds of some works that he had sold previously.

And yet, finding the bag of white powder at the back of the cupboard had not been a complete surprise. Dropping it lightly on the table, she had stared at it for a while. She thought about tasting it, but realized that would simply rule out sugar or salt. Not the confirmation she was looking for.

Confronted, he was unrepentant. "I do it for the money. For canvas, for paints, for brushes, for rent. I do what I need to do."

"Is that it, then? A noble end justifies the means?"

"I don't need to justify myself to anyone." He paused and when he continued he spoke slowly and deliberately. "Listen to me. What I want, more than anything, is to be great. To be remembered. More than rich or famous, or even happy. That is what I care about. And I am willing to do whatever is necessary for it."

"Maybe you need an agent."

He had stiffened. "I'm not interested in playing that game. Meeting with buyers, explaining my work, telling them what they want to hear, playing the artist. I don't care about any of that. I want to paint. I don't care about selling."

Kat picked up the bag of white powder from the table, feeling its scant weight in her palm. "We all sell something. Why not sell something you believe in?"

It was autumn in Paris. She could smell it in the air. That little hint of something almost like cold apples. Kat waited at the front window of the gallery. Dusk was gathering together into night and the shadows were disappearing. Daniel was not there, as she had known he would not be. A small student exhibit in an obscure gallery in a far corner of the Marais; she had seen a call for submissions for it on a board at school. Daniel had disdained to submit, but had not stopped her from doing so. His piece had been accepted.

The man she was expecting was the sixth attendee. Besides the artists themselves, there had been only five visitors that evening. Kat had counted. Although surprised to hear from her, he had agreed to come to the show and had not asked any questions. Harry Harper was a lion in the New York art world and an old friend of her mother's. Kat remembered him vaguely from her childhood, but had not seen him in many years. After all that time, he was little more than a familiar name in her memory, but she recognized him immediately when he came in through the door. An older man with un-likely dark hair, he did not smile, but greeted her cordially, taking her hand between his large smooth ones.

"Hello, Katherine."

"Mr. Harper. Thank you so much for coming."

He dismissed her sentiments. "Not at all. How is your mother? How unfortunate that I was unaware you were in Paris. Marie-Claire and I would have had you to dinner."

"That is very kind of you." She smiled at him and the con-versation abruptly stopped, as they moved from the darkness into the brightly lit gallery. She was uncomfortably aware of how he was now staring intently at her face in the sudden bright light. He seemed not to be fully conscious.

"Shall I show you the paintings?"

Shaking off the spell, he waved her off.

"If I may? Let me have a look around and I will tell you

whether anything catches my eye. That way, we will all know there is no favoritism at play." He spoke seriously, his expression grave.

As he moved toward the first wall of paintings, she returned to the window.

She was watching the streetlights come on as darkness set in when his reflection caught her eye in the glass. She followed his small, measured steps against the dim backdrop of the empty street. She saw the way he paused when he came to Daniel's work and stood back from it for a long moment, as if everything else in the room had suddenly become invisible. He continued around the room at the same measured pace, all the while sneaking glances back at Daniel's canvas. Flirting with it. Completing his slow circuit of the room, he returned to Kat. He indicated Daniel's painting on the far wall. "Is that the young artist you rang me about?"

"Yes." She smiled. "Daniel Blake."

"I see." He nodded. "Here is what I am going to do. I am going to put him in touch with an agent I know in the city who specializes in this sort of thing. Someone who has the collector base to support this type of work."

Extracting a business card from his breast pocket, he turned it over and wrote out a name and a phone number, speaking as he wrote. "He's an eager young fellow, but particularly good at nurturing the fragile temperament of the young artist. And this . . ." He looked toward Daniel's painting. ". . . deserves to be nurtured. I am quite surprised that he does not have representation. He is at the École, you said?"

"He was at the École."

He held out the card to her. "Of course."

Kat reached to take the card from his fingers. "I can't thank you enough for this."

But he was no longer listening to her. Still grasping the card with one hand, he reached up in a fluid motion with the other and touched her cheek softly. His eyes were no longer focused on her, but rather seemed to be looking through her, somewhere into the dark street behind her, his intent gaze impossible to define. She thought she detected the faintest trace of a smile on his face, but when she looked closer it was gone.

Just as Kat was about to fill the silence, he abruptly dropped his hand from her face and relinquished the card. "I am sure that many people have told you that you have your mother's eyes. As you do. But it would seem that you also have your mother's eye."

He smiled. A little sadly, she thought. "Give her my regards."

Kat had collected her coat and was about to leave when the seventh visitor came through the door. She saw Kat and for the smallest moment her face registered what looked like disappointment, but it was replaced immediately by something else. Something she had prepared earlier.

Elizabeth smiled and made her way across the empty room, pulling at the fingers of her gloves. Kat was struck by how different she looked. Her ample curves swathed in a stylish long black coat, she seemed slighter.

"Kat!" she exclaimed, leaning in to kiss her on both cheeks.

"I saw some flyers for the show at school and I took a chance you would be here."

"I didn't realize there were flyers done for this show."

Elizabeth dismissed the comment blithely. "Oh, well, maybe one of the other artists had them done. Never mind." She smiled brightly, her face flushed from the cold. "I came to see you. How are you?"

"Well," Kat replied. The word hung in the air between her and the expectant look on Elizabeth's face until Kat caved. "How are you?"

"Fantastic." Elizabeth exhaled. "Just finished my paper on Rimbaud. Early, if you can believe that! So now I'm free to have a little fun."

Kat suppressed a smile. Elizabeth finished every assignment early.

"I've come to make you an offer you cannot refuse. Some of us are going to Prague this weekend. If we catch a flight after class tomorrow afternoon, we can be there in time for dinner. Jean-Paul has a cousin whose flat we can use. You should come."

"This weekend?"

"This weekend."

Kat pursed her lips in the manner of someone considering something and waited what seemed to her to be the appropriate amount of time before replying.

"Thanks. It sounds fun, but I think I am going to pass."

"Oh, come on. It will be divine. The flat is in the Castle District. Jean-Paul says it has the most fantastic view of the

Charles Bridge and the city." She grinned at Kat. "If all of that doesn't convince you, I hear that a certain aspiring senator may be in Prague this weekend . . . . Who knows? If you aren't there, someone else may very well snap him up. Come on, what else are you going to do this weekend?"

"Thanks, but I still think I am going to say no."

Elizabeth paused and regarded her for a long moment. She seemed to be choosing her next words carefully.

"What are you doing, Kat?"

"What do you mean?"

"I mean, what are you doing? You do realize that you have not been out of Paris since we got here in April?" Elizabeth's tone was accusatory. "You are barely present in classes and no one ever sees you outside of school. I just don't get it. You come three thousand miles to Paris and spend all your time locked up in a studio."

Elizabeth paused momentarily before continuing. "You must know who he is by now."

Kat held her gaze. "I do."

Elizabeth shook her head and adjusted her handbag, slipping its delicate chain-link strap farther up on her shoulder. She turned and took a step away, but stopped and looked back, a rueful smile on her face. "Suit yourself. I just think you are going to regret this—not traveling, not taking advantage of being here and experiencing everything."

As she heard the words, she knew that Elizabeth was right. Paris was meant to have been about her. The program, travel, adventure. Although she was doing well in school, she was aware that rather than immersing herself in it, she was focusing on it impatiently in order to devote the remainder of her time to Daniel.

She had come all this way to Paris only to see the inside of her classrooms and a small studio tucked under the eaves on the rue Garancière. To rush from one to the other through the sunlight on the wide boulevards and to gaze out at the rooftops of the city at night through a grimy window. Paris, which had been her focus for so long, had become peripheral. Certainly her plans for travel had fallen away. Rome, Barcelona, Prague—were all abandoned. She gave them up for something that burned more brightly.

After that day, Elizabeth stopped trying.

Daniel had taken the business card with the name and phone number scrawled on the back in Harry Harper's angular hand. He didn't ask how or where she had gotten it. She did not tell him. She had not waited for, nor had she expected, any response from him. She simply wanted him to have it and now he did. Some months later she had seen the card, streaked and creased, under some crushed tubes of paint in a bowl on the windowsill. She had been pleasantly surprised that he still had it.

chapter nine

The downstairs dining room at the Stanhope was more formal than Kat remembered, although she was sure that it was the fault of her memory and not due to any change in the decor. The Mayfair institution remained utterly indifferent to fashion. She was one of only three women seated in the dimly lit room and the only one not clad entirely in shades of black or gray. A tall waiter in a white jacket approached and leaned down into the incandescent glow of the white tablecloth to take her drink order, his eyes catching momentarily on her brightly patterned scarf. After he left, she removed the scarf, tucking it into her handbag. However, she could do nothing about her hair color, which remained an affront to the muted color scheme.

Kat saw there was a message from Jonathan's parents' number. Willfully defying the Stanhope's ban on mobile phones in the dining room, she brought hers to her ear to listen. It was a chatty message from Will, but she was unable to make out everything he was saying. She pressed the phone closer to her ear in an effort to compensate for the distance between the phone and his mouth.

Secreting the phone back in her bag, she waited, cocooned in the plush brown banquette and the hushed tones of conversation, brought low by the ecclesiastic atmosphere of the room. She could actually feel the heat from the lamp above her. In the whispered voices around her, she thought she might have heard her name. She pushed back further into her cushion.

A few tables away, a young couple was seated opposite each other in high-backed, mushroom-colored fabric chairs. They talked quietly in a Slavic language Kat could not identify, leaning toward each other into the glow of the lamp that hung low above the table. The man seemed to be endeavoring to explain something, while the woman nodded solemnly, interjecting the occasional syllable. Although Kat could not understand what they were saying, she noted the way that their hands remained on their respective sides of the table, and how the woman toyed with the stem of her water glass.

She remembered another overheard conversation in a foreign tongue. She and Daniel had stopped briefly at a small café on a side street in Saint-Germain. It was early in the afternoon and only one other table was occupied. A young couple sat tucked against the side of the building. As their voices rose with emotion in the nearly empty café, Kat could not help but hear.

"But you love me . . . ." The girl said it over and over in French.

Glancing around the empty café, the boy shushed her, half soothing, half smothering.

After some more hushed conversation, the boy left. The girl sat alone in silence for a while, and then rose and made her way out of the café, blinking in the bright sunlight, her tears still wet on her cheeks. Wounded, she moved slowly down the street while people flowed around her. Seeing her watch the girl leave, Daniel asked what was wrong.

"It's just sad."

"What?"

Kat regarded him, suddenly wide-eyed. "You don't speak French."

He appeared unbowed by her incredulity. "I know enough to get by."

"I could teach you."

"I don't want to learn. I like that I am disconnected. I think I see things differently that way."

"Perhaps. But speaking another language is also a disconnection. It's like a mask. The things that I say in French, even the things that I think, are all slightly different from what they are in English, and so while it's still me, it's a slightly different version of me."

He had looked at her quizzically. "There are no other versions of me."

A slight rustling noise brought Kat back to the red brick town house on Upper Brook Street. She looked up, suddenly aware of a large fur coat motionless next to the table. Long slim claws clutched at its edges. Were it not for the manicure, they might very well have been feline. A waiter appeared and grasped the edge of the low-hanging pendant light above the table, moving it aside to allow the coat and the small, slender woman inside it to slide in beside Kat, trapping them together.

"Christ, it is cold," Jorie said by way of greeting.

Satisfied that she had been seen in the coat, Jorie divested herself of it, relinquishing it to a waiter along with her drink order. She appeared unfazed by Kat's confession, delivered in hushed, rushed tones. Kat didn't tell her everything there was to tell. But she told her some things, which was more than she had ever done.

"Well, of course it is you in the paintings, my dear. I knew that the minute I saw them."

Kat pulled her hands into the sleeves of her sweater as the waiter returned with their drinks. "Is it that obvious?"

"Maybe not if you don't know that you two have a history. After all, it has been a while and even you have aged." Kat let the comment pass. "Although in future it's probably best to avoid standing next to them."

"Do you think Daniel knew what Martin was going to say to me? Do you think he sent him to say those things?"

Jorie swirled the wine in her glass, the bright ruby liquid passing dangerously close to the rim. "Depends. Do you think he could hate you that much?"

Kat looked down, unwilling to answer. Jorie waited, taking a sip from her glass before setting it down on the table. "What exactly went down with you two?"

Kat watched a single drop of Bordeaux slip slowly down the outside of Jorie's glass, tracing the gentle curve of the bowl, then sliding elegantly down the stem and out onto the foot before sinking into the parched tablecloth, its bright hue immediately reduced to a spreading suggestion of pink, half hidden under the edge of the glass.

"Kat? Hello?" Jorie was waving her hand back and forth in front of her, a vexed expression on her face.

Looking up to meet her friend's eyes, Kat opted for the lesser of the questions.

"Yes, I think it is entirely possible that he hates me that much."

"I saw the paintings. Hate is not the emotion that comes immediately to mind."

Smoothing the folded newspaper on the starched white tablecloth between them, Kat's hand brushed lightly over the image of the painting of herself on the unmade bed. She turned the paper around so that it faced Jorie. The painting appeared both small and significant inside the bright white circle of light.

"If I asked you how I was different from the girl in this painting, what would you say?"

Jorie raised an eyebrow and then glanced down at the picture. "Well, clothed springs immediately to mind . . . ."

"Just, please. Tell me what you see."

Jorie sighed and pulled the paper closer to her, looking intently at it for a moment. "I don't know." She pushed it back at Kat. "Young."

"Can you tell that I'm in love?"

"I don't think love is an emotion you can see on someone's face. I mean, happiness or anger or fear, yes. But love? I don't know what love looks like."

Jorie paused on hearing her words and laughed lightly. "Maybe that is my problem."

Neither one of them spoke for a moment. "At the gallery . . ." Kat began hesitantly. "It was like seeing someone I hadn't seen in such a long time . . ."

"Well, yes . . . . When did you last see him?"

"No. Not Daniel."

Kat looked at her friend for a moment, considering whether to go on. Jorie regarded her over the rim of her wineglass, waiting.

"Honestly, what is with you lately? It's like talking to a mute."

"It's just that I remember everything." Kat let the words tumble out of her. "I remember every moment. Every day. Every night. I remember every inch of his body, the way he felt, the way he tasted, the smell of his skin. But even more than all of that, and even more clearly, I remember the girl in the paintings. Who she was and what she wanted and what she knew for sure. And I don't know that anymore. Not lately, anyhow."

Jorie was silent long enough for Kat to begin to regret what she had said.

"I haven't asked you how you are doing. About your mother."

Kat hesitated, caught off guard by the sudden shift in subject. "Haven't you?"

Jorie shook her head.

"I'm fine."

"Yes. I can see."

Kat sat in the awkward silence. Silhouettes of waiters glided silently among the tables.

When Jorie spoke again her voice was impatient. "What is it that you want from him?"

"I don't want anything. Certainly not money."

"Brilliant. Sign the papers and it's over." Jorie tilted her head back and drained the remainder of the wine from her glass, replacing it firmly on the table as if to signal that it was sorted. There was something in her eyes that Kat did not recognize. Not quite anger, but its close kin.

"It was over a long time ago," Kat mumbled, leaning back into the banquette, away from the light.

THERE WERE SURPRISINGLY few questions about her early return from Paris that spring. People seemed all too willing to make their own assumptions. Homesickness, trouble with the academic program, a simple change of heart. Any one of the fickle reasons of youth.

Her time there had always hovered noiselessly over her history. A gap defined only as her year in Paris. Eliciting wistful smiles and nods of understanding, it seldom called for any additional explanation. People were happy to fill it in with their own memories, their own fantasies. Talking of the food and the wine and the cafés, all the things that had existed in the background of her time there.

Although no one ever admitted it, she was fairly certain that she had some help getting into business school. After all, while her grades were good, she doubted that as a French-literature major she was at the top of their wish list. To this day, she couldn't fully answer why she had chosen business school, but it probably had something to do with the fact that it was the furthest thing from what she had thought she wanted.

She had been more surprised than most to find that she excelled at it. Once she realized that the quantitative aspect was in fact only a small part of it, it had come quite easily to her. But the real key, she knew, was that she had let go of fear. On some basic level, she understood that it couldn't hurt her. That none of it was real.

After Paris, New York provided the chaos that she needed to hide herself in. It seemed at first to be peopled not by individuals, but by archetypes. Were one to vanish, she felt certain that another would simply take its place. In the beginning, she found it nearly impossible to do things that required stillness or reflection. Listening to music, reading, going to the theater. The nights were the most difficult. There was only the sound of the cars moving unseen in the streets below her window. In her second year of school she took on an internship with a large bank and threw herself into it. She was looking for something to fill her up. To fill up the hole that she could feel inside of her.

She had several offers on graduation. She took the riskiest and most demanding one with a precocious, precarious start-up. Things moved quickly. There was ample room for creativity and little time for fear. It ate up her days and her nights and she became hooked. Addicted to the adrenaline and to the constant future focus. There was no today and there had certainly not been a yesterday. What mattered was only tomorrow and tomorrow.

SHE HAD SEEN Elizabeth at a party in New York about a year after she came back from Paris. Someone's birthday at the Plaza. Elizabeth had just returned, having stayed on to complete the second year of the program. Kat had almost not recognized the slender, elegant blonde who had greeted her. There was considerably less of her than there had been in Paris. The two had made small talk, discussing their summer plans and sharing information about people they knew in common, politely skirting around the edges of her early departure. Kat noticed that almost all traces of her Southern accent were gone. She seemed to be, Kat thought with a smile, the epitome of

New York style. Later on, as Kat was leaving the party, Elizabeth intercepted her by the door.

"I don't know if telling you this is the right thing to do." Elizabeth spoke quickly. "I saw Daniel."

Kat didn't respond immediately. It had been so long since she had heard his name spoken out loud. Elizabeth hesitated, her hands clasped in front of her. She seemed to be looking for an indication of whether she should go on. Kat wasn't sure whether she should give it to her, but the lure of hearing something—anything—about him proved too strong to resist.

"It didn't end well."

Kat surprised herself. A very tidy dismissal.

Elizabeth nodded sympathetically. After all, she had warned her of as much. "It was a few weeks after you left. He came to the flat. At first I wasn't sure it was him. He looked so . . . different."

She glanced at Kat and gave a small nervous laugh before looking away again. "Anyway, like I said, he came to the flat. It was late. He asked for you and I told him you weren't there—that you had gone back home. I didn't tell him where you were, just like you asked. And he left."

Here she paused again, eyes still downcast, the color rising in her cheeks. "And then about an hour later he came back, asking for you again. I assumed he was drunk or something. Obviously. And that maybe he had forgotten that he had been there before and so I told him again. That you were not there. That you had gone home. And he left." Elizabeth's voice was increasing in pitch, but her words were slowing down, as if they somehow weighed more now than when she had begun the story and she was having trouble getting them out.

"And then there was another knock on the door, just seconds after I had closed it. And there he was, just standing there, like it was the first time." She was no longer looking at Kat, but instead looking down as she clasped and unclasped her hands. "He just kept coming back . . . ."

Kat shivered, but said nothing, thinking of Daniel at the door, playing out the scene over and over again. Elizabeth looked up at her, finally meeting her eyes. And in the small silence between them, two things happened at once. Elizabeth decided not to finish her story and Kat guessed its ending. That Daniel would have continued to come back until he found a different conclusion.

"Oh Kat, I didn't mean for it to happen. Really, I didn't. I honestly don't know what got into me." Her face furrowed with desperation. "You won't . . . you won't say anything, will you? I mean, you wouldn't, would you?"

After a moment, the music started up again in the ballroom and Elizabeth looked toward it, regaining her composure. "I never saw him after that." She shrugged, in a small, quick way that looked like a twitch. "I thought you should know . . ." Her voice trailed off as she stood, sad and triumphant, uncharacteristically still inside the warm embrace of the Plaza's gilded grand ballroom, under the soft glow of its glittering chandeliers. After a moment, a small smile returned to Elizabeth's face and she turned back to Kat.

"Anyway. I guess you made the right choice."

Kat nodded. She should say something. It was her turn to do so. But she couldn't think what. A man in a dark suit hovered near them for a moment, slightly agitated, and then approached, placing a hand proprietarily on Elizabeth's shoulder. Kat looked up into a familiar face.

"There you are," Elizabeth said delightedly, reaching up to squeeze his hand. "Christopher, you remember Kat?"

"I do. Kat Lind. How are you? Haven't seen you since Paris." Kat leaned in for the obligatory double-kiss greeting of the recently repatriated. "Sorry to interrupt. Darling, would you come say hello to the Fiskes before they leave?"

Elizabeth startled at the name and hurried to excuse herself. Kat watched the pair dissolve into the crowded ballroom and turned to leave, letting go of the back of the delicate gilt cane chair she had been clutching.

It was at about this time that she had come upon her old camera in the back of her closet in her mother's house. There was unprocessed film in it. Standing in the darkroom, she watched as the curtain of rain appeared under the bath of chemicals. The last photos she had taken. She hadn't used her camera again after that day in the Tuileries. There were several shots like that, followed by a number that she had taken at high speed with the wider aperture. These were completely different, showing the shape of the individual raindrops. Elongated on the way down and fat and round as they bounced off the ground. All that had not been apparent in the moment.

The last photo on the roll showed the clear lines of trees against a fence as ghostlike figures moved in the foreground.

She studied it closely. The focal point of the photo was beyond the figures, rendering them oddly distant despite their relative proximity. She knew that one of the blurred figures was Daniel, leaving the Tuileries after their brief shelter under the tree. But she couldn't tell which one.

chapter ten

Kat noticed the silver sports car, parked at an angle and too far from the curb, before she noticed him. He leaned back on the car easily, arms folded across his chest, eyes on the house in front of him. It was partially hidden under a cobweb of scaffolding, while being repainted in the approved shade of eggshell white. He hadn't seen her yet, but it was too late for her to turn around. She glanced down the street. No sign of the neighbor or of the neighbor's driver. No sign of the security guard at the Greek embassy. The road was empty of traffic. He was still staring at the house when she stopped in front of him.

"What are you doing here?"

"Kat." His eyes came upon her slowly. Despite where he was, he seemed surprised to see her. "I came to see you. You live here?" He said the last word with emphasis.

"Yes."

He smiled.

"What?"

"It just seems like we are both a lot more than two hours away from Paris."

Kat regarded him silently, not moving from her spot on the pavement. He squinted at her for a moment with an expression that seemed equal parts contrite and amused. "I came to say I am sorry."

"Yes. I imagine you are."

He shook his head and smiled ruefully at her. "Listen, do you think we could lay down our weapons for just a moment? Or do you need to take a few more shots at me for yesterday?"

Kat was unbalanced by his breeziness. Where was the rage she had seen in his eyes yesterday? She could not figure out exactly what circumstances had rendered her the angry one and him the rational one. She remembered it being the other way around.

Across the street, the security guard at the Greek embassy eyed them lazily as he emerged from the side of the building, a paper cup clutched in his hand. His blue jacket, emboldened by its official crest, was pulled taut across his middle, secured by a single, brave button. She had trouble imagining him springing into action to fend off an invasion by Troy or some other crisis.

Turning back to Daniel, she cocked her head and regarded him. "Where's Martin? I'm surprised he let you out by yourself."

"Funny girl." He said it as if he were discovering, in that moment, that she was, in fact, a funny girl. That in remembering other things about her, he had forgotten that detail.

Kat shifted the flowers in her arms. She should really put them in water. A car drove down the road and she noted with alarm that it slowed as it passed by. Had the driver recognized her? Or him? She watched the next car nervously as it passed and noticed that as it slowed, it swerved slightly toward the center of the road. She realized with relief that it had slowed simply in order to avoid Daniel's car, the side of which was sticking out into the road.

She turned her attention back to Daniel. Of course she could not invite him in, but she was beginning to realize that the pavement in front of her house was not the place for this conversation either.

"What do you want, Daniel?"

"There is something that I want to show you. Will you come with me?"

Kat intended to refuse. Daniel pushed himself off the car and bent down toward that door. There was no reason that she should go with him. His shirt pulled taut across his shoulders as he turned sideways and bent slightly to catch the handle. His other hand reached for her, palm up, fingers slightly curled. She wondered what it was that he could want her to see.

She stole a glance across the street at the security guard, who had settled into his chair by the embassy's front door and was sipping from the paper cup while perusing what was likely today's Page Three girl. Wouldn't he, a trained professional, spring into action if there was anything untoward in the invitation? Wrestle Daniel to the ground if his highly honed senses detected anything amiss? And anyway, she would just be getting in the car with him. Going to see . . . something. Where was the harm in that?

Stealthy and feline, the neighbor's black Bentley poured itself into the driveway. The surface was so shiny it seemed liquid, as if the car would simply melt into a slick puddle when it stopped. It was only upon seeing her reflection in the car's surface that she realized that she had, in fact, already taken Daniel's hand and was allowing herself to be guided into the small, low red leather seat. His fingers intertwined with hers in a way that was so familiar that she wasn't aware of it until he let go. The driver met her eyes and nodded briefly at her, as if in approval.

They drove in silence. She could not remember the last time she had ridden in a car without any idea of where she was going. She could not remember ever having been in a car with Daniel. She didn't even know he could drive. There were so many normal, daily things that she had never done with him.

As he guided the car through Notting Hill Gate and along the northern edge of Kensington Gardens and then Hyde Park, silence settled into the spaces between them. He took them up Portland Place, under the imposing facades and past the Georgian terraced houses on Park Crescent where Regent's Park dips its toe into Marylebone.

She wondered what would happen if there was an accident and they were both killed. How would anyone make sense of their being in the car together? The most logical conclusion would be that she was considering buying one of his paintings. She had been at his opening, after all. That would be easily discovered. And she had both money and bare walls.

Would it be assumed that that was the extent of their connection? Would they examine CCTV footage of her last days or hours the way they did when there had been a crime? Looking for clues or souvenirs in the last moments of a life. With all the embassies and large homes in her neighborhood, there were myriad security cameras. She thought of their conversation outside the house. What would that look like on camera? They would likely interview both the security guard and the neighbor's driver, as they would have been the last people to have seen them alive. Of course, she reminded herself, there would have been no crime in this instance.

The car was small and the stick shift meant that his arm regularly moved rather close to hers, occasionally brushing lightly against it. She concentrated on ignoring this, focusing instead on the interior of the car, which was very tidy. From the lack of personal items or clutter, she concluded that it probably wasn't his. Rented? Unlikely—such a beautiful and unique car. Martin's? Possibly. It started to rain. Daniel fumbled to find the windshield-wiper controls.

The scent of the flowers had quickly permeated the small space, the stiff green paper crinkling softly under her touch every time she shifted in her seat. It was her ritual to buy a bunch of lilies every week. She found something so fragile and beautiful, so very unlikely and heroic in the way they bloomed, literally turning themselves inside out. She should have left them at home before getting into the car. Put them in water.

She glanced out the window. By now, they had moved out of the London that she knew well. The buildings here were larger and more industrial. There were fewer trees. Although there was a familiar sense of place, she recognized none of the streets. It seemed as though it was a different possibility of what London could be. She thought that it was always surprising how close the unknown was. How short a distance you had to go from the familiar to be lost. She relaxed. There was no one here to recognize her.

Listening to the steady sound of the rain hitting the windshield, punctuated by the low rhythmic swish of the wiper blades, she surreptitiously studied his profile while his eyes watched the road. His closely cropped hair had hints of gray mixed in with the dark blond. Gone were the long, slightly wavy locks that used to frame his eyes and brush the back of his neck. His face was more exposed and seemed larger somehow, especially in the small space of the car. She had long ago lost any ability to judge whether he was handsome or not. His cheeks were more lined than she remembered and were covered with the beginnings of stubble that was not yet long enough to be soft.

He was more muscular than she remembered. His thighs and his forearms were thicker. He had always been lean and sinewy. She smiled to herself—the starving artist no more. His sleeves were pushed up and she watched the tendons moving under his skin as he changed gears. His hands were the same. His left hand rested lightly on the gear shift next to her. Traces of paint embedded in the creases and under his nails. No ring. She felt for hers. It lay flat against her finger. She used to be under his nails, with the paint.

"You all right?" He spoke softly, but his voice startled her, the stiff paper around the lilies crinkling loudly under her hands, betraying her sudden movement. She looked up to meet his eyes.

"Fine."

"Almost there." He smiled, turning back to the road ahead. The corners of his mouth stretched sideways, making creases back toward his ears.

They drove on through Clerkenwell and into Shoreditch with its hulking red brick buildings from another age. Daniel parked in front of a nondescript brick building. A former factory, she guessed. Like many in this area that had been converted into lofts and studios, it deliberately retained its rough edges. Inside, they entered a large goods lift. As they stood on opposite sides of the wide space, she listened to the din of the ancient machinery straining to lift them to the top floor. Stained brick walls slid down the front of the lift—visible between the slats of the cage. Kat followed him out of the lift and as they walked down the tall, wide hall she heard it returning noisily to the ground floor, leaving them stranded in the dusty space.

Reaching into his pocket to retrieve his keys, Daniel stopped in front of a large brushed-metal doorway at the end of the hall. Its surface reflected nothing. She stood apart from him, regarding him from the opposite side of the doorframe with a familiarity she could no longer help.

"So, are you taking me to see your etchings?"

Daniel smiled without looking at her and pushed open the heavy door. Immediately, the smells of paint and turpentine brushed past Kat's face, making their escape from the darkened room. As they stepped inside, the door swung closed behind them with a heavy thunk, trapping them in semidarkness. Daniel made his way along the inside wall. In his footsteps, she recognized the familiar way sound echoed in large, mostly empty spaces. Seconds later, this was confirmed, as lights revealed a pale, cavernous studio with scarred concrete floors and whitewashed cinder-block walls.

Large fans stood like sentinels in the four corners of the room—circulating air and emitting a low, steady purr that made the vast space seem volatile and alive. As she moved deeper into the room, several intricately colored canvases caught her eye. The largest, resting on paint cans and leaning back against the wall directly in front of her, was a mixture of fine, delicate lines in grays and yellows. It looked like feathers and it seemed to have been made by small, sharp knives. To its right was a winter landscape. The stark outline of tapering branches was shaped solely by what surrounded it—thick ribbons of paint pulled taut against the canvas. A thing defined entirely by its absence. It seemed to Kat to be perfect.

Shrugging off his coat, Daniel tossed his keys on a table. He turned back to Kat and gestured to the paintings, his hand brushing lightly against the edge of the winter landscape.

"You see, I paint other things as well. They just didn't want them for this show. Martin wanted to keep it cohesive."

The room suddenly stilled. Glancing back, she saw that he had switched off the large fans. He frowned, shaking his head.

"I can't stand the noise. Do you want anything?"

She could not help a small smile as she held his gaze over her shoulder.

"Got any pie?"

He smiled back. Turning her back on him, Kat stopped in front of the unfinished winter landscape. Without the fans, the odor of paint settled comfortably around her and she breathed it in deeply. The studio's large, high windows provided no context. Letting in only light and revealing only sky.

She turned her attention back to the winter landscape. "I think my biggest problem would be knowing when it was finished."

"That's only because you can't see what is missing."

As she left the landscape and moved farther into the room, Kat's gaze fell on the low line of a narrow bed crouched against the far wall. Looking up, she saw that the wall was in fact an enormous vertical blank canvas, reaching almost to the ceiling. The lower part of the wall adjacent to it was papered with sketches—overlapping studies of a young woman's body, held up with blue tape. Pieces of a girl—the curve of a breast, the nape of a neck, fingers wound around a section of hair. Rough and ragged, but alive.

She turned to Daniel, the question in her eyes remaining unspoken. He looked up at the canvas and the sketches, taking them in as if he were seeing them for the first time as well.

"It's not you. It's a commission. It's not certain yet. I don't know if I want to do it. Martin thinks I should." He paused. "I shouldn't be telling you this." His eyes found hers. "But I know you're good at keeping secrets."

She turned away from him, taking in the rest of the studio. The long, low tables. The brace of brushes, standing at the ready in their jar. Round, bright, flat, filbert. The words came out of her memory stiff with disuse. The palette knives arrayed on trays like weapons, smudged with the remains of their last victims. Their various sizes and shapes—broad and flat, long with a rounded nose, small sharp diamond. The linseed oil and the smudged and dimpled tubes of paint. Their names long since forgotten, but at once immediately familiar to her—cadmium red light, rose madder, cobalt blue, Prussian blue, yellow ocher. Who said she had not seen Europe that year? She had seen all the colors of the hills above Florence, the flesh of odalisques, the Arno at sunset, and the soft verdant gardens at Giverny.

And the canvases. What she had loved most of all in the studio on the rue Garancière were the blank canvases. Stacked neatly against the wall, they were possibility incarnate. His ability to fill them amazed and delighted her. And what he had filled them with, that long dusty summer, was her. She had imagined that in order for it to be possible for him to transfer her to the canvas, she must exist—if only fleetingly—inside him. She entered him through his eyes and then escaped via his hands. She could feel him take possession of her as he painted her. It was, she thought, more intimate than sex.

For a moment, she watched him moving around the studio, remembering more than seeing the way that his hands remained at his sides, how he seemed reluctant to use them. As if he had seen what they could do and was chastened by it. A deliberate, self-imposed impulse, born of its opposite.

As she watched, he turned suddenly to face her. He reached behind his head and pulled his sweater off with one swift movement, momentarily lifting the shirt underneath it to reveal the bare skin above his waist. The sudden movement and the brief flash of flesh panicked her, and she turned away abruptly. The gesture was so familiar that it felt aggressive. In the silence, she heard the faraway sound of her heart beating.

Turning her back on him, she was confronted by an unfinished canvas propped up against the wall, partially hidden behind an empty vase. She took in the smooth, sleek thighs and the long, impossibly slender waist. The long line of her torso. The improbable red hair against the undeniably white skin. The details of her incomplete body captivated her. Looking at herself unfinished, she saw what could have been as clearly as she saw what had been.

How many times had he traced the contours of her body over these past years? Contemplated the fine hairs at the nape of her neck and the stippled trail of freckles on her shoulders, and recalled the exact way that the lines formed at the corners of her eyes? As he had consumed her in his presence, so she had consumed him in her absence. But perhaps no longer. What was she doing behind the vase? Who was the girl in the sketches? Was she the girl from the gallery?

In an effort to drown out her thoughts, Kat spoke. "So, did you bring me here to paint me?"

"I can paint you anytime I want."

She turned and looked over her shoulder at him as he tapped his head and smiled. She had forgotten how boyish he looked when he smiled. A real one—connecting the corners of his mouth to his eyes. She smiled back.

"Right. Memory is far better than the real thing, I suppose."

"Unless I have a choice."

She turned back to the painting, addressing it.

"I used to wonder what it would be like to see you again."

His ghost had walked the streets of New York when she had returned that spring. In the wide avenues so full of empty faces, she would feel his eyes on her. She could feel his eyes on her now. After a moment, he spoke. His voice was low, as if he was uncertain whether he wanted to be heard.

"The thing is, you are all that I paint, really. I think maybe you are all that I can paint."

"Don't be ridiculous. You can paint whatever you want to paint." She gestured vaguely to the canvases on the opposite wall, but did not turn around to look at him.

"Can I?" His voice contained a quiet note of sarcasm now. "How would you know?"

She turned to face him. He was nearer than she had thought. She immediately averted her eyes, looking down at a neat stack of unread newspapers that sat under the table. She remembered the yellowing pages of *Le Monde* that Daniel had used for cleaning brushes in Paris. The distinctive curving type of its masthead brazenly announcing its intent—to bring the world to her. How instead of turning away, she had stared directly at it. Willfully transforming the rounded letters into decoration. Until they became, to her eyes, part of the scenery, dancing black forms dressed in crude smears of color.

She kept her eyes on the newspapers. The words they were saying now seemed to demand a degree of privacy. "You're right. I'm sorry. I guess I wouldn't know."

In fact she knew nothing about his life now or his life for the past twenty years. And yet, she found that she wasn't interested. It hadn't mattered then and it didn't matter now.

She looked up again and he met her eyes. "You know, there was a lot you didn't know about me even in Paris. You never asked too many questions."

"You didn't seem to like questions very much."

"That stopped you?"

She was silent. When he spoke again, his voice was low. "Don't pity me, Kat. You didn't break me, if that is what you think."

"Of course not."

"And I didn't break you." He looked closely at her, examining her in the reflected glow off the walls. "Didn't even make a dent. To be honest, sometimes I think I did my best work after you left." His face was thoughtful. The remark was not meant to be anything but truthful.

"Just as well. That girl in your paintings—she's gone now." She felt her words melt into the large silence in the room.

"I don't believe that."

And maybe he was right. When he looked at her like that, she wasn't gone. In his eyes, she was still the girl in his paintings. The girl with the knowing eyes and the smooth skin and the impossibly slender waist. The girl who was all white flesh and red hair and possibility and passion.

They were straying into dangerous territory. She could barely make out the warning signs as they sped past them. She was aware only of the narrow corridor of his gaze, as if there was nothing outside of it. The shadows of clouds moved slowly over his face. She spoke, trying to fill the space between them with her words—but empty and brittle, they fell to the ground as soon as they passed her lips.

"Where did you go after . . . Did you stay in Paris?"

"After you left? Does it matter?"

He was moving closer to her now. Holding her in place with his pale blue eyes and his still hands that hung at his sides. She knew that maybe she should go. But she also knew that maybe it was too late. He moved slowly. He knew it, too.

Somehow, in this place—with the taste of paint on her tongue and a view of only sky. With the blank canvases stacked against the wall and the thick metal bolt holding the door shut, it seemed all things were possible again.

He took another step toward her. Rain drummed impatiently on the windows. Time was slipping away and she could do nothing to stop it. All of this would be gone. Or maybe it already was. And then his hands were in her hair. She could feel his heart beating through his fingertips. He was so close she could smell him now. Not the paint, not coffee, but Daniel.

She took a step back to steady herself against the table. As she reached behind her, her hands collided noisily with the crisp, dry tissue surrounding the lilies. The sudden crunching sound arrested her movement. They didn't belong here. They belonged in the vase on the side table in the drawing room. She didn't belong here either. She pulled away from him, his fingers brushing the side of her face before she turned and made her way out into the hallway. The metal door was heavy, but the lift was waiting for her. As it descended, she glimpsed the triangle of light extruded from the still-open door and realized that she had left the flowers behind. She did not go back.

chapter eleven

Sitting alone in the half-light of her empty house, Kat wondered at how close she had allowed herself to come to it before regaining her senses. She blamed the studio and its attendant vapors. That familiar light-headedness. Maybe it had all been a kind of delirium, even all those years ago. An intoxication brought about by the fumes. She thought about the way it had been in Paris. The two of them, alone in that small airless room for hours, for days. Seeing no one but each other. She shook her head. It had passed now.

On the phone later that afternoon, she asked if he had made a decision.

"You know what the absurd thing is? It's not mine anymore.

Any of it. The decision, the company—it belongs to the board. To the shareholders."

"You knew that." Kat said it quietly.

"I did. I knew it so clearly when we did the IPO. But you forget. You live with something every day and it just feels like it's yours. Although, apparently I am not the only one to have made that mistake. According to the *Mail*, not only was I the lone savior of the British tech industry, I am now also solely responsible for its demise." The anger was gone from his voice. Replaced by an uncharacteristic weariness.

Before she could respond, he continued. "Listen, I want to say I am sorry. I've not been there for you."

"It's okay. I understand."

"I know you do. But I don't want you to have to. This whole thing . . . everything . . . has made me realize what matters and it is not the company and it is not the deal."

"So, you're coming home?"

"Yes."

"When?" She took note of her quickening pulse and the overwhelming disorientation about what answer she was hoping for.

"Soon." A brief pause elongated into something else altogether, prompting him to speak again. "You're so quiet. Are you still there?"

"I'm still here."

"We can keep the house. We'll be in London, most likely, for some of the year."

It would become another place where she half belonged.

She thought of all the places that she belonged more than she belonged here. She belonged to the cold, hard edges of New York; the soft, bruised Paris mornings; the salt air on her tongue and the tickle of sand on her skin. She belonged with her mother. She belonged pressed up against Will's back, feeling the sweet swell of his breath. But where did she belong now?

Kat put the phone down and glanced at the clock, amazed to find that it was late afternoon. The black-tie fund-raiser for the British Cancer Foundation was tonight.

On her way out of the kitchen to get dressed upstairs, her eye caught on the bright spot provided by a colorful drawing of Will's taped to the kitchen wall, and she smiled. A rare decorative touch, it provided a sharp contrast to the expanse of empty walls, punctuated only by the four squares of dried paint in the drawing room, their differences indistinguishable in the low light of morning. Underneath it on the counter was a thick green file folder. Her smile disappeared.

A reminder. A relic. She picked it up and carried it upstairs, determined to find a place for it. To put it away somewhere that she did not have to see it. It was all in there. The test results, MRIs, blood work, prescriptions, and chemo schedules traced the arc of her mother's illness from shock to hope to despair. From the first nagging symptoms and the resulting tests, to the diagnosis, delivered along with a heavy measure of hope—optimistic percentages and new drugs were cited. To the relief from the initial success of treatment, to the despair at its subsequent failure, to the more extreme treatment options—followed by the slow, creeping dawn of realization—heels dug firmly into the ground on the excruciating slide into the end. She knew how this story ended, although the ending itself was not in the file.

The obituary had made her angry. One hundred and fifty-three black words in eight-point type. The number of words, the size of the words, but mostly, the words themselves. Words that had little to do with her mother and the extraordinary woman she had been.

This was a woman who had learned how to ride a bicycle at the age of fifty, who had told bedtime stories so vividly that as a child Kat could still hear the wail of the wind in the trees and smell the yeasty smell of the forest floor while drifting to sleep. A woman whose face, in repose, had an expression that she had only ever seen on the tall porcelain statues in church alcoves. A new bride who had found herself widowed at the age of twenty-nine. Two weeks later, she had discovered that she was pregnant. A woman whose smile hid nothing and whose laughter was so clear to her now, but would fade, she knew.

It is a formula, Jonathan would say to her. There are rules for writing these things. No one expected an obituary to be the measure of a person. It was not even a eulogy. It was simply meant to report certain facts. It did not matter. But it did matter. The audacity of it—these marks on paper—trying to convey a lifetime, or even a moment.

She just wanted them to know all that had been lost on that cold December morning in the sun-filled room with the dark green wallpaper overlooking the park. In the big bed, next to the table filled with the framed photos. Her mother had died on December 21. The winter solstice. She knew from studying Latin that the literal translation of solstice was that the sun stood still. The sun had stood still on the day her mother died. Why hadn't they said that in the obituary?

chapter twelve

Opening her closet, Kat was surprised to find that one of her gowns had been steamed and left out, as well as shoes and accessories to go with it. The housekeeper must have done it that morning. There beside the long jade-green dress was a neat list—gown, jewelry, shoes, bag—in her own handwriting. She had written it before she had gone to New York. She looked at it curiously. An artifact of another time. A time when her mother was still alive.

Impulsively, Kat retrieved the green file from the bottom drawer where she had placed it just moments before. She opened it to reveal an MRI. Maybe the last one? Kat looked down at the filmy white shadows. The cold, austere, pure beauty of science. Beauty that hid in soft and secret places. Places that defined her, that sustained her and that had failed her. Places that she would never see and that held mysteries only a stranger could divine. Kat thought that she was not what others saw when they looked at her. She was not what she saw in the mirror. There were shapes and shades in her that she would never know. Kat closed the file and dropped it back in the open drawer.

She usually wore her hair up to these events, but there was no time. She showered quickly and left it loose around her face. She paused briefly before the mirror in the front hallway, momentarily halted by her fading resemblance to the girl in the paintings. She had thought that she would skip the event. It was likely that many of the same people who had been at Daniel's opening would be there this evening. But this was, after all, an important cause.

She retrieved the invitation from its resting place on the corner of the mirror and glanced at it. The Dorchester. The ball was at the Dorchester. She laughed, the unfamiliar noise echoing off the walls.

Kat left her car with the valet and crossed the smooth semi-circular drive of the hotel. She walked quickly past the small group of photographers, their flashbulbs a fraction of what they would have been had Jonathan been with her.

Was Daniel upstairs in the suite overlooking the park? Walking though the lobby she was suddenly certain he would appear in front of her. She set about deciding how she should handle this. She could pretend not to know him—probably the safest option, but was that level of subterfuge necessary? Perhaps a casual acknowledgment. But what exactly? A smile? A wave? A kiss on both cheeks? She thought of how close he had been last night. She thought of his fingers slipping from her hair and grazing the edge of her jaw as she had stepped back from him.

She was not sure how many times her name had been called, but by the time she became aware of it, other people in the lobby had turned to look. For a woman so skilled in the art of ignoring people, Margaret Browning seemed to have surprisingly little appreciation for being ignored herself and her face puckered with annoyance. Kat tucked her thoughts tidily into place and brought out the most brilliant smile she could find. Her eyes strayed to the pearls the size of a baby's fists around Margaret's neck. All the beauty that money could buy, shining defiantly against her crepey skin.

"Margaret. How are you?"

"Well, I'm fine." Margaret's voice was tight. "I must have called your name five times just now. I saw you from the other side of the lobby, of course. You can't hide with hair that color, you know," she accused.

"It's a wonderful turnout for you tonight. Better than last year."

"Yes. Well, we will just see about that. You might have let me know that your husband wouldn't be here so I could have filled his seat," Margaret scolded her. "Never mind. I'm sure you will make amends during the auction. Or have you spent your allowance already? I saw you at Penfields the other night.

I only ask because Clemmie was desperate to get one and she wasn't able—poor thing." Margaret seemed genuinely delighted by this. "She was after the nude sitting by the window for their new place on Montpelier Square. Her designer thought all the flesh tones would go perfectly with the curtains."

Kat nodded mechanically, willing herself to remain calm as Margaret continued to expound on the nude portrait of her. She and Jonathan had recently made a large donation to the foundation and Kat knew that she was merely a name on a list of people whom Margaret needed to chat with this evening. In point of fact, she knew that the name on the list was actually Jonathan and that she was merely his proxy. If she could just get through her allotted amount of time and conversation, then Margaret would move on to the next name on her list.

"So you did get one?" Margaret's face registered uncharacteristic surprise.

"Oh, no. No."

Margaret seemed relieved. "Shame . . . . Of course, you know how it is—I hear that the good ones were all sold before the show opened anyway. Penfields gives its best customers a preview and everything goes before you can even get a look at it." Margaret pouted.

"Do you know who bought them?"

Margaret considered this for a moment. "The rumor is that Malcolm Jeffries got one. You know how close he is with the gallery. Although one might have hoped Penfields would have better taste. He is so flash with all his new money." She paused and her eyes came to rest on Kat. "Oh, no offense, of course."

Kat smiled, although perhaps a moment too late.

Margaret laid a manicured hand on her arm. "Now, don't be cross with me. I am not belittling what your husband does, it's just that he doesn't create anything, really. He just works out clever ways to do things." Kat could hear Margaret trying on the trace of a British accent. Holding it up against herself, like a posh frock, to see how it fit.

"Right," Kat said. "Except for money. He does create quite a bit of that. I can't imagine that had escaped your notice. It is, after all, the reason you asked us here, is it not?" She smiled sweetly at the older woman.

"Well, isn't the devil in you tonight," Margaret mused, an approving glint in her rheumy eyes. "But any fool can make money. In fact, many of them do, as you can clearly see from the crowd tonight."

"True," Kat agreed, surveying the room and seeing that the older woman was indeed right.

Margaret leaned in closer and smiled wickedly at Kat. "Of course, you know that whole Cinderella story is a bit put on."

"Is it?" Kat was suddenly interested.

"Bearing in mind that this is an artist already known to and indeed owned by some of the top collectors, it is all really rather convenient, when you think about it," Margaret mused. "This 'discovery' of this stash of paintings of a mysterious girl . . . I daresay the value of all his other portraits is going to get quite a bump from this show. Were I a more cynical creature, I might suspect the whole thing to be contrived."

Kat tried momentarily to picture a more cynical Margaret.

Margaret took a step back and squinted at Kat, as if seeing her for the first time. "You know, I had not noticed it before, but there is definitely a resemblance. The girl in the paintings could be the daughter you never had."

Kat flushed, but Margaret's gaze by now was fixed on something behind Kat's back.

Kat turned to see Martin approaching.

"Mrs. Browning, such a marvelous evening—you and the board have outdone yourselves," Martin greeted the older woman deferentially before turning to Kat. "And Miss Lind— you are looking pretty as a picture in that green gown this evening."

Kat glared at him through a tight smile.

"I didn't know you two were acquainted." Margaret frowned.

"Everyone has their secrets. For instance, were you aware that in her younger days Katherine spent a year in Paris studying French literature?" Martin smiled benignly.

Margaret looked slightly betrayed by this disclosure. "I was not."

Kat looked at Margaret—the older woman's face animated under a layer of colors that were not its own. Although her mouth was moving, Kat no longer heard what she was saying.

Margaret didn't notice. Her eyes were once again scanning the area behind Kat and Martin for any signs of other people more worthy of her attention. Spotting someone, she excused herself, tossing a few final words over her shoulder as she left.

"Do make sure you put your paddle to good use this evening. I'll be watching," Margaret warned.

"Yes, of course," Kat managed, addressing Margaret's back as she headed toward a cluster of people who had just arrived in the lobby.

She and Martin stood side by side in silence for a moment before the gilded metal doors swathed in intricate chinoiserie birds and butterflies. Kat waited for him to leave. She would not be run off. She was the one who belonged here, not him. The crowd moved around them. Martin nodded intermittently at select people. After a while, he sighed.

"All this beauty . . . do you think anyone even sees it?"

Through her anger, Kat was surprised. By his words. By the almost mournful expression on his face.

"I know that sometimes all they can see is the price. But what they don't know is the real cost. Look at them." He surveyed the crowd as it moved around them, multiplied in the antique mirrored paneling. "They don't want to know. And maybe they're right. Maybe knowing doesn't make it more beautiful. Maybe knowing makes it less beautiful. But I think you have to know what it cost. What was destroyed or abandoned or forgone for it. You have to know that in order to see it fully."

Kat stood speechless for a moment. Before she could reply, Martin turned toward her gravely.

"You know what being an agent is? Waving your arms about and yelling, 'Look at me! Look at me!' And then, the moment you get someone's attention, pointing at your client and saying, 'Look at him.'"

"Perfect but for the last bit, I suppose," she replied dryly.

"On the contrary, Katherine. I am well aware of my place." He paused, the briefest of smiles passing over his face. "It was Baudelaire, was it not, who said that there are only three things worthy of respect—to know, to kill, and to create? Now Daniel—he creates, obviously. But, I can look at a painting and I know its beauty, its value, immediately." He snapped his pudgy fingers in the air, producing a surprisingly sharp sound. "It is my gift, my curse. Perhaps you and I are similar in that way. We both recognize beauty and value."

"Perhaps. But I know the difference."

"But, my dear." He turned to face her, smiling. "There is no difference. And I am afraid that leaves only one opening."

FOR A WHILE after that Kat had the vague sense that she was invisible. That everyone recognized her, but that no one really saw her. Several acquaintances politely engaged her in conversation, all of which invariably led back to Jonathan and the company. People loved to talk about Jonathan. After many years she was well practiced in the verbal sleight of hand required of a corporate spouse and was well able to engage in conversation without revealing anything about Jonathan's whereabouts, schedule, or general state of being. For the remainder of the cocktail hour, she bobbed silently through the crowd of people, enjoying the relative anonymity that not being accompanied by Jonathan brought her.

It was only as the cocktail hour wound down and she made her way among the tables in search of her seat that she became aware that she was being watched. Like the lone gazelle in the wildlife programs Will favored on the BBC, she was being stalked. He mirrored her movements as she weaved among the tables. She evaded him halfheartedly for a while, but after a quick glance ahead revealed her way to be blocked by a clutch of other attendees in search of their tables, she stopped, marshaling her defenses as he made his approach, an exhausted-looking man with extravagant eyebrows.

"Mrs. Bowen." He bowed slightly, a gesture that she found simultaneously awkward and patronizing.

"Mr. Warre."

"You're alone this evening?"

"I am." A two-word answer. One more than she had found to be prudent with reporters.

"How is your husband enjoying China?"

She smiled her most benevolent smile at him and opted for silence, reasoning that she had already used her quota of words in replying to his last question.

He sighed at her silence, his eyebrows migrating southward in a frown.

"It's impossible to travel undetected these days, is it not?

With all the new regulations and paperwork. Such a shame, really. But I was schooled on Fleet Street, so I admit I am a bit old-fashioned. Nothing beats the long lens."

He paused, allowing for the possibility that she would speak. When she did not, he continued.

"Should you be speaking with your husband, you might remind him that in the event he would like to explain to the British public why he is selling out to the Chinese, the *Mail* would be pleased to provide him the opportunity to do so."

"Enjoy the evening, Mr. Warre," she said as she moved past him.

"I intend to, Mrs. Bowen."

Kat made her way to her table. Jonathan's place card was there next to hers, neatly embossed in thick black letters. She looked at the empty chair. Since she had returned from New York, nothing seemed to be in its proper place. If Jonathan were here, although they would both be in conversation with others most of the time, his hand might wander over and squeeze hers occasionally during the evening. Maybe she would brush the back of his jacket lightly. She thought about going home to her empty house. She should not have let Will go to the country with his grandparents. She needed him like oxygen. She wondered at the absence of a child. So utterly different from any other absence.

A tall gray-haired man pulled out the chair on her left and sat down next to her, eyes alighting almost imperceptibly on her place card as he did.

"Hello, I'm Peter Galbraith." His smile was warm and sincere. She couldn't help but return it.

"Kat Lind."

Kat looked at his place card. Dr. Peter Galbraith. Of course. She had seen his name on the foundation's reports. He ran the research lab. She watched as he introduced himself to the other guests at their table. Smooth, polite, handsome. This was the man who had failed her mother. Dinner was served.

There was a jubilant feel to the evening that she didn't share. What exactly were they celebrating anyway? Certainly not victory. Cancer had not been defeated, as she well knew. It was not even as if they had it on the ropes. As far as she could tell they were losing the battle. She looked around the room at the familiar, smiling faces. What did tonight have to do with cancer anyway? What did any of this have to do with the disease that had stolen her mother's strength, spirit, and dignity before taking her life? She knew the answer was money. But was it? Her mother had the best care that money could buy—the best hospitals, doctors, treatments—and it hadn't been enough.

With the chair on her right empty, Kat was forced to speak with Dr. Galbraith on her left. Throughout dinner, he made polite inquiries about her involvement in the charity. She answered briefly, struggling to remain civil. What was he doing here anyway—picking politely at his salmon en croute and making small talk with her? Shouldn't he be in the lab? Weren't there experiments and investigations and research that needed his attention?

Despite where she was and because of where she was, Kat thought about her mother.

He was about the same age as she had been. She looked at his hands. Long delicate fingers. He wore a thin gold band on the third finger of his right hand. Was he a widower? Had he lost her to cancer? she wondered. Had her death inspired him to do what he was doing now?

Glancing briefly around the large, crowded ballroom, Dr. Galbraith turned and smiled warmly at Kat. She saw that the left cuff of his tuxedo was worn in the place where his watch brushed against it. He must attend a lot of these events. Kat felt something restless begin to expand in the empty spaces inside of her. She took slow, deep breaths in an effort to compose herself.

Despite her clipped answers, he persisted undeterred in his efforts at conversation.

"This really is a wonderful event."

"It's not enough, though, is it?"

"True." He nodded solemnly. "We could always use more."

"How much will it take to find a cure?"

If he was taken aback by this, he didn't show it, meeting her eyes. "I wish I knew, Kat. All I can say for sure is that every little bit takes us a step closer."

"But you're not going fast enough."

"I beg your pardon?"

"I said you are not going fast enough." She saw the heads at the table turn toward her. Her voice was too loud. She was trying to maintain control, but she had to make him understand.

She looked around the room. "Is this really the best we can do to cure this disease? Have a party? Why does everything need to be so removed from its real meaning? Why do we have to dress it up like it is something else? Why can't we just do what needs to be done?"

The doctor looked genuinely concerned. It was a look she knew well, having seen it on the faces of so many medical professionals so recently. He leaned toward Kat, a gesture designed either to make sure that she heard him or to quiet her voice.

"I assure you, we know how urgent this is. And I assure you that events like this do matter. I know it may not seem like it, but they do." He spoke earnestly. "The money from this evening alone will fund our lab for six months. Sometimes in order to get something done, you have to dress it up like something else—because that is sometimes what it takes to get people to part with their money."

"I just don't believe it. It can't just be money. If it is, then why haven't we done it yet? If all it takes is money, then there is probably enough of it in this room."

She looked around at the bright and the beautiful of London. She wondered how much all the jewelry in the room tonight alone was worth. She remembered going through the contents of her mother's jewelry box, feeling the weight of the pieces in her hands. There were fewer pieces than she remembered. All cold stones and metal. She remembered how light and frail her mother had become toward the end. Like a bird. Stripped of all the things that fell away so easily when she lost the strength to hold on to them. She thought about how much strength it took to carry these things. And about how under all the clothes and the jewelry and the perfect wrapping—we were all the same. Frail bodies. Frail egos. Frail lives.

Walking into the green bedroom four weeks ago. Sleeping cocooned among the quilts and oversize pillows on the big bed, her mother had looked so small. So still. Stopping at the edge of the bed, Kat caught her breath. Still the figure in the bed did not move. As Kat bent down closer, her mother suddenly opened her eyes. She must have seen the fear in Kat's face.

"Don't worry, love. I am not going to leave you."

The words were slurred and small—delivered on the back of a shallow breath. But Kat had believed them and had been relieved. An hour later her mother was dead.

Why hadn't she moved back when her mother had first become ill? She should have been there with her. What was she doing in London anyway? Why hadn't she just curled around her mother and stayed with her? What could have been more important than that? It was impossible to accept that she was gone. That there would be no new moments with her. For her.

"Ladies and gentlemen, may I have your attention please?"

The crowd quieted as their host began to introduce the evening's speaker. Dr. Galbraith slid his chair back and made his way through the crowd to the front of the ballroom. As the polite applause died down, he moved to the podium and surveyed his audience. He began speaking, his voice low and warm.

"Everyone in this room will be affected by cancer in their lifetime. More than a quarter of a million people are diagnosed with cancer each year in the UK alone. But even those lucky enough not to be among this number will be touched by the disease through someone whom they know. Maybe someone whom they love."

He found Kat's eyes briefly. Kat looked away, glancing instead around the table. The rather large, red-faced man to the far right of her was engaged in the dogged pursuit of an errant band of petit pois, fleeing erratically across his plate. Across the table, Margaret enthusiastically chatted up her octogenarian companion while just as enthusiastically ignoring his much younger wife. The room buzzed softly with conversation and the faintly musical rhythms of crystal against crystal and silver scraping china.

His voice floated above the noise of the room. As he continued to speak, detailing the specific research projects and goals of the foundation, Kat was surprised to hear what sounded like faint laughter. As she listened, the noise level in the room slowly began to rise until it had returned to the level it had been prior to Dr. Galbraith beginning his speech. Until it was difficult for Kat to make out what he was saying. Perhaps sensing that he was losing his audience, Dr. Galbraith cleared his throat loudly and began to wrap up his speech.

When he resumed speaking, the timbre of his voice had changed. The words he now spoke seemed to originate in a different part of him, a softer part, than the ones he had uttered before. "I look around this room and I see people who have the power to do extraordinary things. People who can build empires, move mountains, truly change the world." He paused and looked up from the podium. "But I'm not asking you for that tonight. Tonight I am asking for only one thing. For money. With that we can and we will move the mountains."

In her final days, her mother had refused pain medication. It had been excruciating for Kat to watch her suffer. But it was all her mother had control over at that stage and, as she told Kat, "I want to feel everything. I don't want to die before I die."

In those last few days her pain had fixed her to the earth like a pin. Holding her fast to each moment, to each breath. Kat wondered if she would make the same choice. To feel pain over feeling nothing. She wondered if she had already.

Kat heard the scattered applause that followed Dr. Galbraith off the dais after the brief pause required for the crowd to register the absence of his voice. She thought about the people who were dying. The mothers and fathers and sons and daughters for whom this would be their last night. Their last moments to feel. She thought about the weight of Daniel's hand at the small of her back.

As she left the ballroom, Kat heard a reverential hush descend as the first auction lot was being described. She pictured the good doctor returning to his seat at the table, and finding the chair on his right empty.

chapter thirteen

She paused outside the Dorchester waiting for the valet to retrieve her car. Shivering under the thin layer of silk, she tried to conjure another destination. But there was only one place. She wondered if she could find her way back. She didn't know the address and it was not exactly an area she was familiar with. She followed the same route he had taken along the top of the parks and then through Marylebone. With the neighborhoods and parks cloaked in darkness, it seemed there was no city outside of the maze of lighted streets. She expected to get lost. She expected an obstacle. A diversion. But there was none. She thought that it should not be so easy.

She parked several blocks away and walked quickly through

the empty streets. She saw no one and there was no one to see her. The sharp sounds of her heels on the pavement dissolved immediately into the silence. The bottom half of her long green gown glowed as she walked through the pools of light under the streetlamps, the sudden flashes of color reminding her that she did not belong—in this place, in this dress.

Reaching the building, she saw Martin's sleek silver car parked in front, gleaming softly under a streetlight. A small pile of broken glass from a shattered car window, or maybe just a bottle, glinted dangerously on the pavement in front of her. She slowed down, stepping easily around the shards. She reached the wooden door, worn smooth, its small glass panels protected behind a metal grid, and pressed the button beside it with a naked finger. Inside, the building appeared empty once more, its silence disturbed only by the sound of the lift as it carried her to the top floor. Leaving the cage, she heard the deadbolt slide open at the end of the hallway. The heavy metal door opened before she reached it. It was that easy.

She entered the darkened studio, breathing in the scent of paint. The ferrous tang clung to the inside of her nose and mouth, insinuating itself into the soft, wet membranes, seeking them out and mixing easily with them.

She felt him move up behind her. She started to turn around, but he caught her shoulders, his strong hands holding her still. Gathering her hair in his hands, he swept it to one side of her neck. He lifted the clasp of the heavy necklace away from her skin and unfastened it. The sudden sound as it hit the floor was dampened by the feel of his fingers moving on her skin. Bringing his hands up the sides of her neck, he removed each of her earrings in turn and they fell from his hands to the floor by her feet. His fingers ran down her arms to find the flat gold band on her limp left hand and wiggled it off over her knuckle. Eyes closed now, she heard it rolling across the concrete as his hands traveled to her back to undo the covered buttons along her spine, starting at the top and moving down.

She thought of her mother in hospital. Stripped of everything, even her wedding band. The most basic things that identify us, that anchor us to our lives. That speak to us and that speak for us. She wondered at how easily even the things that we cling to fall away. So that we cease being mother, daughter, wife. Squeezing her eyes shut to banish the thought, she took a step back and leaned her head against his chest. She felt him nudge the straps of her dress off her shoulders and felt it slip to the floor.

They reclaimed each other. Memory and desire sweeping away time and distance. So that there were only her fingers pulsing in the hair at the back of his neck, the weight of his body pressing down on her. They lay together afterward until one of them moved. Adjusted a leg or turned slightly and the sensation of skin moving on skin set them off again. For an hour, maybe less, she was asleep. She awakened warm and encircled in the narrow bed. Opening her eyes wide, she looked down at their bodies, melted into each other in the murky pre-dawn light.

For a moment, she did not move, did not adjust her

position, savoring the perfect way that they fit together. And then she rolled over so that she was lying on top of him, her hair falling down around the sides of his head, so all she could see was his face. She felt the heat of his body pressing up into her. He was so familiar this way. Close-up, it was so easy to see him. He still turned back into a stranger when they were separate. He opened his eyes.

"Tell me what you see."

They were the first words that had passed between them. She whispered them into the small space between them, breathing in the brief pause before his answer.

He closed his eyes and she moved even closer, so that when he spoke, his lips brushed against hers. "I see the exact shade of blue under your skin, the coppers and pinks in your hair in the morning light, the way the dust moved in your breath, the shadow under your jaw, the curve of your hips."

She closed her eyes, listening as he painted pictures for her.

"But I could never see you whole."

She gave herself up to him as wholly as she gave herself up to the darkness. Both took her without hesitation.

The second time she woke, she surfaced alone. The darkness was already diluted and what little remained was fast escaping through the high windows. It surprised her that while the light in London was so different than it had been in Paris, the darkness would be exactly the same. That specific diffuse quality that reduced things to their elements, as if she were seeing the atoms themselves. She remembered the way the light used to define them in the morning. How they would emerge from the darkness, two fuzzy figures entangled in each other, like the Seurat paintings in the Louvre. In the changing light, she would watch as the particles of darkness slowly moved apart. There was almost no moon. She lay still as the thin light dropped from the windows and crept under the locked door, watching as their figures emerged from the darkness. She thought that she could see time passing.

A faint, familiar dry scratching was just audible in the room. Turning, she saw that Daniel had moved a chair close to the bed and sat sketching her. She felt his eyes running over the contours of her body as his hands had done only hours before. He leaned forward, his left forearm supporting the sketch pad, fingers curled into a fist over its top edge. He gazed at her with such intensity that he seemed not to notice that she had moved.

The bare part of the wall over his shoulder was scarred with the ends of broken brushstrokes begun elsewhere. Trace evidence of what had been there, like blood from erstwhile limbs. So here was the place outside of the frame. She noticed the lilies, still wrapped in their paper, lying on the table by the wall, their limp white petals creased and tinged with brown. Suddenly self-conscious, she sat up and started to pull the sheet around herself.

"Don't." The word was hard and blunt. A single syllable laid at her feet.

Kat watched him turn the page and start a new drawing. The expression of concentration on his face was one she remembered. His hands moved above the paper with a restless energy. The pent-up force of the coiled spring—released. All motion, all control and energy—lit up and alive. It astonished her, igniting a half-forgotten ache that burned just under her skin.

Still feeling his eyes on her, Kat let the sheet drop from her fingers and lay back, snaking her arms over her head, allowing the fear and the freedom of being seen wash over her. Above her a black bird, elongated in flight, passed by the window. The small intermittent sounds of pencil scratching on paper stopped. She smiled, not unaware of the image she presented. She heard him drop the pad and pencil at his feet and turned to see him pulling open drawers, searching for something.

When he found what he was after, he moved past her, one hand curled into a loose fist at his side. What was he doing? Reaching the wall behind the bed he turned back to her. There was no sound, only stillness. She felt the weight of his gaze on her bare skin. Abruptly, he started to move, drawing his hand across the wall in slow, smooth arcs, each scrape of charcoal trailing a shower of black dust that dissipated in the light.

Stretched out on the sheets, Kat watched the rhythm of his body as he began to describe her figure on the rough concrete, eyes flickering between her and the wall. She recognized the gentle curve of her lower back as it rippled across the wall and the loose tangle of arms around her head. She could almost feel the soft edges of the charcoal brush her skin. As each piece was worn away he took up another from his fist. Her body at once weightless and rooted to the spot, her breath began to come quickly and before long she started to stir, driven by some intrinsic impulse, some wave of instinct and appetite.

"Don't move."

Kat stilled herself willfully as she took shape under his fluent hands, the charcoal adhering tenuously to the rough surface, line by line, curve by curve. She felt the distance between them stretching and contracting like a physical thing every time he moved. His long, sweeping strokes became shorter, quicker movements as the restlessness built inside her. The air was cold on her warm skin. His eyes lingered on her body before he turned back to the wall and slowly rubbed the flat of his palm along the line of her thigh. Her pulse quickened.

"Daniel." His name mingled with a breath.

"Wait."

The recumbent figure on the wall beyond him was almost complete now. Anchored at one end by delicate tapering legs bent at the knee, the color of bone inside its edges. As he used his thumb to smudge and thicken the shadows under her chin, she felt the exquisite friction and pushed her head back into the sheets. Just as she thought she couldn't take it any longer, he let the last bits of charcoal drop from his fingers and came toward her, eyes wild, hands smudged with cinders.

KAT WOKE TO Daniel getting out of the bed. Since her arrival they had clung to it like a lifeboat. Never venturing too far from it, always returning to it quickly. She moved into the space he had left, feeling his residual heat on the sheets. From where she lay, she could see the charcoal outline on the wall above the bed. Brushing the hair from her face, she regarded her likeness. The rough silhouette was almost primitive. Not far removed from the prehistoric figures found on the walls of caves in southern France. Cryptic drawings made by the glow of ancient fires, their true meanings obscured by time. She couldn't help but smile, remembering the caves as one of the places she had planned to visit during her student days in Paris. It was the first time since arriving at the studio that she had thought of anything outside of the four walls around her.

She sat up and swung her legs to the floor, wrapping the sheet around her, waiting for the slight spinning sensation to cease. The floor was cold and the soles of her feet felt soft and slightly swollen. The sky was dark through the windows. Could it be late afternoon?

"You hungry?" His voice came from the far corner of the room.

"Starving," she said, realizing that she hadn't eaten since yesterday. Her voice echoed off the walls and she felt herself blush. They had not done much talking in the last few hours, certainly not above a whisper, and the full light of day combined with the distance between them made her suddenly shy. He stood up and she saw that he was dressed in jeans and a T-shirt. She pulled the sheet more tightly around her.

He came toward her, carrying a bowl of apples in one hand. She had seen it in the room before, but assumed it was fake, a decorative prop, so uniformly red and round were the apples.

In his other hand was a short, wooden-handled knife. He sat down on the floor beside the bed. She slid down beside him, pressing her shoulder against his, reestablishing contact.

"Just what every artist needs, a bowl of fruit."

"I've no idea how this got here," he said, taking an apple from the bowl. "I think it's meant to be reference material."

"Right." She smiled. "I imagine there must be some sort of ordinance requiring every studio to have at least one bowl of fruit."

"And now we know why."

Daniel cradled the apple within his palm. She watched as he worked the knife through the fruit, the blade disappearing into its flesh, scant white froth bubbling at the incision. When the blade touched his palm, he withdrew it and raised his hand to his mouth to catch a rivulet of juice that was making its way down his wrist. He extended her half of the apple, balanced lightly on wet fingertips.

She could smell it already, the crisp scent at odds with the other dense odors of the studio. It tasted like the edge of the knife—sharp and hard—the flavor mixing with the taste of him. She tucked her toes underneath his leg and they sat together on the floor, their backs against the bed.

Daniel gestured at the figure on the wall, the knife still in his hand. "That's the first complete figure of you I've been able to do since Paris." He looked stunned.

"I wouldn't say complete."

"Not yet. But whole."

They ate in silence for a moment.

"You told me once that if you really see something, then it never leaves you."

"You remember that?"

"I remember everything."

And she did. A startling sense of clarity had lodged itself behind her heart.

He thought for a moment. "It's different. Painting from memory. You were always there, but just out of reach. I could only see pieces of you. Fragments. A shoulder, a cheek, an open eye. But so clearly." He lightly touched the back of his hand to the side of her face. "It drove me mad at first, but then I started to paint the parts that I could see. I felt like if I did that, then maybe I could bring you back, bit by bit. It was just for me. I never showed anyone." He paused, turning back to the figure on the wall. "Until Martin."

She cringed. Martin. Small and sharp like the man himself, the name produced a precise, narrow rupture in the protective veil they had drawn about themselves. She looked away. It was all so fragile. Didn't he know that?

She finished her half of the apple and stood up. Wrapping the sheet more tightly around herself, she moved over to the drawing on the wall, stopping only inches away. Close-up, it dissolved into the lines themselves, the thin deposit of charcoal on concrete. She wondered at how something could be so altered solely by her relation to it. Drawing her fingers lightly across the uneven surface, she traced the figure, softening the lines. Removing her fingers, she saw faint smudges of black dust on her fingertips. Traces of something that had once burned so brightly, now distilled to its essence. Still organic, even after the fire. Something diminished only by contact. Leaving evidence of itself on whatever it touched. Paper. Skin.

"Are you trying to erase it?"

She turned to him. "What? No. I love it." She watched him finish his apple and lick the juice from his fingers. After a moment she smiled.

"What?"

"We're eating your reference material."

"Yes." One corner of his mouth curved upward. He pushed himself up off the floor with one hand and started toward her, laying the knife down on a table. "What will I paint now?"

He ran his finger up and down her arm. She glanced up at the windows and frowned. Time was passing.

"Dark already."

"It's not dark." He squeezed her shoulder. "Get dressed. I'll show you."

She hesitated. Surely he knew that they shouldn't go out in public. But she pulled on her clothes as he waited. It wasn't likely anyone she knew would be walking the streets of Shoreditch. He handed her his coat and on her way to the door she grabbed her purse, but he shook his head.

"You won't need that."

She followed him down the long hallway away from the lift. Where was he taking her? At the far end of the passage, a metal ladder rose into the ceiling. Daniel stepped onto the second rung and began to climb. Kat watched him vanish into the darkness until a sliver of dim light appeared, waxing into a larger rectangle as he pushed open a hatch to the roof. As he disappeared through it, she took hold of the thick rails and followed him up. Her arms felt weak and her hands scraped against scabs of corroded paint.

When she reached the top of the ladder, Daniel grasped her forearms and pulled her up through the hatch. For an instant she hung suspended, her toes pointed down into the mouth of the passage, the full weight of her body in his hands, before he swung her to the side and set her down gently.

The flat roof was covered in flaking tar paper. So wide and dark that it seemed to lose mass in places. Kat moved instinctively to its center, planting her feet wide and keeping her eyes down. She could hear the distant hum of traffic. The wind rushed past her, lifting her hair off her face. A faint geometric pattern emerged on the ancient tar paper under her feet. A heap of tiles, cracked and chipped around their edges, lay nearby. She matched their shape to the pattern etched on the paper.

After a moment, she realized that she was half crouching and willed herself to stand straight, immediately dizzy under the vaulted gray sky. Daniel stood at the edge of the expanse. She watched him move along the perimeter, his eyes on the horizon. He stopped and kicked lightly at the low wall beside him, the brick flaking and crumbling, and then glanced back at her.

"You have to look hard to find darkness in cities. There is always light. And London is so far north that in the winter you can always see the red glow of the sun just below the horizon."

She forgot that he had grown up here. It was a part of him she knew nothing about. As he rested one foot on the low wall that bordered the roof, he became the darkness, blocking out the lights behind him, his broad shoulders spanning city blocks, obliterating entire neighborhoods. As he leaned out over the edge, Kat found herself involuntarily leaning backward, as if to balance the building.

She took a few steps toward him, wishing he would come away from the edge. After a moment, he turned to face her. He said something, but the wind took the sound.

"What's that?"

"It's changed. The city."

"Maybe you have."

He smirked at her, his face coming into sharper focus as she moved closer to him.

"*Peut-être.*"

She stopped where she stood, mouth open. "*Je ne crois pas!* You learned French!"

"*Je te jure.* Someone once suggested I should."

"How long have you been waiting to show me that?"

He laughed and held out his hand to her. "A long time. Come closer."

She edged nearer to him, lifting her feet deliberately, the roof rough and blistered under them. She felt light-headed. From the elevation or from having eaten only half an apple all day. He stood motionless, watching her. She tried to keep her eyes on him, ignoring the city beyond and below. When she was within reach, he grasped her hand and led her the final few steps. They stood together balanced on the rim of the building. Kat held her breath and looked out over the city. She took in the pale gleam of streetlights, the phosphorescent glow from windows, the sustained voltaic arcs of headlights. Daniel was right. There was light everywhere. The city fizzed and burned with it.

They stayed there for a while watching the city pulse and spark below them, spread out in diminishing detail and increasing familiarity. From decorative cornices atop adjacent warehouses, to the newer steel-and-glass towers in the middle distance, to the immediately recognizable shapes in the city skyline—reduced to the size of tourist souvenirs amid the masts and jibs of tower cranes.

When they grew tired of standing, they sat against the wall of the adjacent taller building, its ancient brickwork blooming with salty efflorescence. She nestled between his legs, his hands resting lightly on her knees, while the sleepless streets coiled around them in incandescent rings.

He talked about the way the light moved differently in London than it did in New York. About the way the August heat there made the buildings shimmer. She listened, feeling the vibrations his words made against her back. The rest of the time they watched the thin edge of young moon that sat low on the horizon. She told him that she thought she would like to live by the ocean for a while. There were other things she wanted to tell him, but not yet. There would be time.

The word that kept running through her mind was "redemption."

They returned to the studio and slept for a while. When Kat opened her eyes again the rectangles of window above her were brighter than the ceiling. Daylight had returned. Daniel sat at one of the tables. He had a sketchpad before him, but he wasn't drawing. His hand rested in his lap while his eyes moved restlessly around the room. Keeping vigil.

The smooth green dress lay where it had fallen by the side of the bed, bold and garish against the rough, used floor. Clutching the sheet around herself, she bent down and grabbed a handful of the slippery fabric, the movement drawing his eye. She managed to find the bottom hem of the dress and work her arms through to the top. In one fluid motion, she stood up and let go of the sheet, feeling it slip from her as she pulled the dress over her head.

Smoothing the dress over her body, she found that it looked just as garish against her pale skin as it had against the floor. She bent down again and retrieved her purse and necklace from the floor. Somewhere in the studio were her earrings and her ring. She did not see them. So small and delicate, they could be anywhere. She imagined the ring, a perfect circle, rolling across the floor the night before.

She finally spoke, her voice low.

"I have to go."

"You don't."

"He's coming home today."

Daniel's expression changed instantly, his face clouding dangerously. Jonathan. He thought she meant Jonathan.

"My son." She said it quickly, her eyes remaining on him.

He allowed his head to drop into his palms before lifting it to look at her.

"Tell me that you're coming back."

"I'm coming back."

As she slipped her feet into her shoes, Daniel came toward her. She watched him reduce the space between them until he could reach out and touch her. Taking her face in his hands, he studied her intently. His gaze shifting downward to the dress, frowning, as if he did not recognize it. The extra height of her shoes put her close to eye level with him and she met his eyes, milky blue in the white room.

"Say it again."

"I'm coming back."

She could feel his warmth through the thin silk. And so, for the second time, the dress glided silently to the rough floor, pooling around her feet like so much paint squeezed from the end of a tube.

SHE DROVE QUICKLY, heading too far north before managing to find her way back down to the Ring Road, which took her back into Kensington. She parked and crossed the wide pavement across the road from her house, passing in front of the Greek embassy. As she did, the guard emerged from the side of the building and started up the driveway toward her. He stopped halfway up the drive. She saw him see her. Alone. In the green dress. In the pallid early-morning glow. This time he did not ask her why. This time he looked away.

She moved through the house like a thief. Turning on no lights. Gliding through the silent rooms. Taking inventory of the strange and ordinary things. Entering the bathroom, she caught sight of her face in the large mirror. The unfamiliar image arrested her. The downward curve of her mouth, with its thin, pale lips. The shadows under her eyes and the thin vein tracing a faint blue line along her left browbone.

She showered quickly, stepping into the stream of water without waiting for it to warm up, gasping at the shock of the cold on her skin. Only the tears were warm on her cheeks. The salt stung her skin. She had been right about the stubble on his face. She was sore everywhere. Rubbed raw. Turned inside out. She felt everything like it was the first time. The cold water, the raw skin on her face, the weakness in her legs, the pain in her heart. His hands on her skin, his mouth, his breath, his heat.

After the shower, Kat dressed and made her way down-stairs. Her whole body ached. She leaned back into the couch cushions. She would close her eyes for just a minute. And then she heard the door being pushed hard against the jamb, as if it might be unlocked, followed shortly by the clatter of the seldom-used knocker being deployed against its brass plate. It was shaped like the head of a lion, and Will used it at every opportunity. She ran to the door, pulling it open with both hands.

And then he is here. Spilling into the front hall. And she is on her knees, his skinny arms encircling her neck. His cheek against her chest, the pulse of life humming under his skin. And they built a dam! With sticks! And Fen helped. And Ollie. And he fell in the stream! Well, his foot. And it was so cold! And there was a thunderstorm—so very loud. He pulls back to demonstrate, pressing his palms flat against his head, his eyes wide. And she is Mummy again.

But now Will is squirming away from her embrace and Jonathan's mother is leaning down to kiss her cheeks and taking the measure of her with concerned eyes. And Jonathan's father is in the doorway with Will's bag. And would you believe the traffic on the M3? This time of day? And Will is kicking off his trainers and heading toward the stairs. And the cousins, Ollie and Fen, have come along and they fill her arms—Is this really your house, Auntie Kat? Do you love it?— before dashing upstairs after Will. And will they stay for tea? They will. And the house seems bigger each time they see it. And it does seem bigger suddenly. Full of noise and motion and people with dark curly hair and eyes like Jonathan's. And she sits back on her heels in the middle of it all until Jonathan's father reaches down with both hands to pull her up. And she wonders how it is that they don't see it on her face.

Kat tidied up the dishes from tea so Will could set out all his crayons and markers on the table. He talked while he drew, lost in the task.

". . . the storm was so big and Grandpa said that'll be the ruin of it then. But Ollie said maybe not. But when we went to look before breakfast the dam was gone."

She sat beside him, examining the rushing stream he had drawn, complete with sharply formed cresting waves threatening to overflow its banks. "The water is brown," he informed her, his eyes serious. "It is pulling the earth into it in great clumps. In this one the dam," he indicated a large, elaborate structure stretching itself across the stream, "is still intact."

She smiled. A new word. From Grandpa, she guessed. Or Ollie, so clever for his age.

She watched him in silence for a while, the tip of his tongue edging out of the side of his mouth in concentration.

"A little fox was here. While you were away."

He glanced at her, but made no reply, reluctant to relinquish his story for hers just yet.

"I think he came to see you, but you weren't home."

"No." His hand passed briefly across his brow to brush aside a wayward lock of hair that had fallen over his eyes. "He came to see you."

"You think?"

"He knows that you're sad."

"You think?"

"I know."

She leaned closer to him so that her head was next to his. He reached up and grabbed a handful of her hair, pulling his fingers through it absently the way he sometimes did. She closed her eyes, feeling the gentle tugs on her scalp. When she opened them, he was looking at her. His face with its wide forehead and dark eyes. So much like Jonathan's face. The similarities becoming even more evident as the roundness in his cheeks waned.

"When is Daddy coming home?"

She swallowed the rising lump in her throat. "Soon."

She sat with him in the quiet, watching him filling in the empty spaces.

Later, after she had sent him upstairs to brush his teeth and get washed up, she heard the sound of a door banging open. Her pulse quickened. Was it Jonathan? She entered the kitchen and saw that the door to the garden was open. Looking out into the gathering dark, she saw Will standing in the center of the garden, arms extended, holding a piece of paper over his head. No coat, bare feet, white shins visible below his short pajamas. Head tilted back, face to the sky. She shook her head in bewilderment. Careful to keep her stocking feet inside, she leaned out into the darkness and called to him.

"Time to come in."

He dropped his arms and turned to her, chewing his bottom lip, his face small and sad.

"What is it, Pie?"

She stepped out into the garden, the wet grass soaking through her socks with each step. He held out the paper to her as she approached. It was one of the drawings he had done earlier. "I made it for Nana. But I don't think she can see it. She's so far away." He raised his arms over his head again to illustrate the inadequacy of their reach.

She looked at his face, his lower lip still held between his teeth. They had talked about this. About how Nana was in heaven now.

"I have an idea."

Kat handed the drawing back to him and kneeled down. Will looked perplexed for a moment before his face brightened and he climbed up her back, hoisting his legs over her shoulders one after the other. She steadied herself, her fingers pushing into the damp ground, and then stood up. His hands were on her forehead. He was heavier than she expected, something she had come to expect. As she straightened up, her hands around his bare feet, he let go. She felt his legs go taut against the sides of her neck as he stretched up, raising his drawing closer to the sky. They stood together like that for a while in the fading light, her feet sinking into the soft ground as he pressed her into the earth, a delicious ache forming in her shoulders.

In the early-evening silence after Will was asleep, she wandered through the house. Light from the streetlamp shone through the drawing-room window, illuminating the four paint samples on the wall. She could not conceive of what any of them would look like spread across the whole of the room. How was she meant to choose from something so small?

The newspaper lay where she had left it on the table, open to the review of Daniel's show. As she reached down for it, her eyes fell on the image of the painting of the jade-green comb in her hair and she remembered where she had seen it.

They had been walking through the Marais late one afternoon when the comb had caught her eye in a shopwindow and
she stopped to admire it. Looking at it through the thin glass,
she could see it in her hair, could see what Daniel would see.
Moving on from the shop, she realized suddenly that she was
alone. Turning back, she had seen Daniel, still at the shopwindow. His face close to the glass, eyes concentrating intently
on the comb. Now it was there. In her hair. She folded the
paper carefully and carried it to the kitchen, pushing it down
the side of the bin under the rubbish.

Kat climbed the stairs to Will's room. It was by far the
most densely furnished room in the entire house. In the soft
glow of the night-light, she saw his plush animals arranged
along the floor beside his bed, their positions reflecting their
standing in his heart. A surprisingly gaunt gray elephant occupied pride of place at the center of the arrangement, his large
limp ears, the recipients of countless secrets, draped loosely
over his companions.

She leaned down to watch his face in sleep, knowing that
there was nothing that she wouldn't sacrifice for him. A truth
that at once sustained and haunted her. Exhausted, she sank
into the overstuffed chair in the corner.

chapter fourteen

It was, perhaps, the smallest measure of time. The moment between sleeping and waking when everything was as it had been before. It was gone before she took her first conscious breath. Replaced in a rush of memory. In the near darkness of the early morning, she kept her eyes shut and willed herself to remain still as it broke over her. But her body betrayed her, calling up sensations, playing them out on her motionless limbs like a movie flickering on a screen. For a while she was unsure if it was memory or desire. And then she wanted to sleep again. Just to have him once more. Just to feel him leave her. Just to lose him again.

And then Will's voice. "Mummy, did you sleep in my room for all of the night?"

She opened her eyes.

That morning, she made Will egg and soldiers for breakfast and then walked him to school, one hand in his, her other hand empty. Returning home, she climbed the steps outside the house, stopping before the front door, toes balanced on the top step, heels hanging off the edge, the polished lion staring back at her, brass ring clenched tightly between bared teeth. Not a hundred yards away on the opposite side of the road, she had spied the distinctive low haunch of the silver sports car. Surprise was not what she felt. She couldn't see him, but she felt him watching her.

After a moment, she turned and walked back down the steps. As she reached her car she heard the hollow growl of an engine revving to life. She didn't have to look in her mirror to know he was behind her as she drove into Shoreditch. She concentrated instead on the roads, gripping the wheel tightly as a black cab stopped short in front of her and lorries edged dangerously close to her lane. A bicyclist ran a stoplight just in front of King's Cross and she caught her breath as a car missed him by inches. All around her the city was suddenly crowded and dangerous.

She parked her car within sight of the entrance and watched him enter the building. She sat in the car, hands still on the wheel. There didn't seem to be anyone about, but she let five minutes pass before following him inside.

"You shouldn't have done that. Someone might have seen you."

He pulled her to him. She pushed back, but his arms were already around her waist. She gasped as his hands slipped under her sweater and up her back.

"No one saw me."

"Someone might have."

"No one did."

"It's reckless."

He leaned his forehead against hers. He knew that her words were not intended for him.

"I know."

His head slipped lower, his mouth moving on her neck. She tilted her head back, her body rising to meet his. And then he was pulling the sweater up over her head.

Later, resting under his hands, she looked down at the layered composition of their convergence. In the foreground the span of his arm across her waist. Below that, the long gentle camber of her thigh flung over his hip. Listening to his heart beating against her chest, she knew that it was worth the risk.

She scanned the room, taking in the well-organized space with its industrial furniture and fans and neatly labeled shallow drawers. The sleek metal tubes of paint, dangerously sharp pencils in their clean glass jars, unopened boxes of charcoal, pads of sketching paper, and different-size brushes and knives, laid out like in a surgery. The bright, neat space was far away from the rue Garancière. This building had originally been a factory. An efficient space designed to produce things. A place of expediency and of quotas, not of passion and creativity. It all seemed cold and contrived. Borrowed and temporary, like the car. Separate and distinct from Daniel. Above her, clouds swirled in the milky sky. Daniel shifted beside her. He was awake.

"Did they sell? The paintings in the show." Her voice seemed insubstantial and small in the large space.

"Yes." She felt him breathe the word into her hair.

"All of them?"

"Nearly. Martin wanted to save some for New York." She tensed at the name, but Daniel didn't seem to notice. His hands moved slowly, deliberately, over her skin.

She thought of the paintings and of what they represented. Arranged on the walls of the gallery, tracing the arc of their story. Now where would they go? Scattered in various strangers' homes and offices and galleries. Separate. Out of context. She imagined the painting of her in the blue bath hanging over Malcolm Jeffries's desk. What would their new owners see in them? They would never know their entire story, but maybe they would see pieces of the passion—both bright and dark.

She wondered if anyone would really know the entire story. Or if they would simply be drawn to the parts of it that appealed to them. And once they had found what they needed, they would stop looking for more. Had Daniel stopped looking after finding her? By leaving him had she given him back something to search for?

She closed her eyes and concentrated on his hands on her skin. She thought about how the paintings had become something other than what she had known them to be.

"It doesn't bother you to give them up?" she asked, her eyes still closed. His fingertips did not leave her skin, tracing her shoulders, her neck, her jaw, mapping the constellations of freckles.

"No. They brought you back. What more could they owe me?"

Watching as the whole sky drifted past piece by piece framed within the windows above them, she moved the flat of her hand over the scarred topography of his body, reading it like Braille. She was sure that she remembered every last scar, but there were new ones now. She lingered on the thick, raised lines that ran along his wrist above his veins. And then slowly, deliberately, she drew her hand across the line of his shoulder into the hollow of his throat and then down his chest and felt him turn in to her, his hands seeking her instinctively.

He lingered just inside the door as she was preparing to leave that afternoon. As she came toward him he hesitated, his eyes on her face.

"Look. I've got some money coming. Enough for us. Enough for a long time. So you don't need to worry about that. We can get a place. Maybe in Hoxton. Or in the country. Wherever you want."

Kat wondered briefly where the money was coming from. If the bulk of the paintings had sold before the show had gained momentum, then the real money would be made in the aftermarket. The early buyers would be the true beneficiaries of Daniel's success.

In the days that followed, she moved between them, the two halves of her heart. Each one perfectly formed, each whole within its own world, overlapping only on her body. The faint heat of breath on her skin. The feel of a hand in hers. A half-heard whisper. She was overcome by each, forsaking all others, but faithful to neither.

They didn't have long. Only a few hours. She learned to tell time by the spreading shadows on the studio walls. She would go to Daniel after dropping Will at school, leaving in time to make it back down to Kensington to park the car on the street outside the house and then dash to collect Will from school. The two of them would walk home through the park, stopping to feed the ducks at Round Pond—shunning the swans that hissed at them. The darkness came so early that sometimes the side gates would be closed and they would have to walk up to Lancaster Gate to exit. As they made their way along the top of the park in the gathering dark, Will gripped her hand a little tighter and Kat wondered where all the lights she had seen from the rooftop had gone.

It was far from routine, but every time she made the journey, retracing the circle from one to the other and then back again, she felt the momentum behind her movements. She was aware that the lines between them were being built up. It was within these lines that Kat began to think about a house in the country. Somewhere with a good school for Will. Maybe somewhere by the sea. The images flashed across her consciousness, leaving trails of light in their wake. She knew that it wasn't that simple, but maybe it wasn't that complicated either.

It was only at night that she was alone. She slept soundly, a fact that surprised her, and if she had dreams, she didn't remember them. She wondered at how quickly it became familiar. How easily he had returned to her. So that she was not entirely sure what she remembered from the day before and what she remembered from twenty years ago. She wondered where he slept. If he stayed at the studio or spent his nights at the Dorchester.

DANIEL WAS BENT over his phone when Kat arrived the next morning, checking his messages, she guessed. She walked around the edges of the studio surveying the canvases leaning against the walls in various stages of completion. She noted that there were no figures, only abstractions. The sketches of the girl that had been on the wall were gone. She picked an apple out of the bowl on the table and rubbed it absently on the fabric of her sleeve. A white paper coffee cup that hadn't been there yesterday sat next to the bowl, a stack of unopened post beside it. She ran her finger along the top envelope as she passed by. The return address was the Tate.

"What's the story with this?"

Across the room, Daniel lifted his head as she indicated the winter landscape. Its accretions of pigment pulled flat into thick, overlapping strips on the canvas.

He told her that he had found nature in New York City. That he had become captivated by certain trees in Central Park. Looking closer at the canvas, she noticed the long vaulted canopy of branches receding into the background of the painting and recognized the twin stands of elms lining the

Promenade. The only straight path in Central Park. Seeing such a familiar place through his eyes delighted her.

"Do you like it?"

"I do."

"It's yours," he said without hesitation.

For an instant she pictured it on the wide wall above the hearth in the drawing room. She caught herself almost immediately, but not before noting how the stark branches and bold shades would have provided an elegant counterpoint to the scene outside the window. As she turned away from it, her eyes came to rest on her parietal silhouette, suspended above the ground. He must have seen her looking at it.

"You'll like that one better once I finish it."

"What will you do with it?"

"Haven't decided yet."

"Maybe you should leave it the way it is."

"On the wall?" He raised an eyebrow. "It won't last long there."

"I like it there. I like that only we can see it."

He stood and came toward her. His hands found hers, lifting them above her head and pressing them lightly against the wall.

"Of course, if I were to do something with it, the next step would be color."

His fingertips stroked her open palm, moving down the inside of her forearm, flattening it against the wall. His other hand moving down the side of her neck, his fingers on her warm skin. She knew what he was doing. Seeking out all her colors. Arranging the progression of shades on his palette from light to dark. From the palm of her hand to all her shadowed places.

THE NEXT DAY Kat pulled the door shut behind her and hurried down the steps. Under her arm was a paper bag containing bread and cheese. They couldn't live on apples alone. It was the same food she used to bring home for them in Paris. Tourist food, he had called it. Smiling at the memory, she was only partially aware of the sound of a car door being opened and her name being spoken.

"Where to, Mrs. Bowen?"

She stopped short, coming face-to-face with Jonathan's driver, who stood on the pavement beside the black car. Farther down the road behind him a gate creaked open and a lithe figure emerged trailing several sleek brown dachshunds.

"Oh. Hello. I didn't know you were working today. Jonathan is still out of town, I'm afraid."

"His office rang me yesterday to say he would be returning sometime later this week."

"Right." Kat felt his words detonate around her.

"Is there somewhere I can take you this morning?"

"I think I'm going to drive myself. Thank you." She attempted a smile, indicated her car parked behind his, and started away from him.

"Don't think I don't know your secret."

Kat froze on the pavement and turned slowly back to him.

"Oh, and it pains me, it does." He shook his head and then winked at her. "You taking the bus."

She managed a strained smile to accompany his expression of sly amusement, backing away from him as the dogs passed between them, their tiny legs blurs of motion.

Kat checked her phone when she got to the car. Two missed calls from Jonathan. No messages. They had not talked in days. He would be back this week. A sense of urgency gripped her and she started the car and pulled away from the curb.

KAT WASN'T QUITE asleep when a steady knocking filled her senses. She sat up, panic spreading in her chest. It took her a moment to realize where she was. Was someone at the door? After a moment she realized it was just the radiator. She rubbed her eyes and looked around. The shadows on the wall told her it was late. The studio was cold. Daniel was on the opposite side of the room. She could hear him speaking in a low voice on the phone. She hadn't had to tell him that morning. He had seen it on her face as soon as he opened the door. He hadn't said anything, had just pulled her to him.

She stood up and dressed, moving into a patch of weak sunlight against the rough wall. She avoided looking at the charcoal silhouette. Daniel followed her as she moved around the room. Not so much with his eyes as with his body position. Conscious of where she was at all times even if he wasn't looking at her.

She waited by the door. He put down the phone and crossed the room, stopping just out of her reach.

"I'm coming back, Daniel. I am."

She saw a muscle twitch in his jaw.

"You'll come tomorrow."

"I can't. It's too risky."

"It's only a risk if you're afraid of losing something."

"It's not that simple."

"It is for me." He stopped speaking and stood quietly for a moment. "Everything I want is in this room."

She thought of what she wanted, what she needed, that was outside of the room. That at this very moment was in a small Victorian schoolhouse the color of clotted cream on a quiet road in Kensington.

It was cloudy when they left the studio. Stepping onto the pavement outside the building, she noticed that the glass shards were still on the ground. They had not been cleared away. A squat blue Renault was parked behind Martin's car, its engine idling in the cold.

As she stepped sideways toward him to avoid the glass, Daniel reached his arm around her, pulling her into him until they were joined at the edges. As he moved in closer, she saw the flash of light, reflected in the glass by her feet. By the time it reached her, it had already happened. Like light from a distant star.

Time slowed, moving only in the spaces between her heartbeats. She heard the sudden growl of a car engine. They turned in unison to see the Renault start haltingly and then accelerate loudly out of sight down a narrow street. As the sound disappeared after it, he reached for her. But she backed away, her eyes fixed on the street behind him down which the car had disappeared. Her hands covering her mouth in a childlike pose of horror. She imagined the photograph in all its damning detail. His arm around her shoulders. His face next to hers.

"Oh God."

"Kat . . ." He reached for her again.

She felt panic rising in her chest. "I told you. I told you it was risky."

They stood under the unblinking stare of so many empty windows. After a moment, it occurred to her that the photographer might return and she turned and began to walk in the direction of her car.

She heard his voice behind her. "Was it so different?"

She did not turn to look at him.

"Was it so different when only we could see it?"

She kept walking.

She drove quickly, the route familiar now. She was angry. Daniel's newfound fame had put her directly in the line of fire. The flash had obviously been a paparazzo looking to get a shot of the London art world's latest darling with his latest darling. Her only hope was that the photographer would not realize what he had, but she knew that hers was a face not entirely unfamiliar to the London media. The thought crossed her mind that Martin might have tipped off the photographer. How much had Daniel told him about her? About them?

She parked on the side of Holland Park. She would cut through on foot, in case she had been followed. She waited in the car for a moment. It was quiet save for the occasional distinctive low diesel growl of a black cab in the distance. She opened the car door and stepped out into the cold air, gasping as it closed around her like a fist. She had no coat.

She left the path to cut across the uneven, barren landscape, moving deeper inside the empty, frozen place. Her shadow moved before her on the rimy ground. How well she knew this place in the summertime. Altered by season alone, it seemed foreign to her now. The fragile blue sky was empty, swept clean by the wind. Even the air was devoid of any familiar smells. There were no places to hide and nothing familiar. If not for her memory of it—of having seen it—she could not imagine what awaited this winter landscape. The riot of color and life that lay sleeping in the frozen ground.

As she moved deeper into the park, there was no noise. Here nothing moved except the wind. Thin and cold and knife-edged, slicing through the naked trees, racing above the frozen ground around her, through her—making her solid and brittle, until she was sure she would shatter if she fell on the ground. Her breath came quickly. The sound of her footsteps as they crunched on the frosty grass seemed indecently loud. With every footfall she heard the sound of something breaking.

When the phone rang later that afternoon, she answered it immediately.

"Tell me, Mrs. Bowen, do you read the newspapers?"

Recognizing the voice after a moment, she stiffened.

"As I have told you, Mr. Warre, I have nothing to say to you at this time."

"Have you read the one about the wife of a prominent businessman caught in a compromising position?"

She was silent, as she had learned to be. It hadn't been Daniel they were after. It had been her.

"The thing about stories—they can be told in many ways, from many different points of view. Or they need not be told at all." He paused and she could hear his raspy breath. "This particular story hasn't run yet and it's of little interest to me. It would be very easy for me to forget all about it. But, as you are aware, there is another story that is of great interest to me. You get to decide which one is told."

He waited. It was her move and they both knew it.

"Mrs. Bowen?" he pressed.

"You know as well as I do that the *Mail* is not going to print it. Nobody cares about this."

He started to say something, but she cut him off. "Nobody cares."

She put the phone down hard and caught her breath. It was true. She knew that it was unlikely that the *Daily Mail* would print the story. But she also knew that the city was rife with publications that specialized in stories just like it.

Clasping her hands together, she rubbed at the unfamiliar soft circle of skin around the base of a finger on her left hand. It took a single heartbeat for her to register the fact that her ring was gone and one more for her to remember where it was.

chapter fifteen

Will wandered through the newsagent's, clutching his prize. The lollypop looked so big in his tiny hand. She smiled. She didn't usually indulge him like this, but she was feeling, well, indulgent.

As they left the till, a glossy magazine cover caught her eye. On it was a photo of Daniel. Still holding Will's hand, she slowed down to look at it. His face was intent, his gaze fixed some distance ahead of him. From the direction of his eyes and from his expression, it was obvious that he hadn't seen the photographer. He was wearing that same soft gray sweater he had been wearing the other night. She smiled slightly, involuntarily, recalling him pulling it off over his head and the soft silence as it hit the floor. She thought of the way he had kissed her. She thought of the way he tasted. She felt him pulling his fingers through her melting skin. It took only an instant for her to see the woman on the edge of the photograph. He clutched her tightly, his arm wrapped around her waist, his hand resting on her hip. Her dark red hair partially obscured her face, but did little to hide her identity.

"Mummy!" She looked down to see Will smiling up at her, as he pointed to the photo.

Kat sat in the park, unable to move, her eyes following Will as he played on the slide in front of her. Had there been a head-line over the photo? She hadn't noticed. Were there more pictures? She hadn't bought the magazine for fear of having to further explain it to Will. She had simply told him that it must be a lady who looked very much like her.

She looked at Will's face as he played happily in front of her. Her mobile phone was ringing. There were two missed calls. She recognized this new number. She picked up.

"I just saw . . ." She tried to control her voice, her eyes fixed on Will as he climbed to the top of the slide.

Daniel interrupted her. He knew. It was all right. Her name had not been printed. He would take care of it.

She could not imagine how this could be taken care of.

"What should I do?"

"Don't do anything. I'll talk to Martin."

"Not him. Please." The last word came out as a long, low breath, barely audible over the noise of the playground.

"This is what Martin does. He'll find a way to fix this."

She said nothing.

"Kat? Are you still there?"

"Yes."

"I'll come to you. Where are you?"

"No. I'll come to you."

"Come to the hotel. We'll figure this out together. Kat? Will you?"

"Yes." Will had a tennis lesson at the Pavilion in Hyde Park later that afternoon. She had been meaning to cancel it, but had forgotten to do so. She could dash over to the hotel while he was playing.

She hung up the phone and glanced around the playground uneasily. She felt a rising panic in her chest as she noticed the nanny across from her, one hand gently rocking a pram, the other flipping through the pages of a glossy magazine on her lap. It was only a matter of time before someone recognized her, if they hadn't already.

She thought about what Daniel had said. That this was what Martin did. She wondered how many times he had been called upon to fix a situation like this. Kat needed to talk to someone. She had few options.

"While it is unlikely that anyone is going to recognize your ass in the Penfield Gallery, your face on the cover of *Hello* magazine is an entirely different story."

Jorie's voice was difficult to hear over the din of the playground. Kat hunched forward on the low bench, phone clutched to her ear.

"Honestly, Kat. What were you thinking?"

"It never occurred to me that there would be photographers following us."

"I'm not talking about the photo. I'm talking about Daniel."

"I thought you would understand."

"Did you now?" Jorie's voice was suddenly indignant. "And why is that? Contrary to reputation, I've never cheated on any of my husbands, despite the fact that many of them deserved it, certainly a lot more than Jonathan. That's what I don't get. What was wrong anyway? Because I've been thinking about it and I can't think what it was. You weren't unhappy. You weren't unloved or ill-treated. That's what baffles me." There was static on the line for a moment and then she spoke again. "Or is it because he's your soul mate? Your one true love?" Kat heard the quiet mockery in her voice.

"Maybe he is," Kat said, suddenly defiant.

"You think? I did a bit of checking up on your soul mate. Apparently, he has cut quite a wide swath through his subjects. Rumor has it that is part of the reason he is now in London—too many pissed-off husbands in New York. So you've got to ask yourself. Were you different? Or were you just first?"

Jorie let the silence remain for a moment before she continued. "You know, I look back at the great loves of my youth and it turns out they were mostly about sex. Explain to me how you were better then than you are now? What are you going to do when Jonathan sees the photo? Because he is going to see it, Kat. And you need to figure this out before he does."

"I don't know what to do."

When Jorie spoke again, her voice was softer.

"Listen, you're a clever girl. Right about now, you are probably realizing the trap you are in. You think that you need this to be true. That you need this to matter more than all that you destroyed to have it. But, it doesn't have to be like that. This can still be a mistake."

"What if it isn't a mistake?" Kat said, her words diminished by the playground noise around her.

Jorie sighed. A deep sigh of not only sadness, but of lost hope. It was a sound Kat had never heard from her before.

"Then I can't tell you what to do. If there is one thing I know, it's that in the end, people do what they want. But I will tell you this—if you go back to Jonathan, it can't be just for Will."

Kat's voice, when she found it, came from somewhere deep inside of her.

"Why not? Why can't it be for Will? What better reason is there? What other reason is there?"

After the phone call, Kat sat on the bench and watched Will waving to her from where he sat atop the slide. For a brief instant, his small face set in determination as he readied himself for his descent, before dissolving into a breathless smile as he slipped down, the wind catching his dark curls and lifting them up and away from his face. Like so much of what she cherished as a mother, it was a small moment. She thought of how it is the small moments that change everything. Moments easily lost or found in the blink of her eye. Looking down at her hands, she saw the empty space where her ring used to be.

Kat shivered, remembering how cold the studio had been that morning. Spring had not yet arrived in Paris, but the heat had already been turned off for the season. The air felt raw and clammy and she could smell bitter, heavy rain through the closed windows. She had bought two tests, but she had only used one. She already knew. She thought at first that maybe she would not tell him. That she would just leave Paris. Just go back home. But she needed to see his reaction. She knew what she was looking for. And so she had said the words to him.

She had watched his face closely. So very closely. And there it was. She had seen it.

In the instant that she had told him. He had winced. It was so quick that she might very well have missed it if she had happened to blink at that exact moment. But she had not blinked. In the next moment, he had pulled her to him, roughly, and they had held each other. Neither trusting their faces. She felt his breath coming quickly.

He had said other things on that afternoon. Vague, reassuring words that she could no longer remember. But pressed hard against his chest, she had known that this was the way it ended. In the airless space, she had recognized the familiar shape of it, if not the detail. She told herself that it had been there all along. Biding its time within the ample shelter of the unasked questions, the unknown history, the unshared dreams. But had she been looking for it? Had she only seen what she had wanted to see?

Later that same night, she had woken to the sound of the

floorboards creaking and early-spring rain on the window and had lain silently, as he paced in the small space by the bed. Two steps one way and then two steps back. Adjusting his stride to fit the confined space. Already trapped. Much later that night she had woken to hear the catch on the window being released and smell the fresh air entering the room.

The next morning, she had woken early. The weak sun streamed through the dusty windows of the studio. Kat squeezed her eyes shut against the light. Closing her eyes, the ghost image of the window appeared before her—darkness where light had been. Daniel was already awake and dressed. Opening her eyes again, she watched him as he moved stealthily around the small room. He stood silently for a while in the center of the room, surveying the paintings arrayed around him, almost invisible in his stillness. Finally he spoke.

"You choose."

She did not hesitate.

"*The Blue Bath.*"

He was silent for a moment.

"I thought it was your favorite."

"You'll make more."

She closed her eyes. In place of a reply, she heard the soft crinkling noise of the canvas being wrapped in paper. She stayed in bed under the covers, feigning sleep. Before leaving, he had lain down on top of the blankets next to her, his hand stroking her hair softly. She felt the shape of his body, but not his warmth, not his skin on hers. And then his hand slipped from her hair and he was gone.

He returned several hours later. The gathering clouds had finally burst. She heard drops falling onto the studio floor and turned to the window to pull it closed. When she turned back, Daniel was holding it between his thumb and forefinger. A small patch of color. A single opaque green stone suspended in a thin lattice of silver, its shallow facets reflecting light from the overcast sky. A pretty thing.

She looked from the ring to his face.

"For you."

Before she could say anything, he pressed it into her hand and enfolded her in his arms. Outside the city dripped with spring.

After he was asleep, she examined it, snug on her finger. It was the first thing he had given her, but she doubted it was the first time it had been given. The inside felt soft, and the bottom bit was scratched and worn thin. She wondered whose fingers it had graced before hers and what long-forgotten promises it represented. Had it been extravagance or trifle? Affection or atonement? Had someone looked at it and thought forever?

She thought about what he had traded for it. One object for another. The murky blue water for a single spark of green clarity.

It was several days after the departure of *The Blue Bath* and the arrival of the ring. Alone in the studio, she had sat in the middle of the bed and, turning as one following the sun, made a complete circuit, viewing all of the paintings. Some in shadow, some in light, some half hidden behind things, some right side up, some sideways. She sometimes felt that without the pressure of her gaze affixing the paint to the canvas, it would simply slip off. She wondered if without Daniel's gaze, the girl in the paintings would slip from her as well.

Looking around the studio at the remaining paintings, she had thought that they were more than pretty pictures. That they were important. That they had value. But something was different. The easel was gone. An unfinished painting of her lay on the table. He had stopped working on it. She sat alone in the studio that afternoon, watching the setting sun draw lengthening shadows on the walls. By the time he returned, all light was gone.

Standing at the sink, he pushed up his sleeves and answered her unasked question.

"It's a commission. A portrait."

She hesitated. "Is that what you want to be doing?"

He turned from the sink to look at her. In the dim glow of the one lamp, she saw that his hands and arms were streaked with colors she did not recognize.

"You were the one who wanted me to do this. To sell something. Remember? Something I believed in."

"Yes, but . . ."

"Well, this is what they wanted to buy."

He turned his back to her and bent over the sink. He was already compromising. Doing what was expected. She saw that the streaks of paint extended up his forearms. Colors that did not belong. Soft dove gray and ruddy brown. Some yellow and flecks of red near his elbow. She pictured him rolling up his sleeves in a dove-gray drawing room. The same color that now streaked his arm. Taking care not to drip any excess paint, he had deferred to using his arm to wipe the brushes on.

As Kat watched, his subject began to materialize out of the various colors on his skin. She saw her thick dark brown hair. It must be long—falling past her shoulders. She wore a dark red blouse that complemented her warm skin. Had he suggested it? Had he volunteered that as a flattering color? Or had he been presented with a choice from her wardrobe? Several silken garments laid before him. She pictured him looking them over, selecting one and moving it to where she would be sitting, perhaps holding it up to her face, watching to see how the color looked in the light, feeling its soft-as-air texture, noting the way her skin glowed next to it.

In Kat's mind, the girl sat straight-backed on a wooden chair, the top of its delicate reddish brown curves just visible over her right shoulder. She looked sideways at him as he took into account the different hues in her hair. Noticing how it contained some red and even some black, but that in certain light looked nearly blue. How her skin was an altogether different shade of brown, and the light sheen it acquired later in the day, when it seemed to gleam around her brow. The contrast to the white of her eyes and teeth when she smiled. A shy smile, she thought. Something fragile. Something rare.

The faucet made a whining sound as he turned on the tap,

rising to a familiar high pitch when he added the hot water. Pushing his sleeves farther up, he reached for the soap above the sink.

Was she silent while he painted her? Or did she talk to him? What did they speak of in that cool drawing room with its pristine dove-gray walls? Kat pictured him unpacking his easel and setting out his brushes and paints. Had she been curious? Asked questions? How long would it take? Would she need to be entirely still or could she move? Where did he want her? How did he want her?

His shoulders shook slightly as he lathered up, his hands reaching up his arms as he scrubbed at the paint and then bent down and turned slightly to rinse it off. As he straightened, she saw that the water had reached almost to his elbow, leaving only a few flecks of red behind. The color of blood. The color of wine. Outside newly illuminated windows made small rectangles of light against the darkening sky. He had been gone most of the day. Even in the best of circumstances, the light would only have been good for a few hours.

KAT MADE HER way along the soft, empty corridor of the Dorchester toward Daniel's room. Even before she reached the door, she heard the voices. They grew louder as she moved closer. She slowed down.

"For Christ's sake, Martin, they talk about it in square feet—four hundred square feet of art." She could hear the indignation in Daniel's voice through the door. "It's wallpaper. They should just put their money on the wall—that's all this is about."

"You signed the contract!" Martin was shouting. She was surprised at how loud the small man's voice could get. "After a lifetime of anonymous work, someone wants to give you three million pounds and now you're jeopardizing it because of a little creative difference of opinion?"

"Look, it's me they want, right?" Daniel again. "They don't care what I paint, they just want to have a Daniel Blake on their walls. They'll change their minds when they see it completed."

When Martin continued, his voice was weary. "I don't know that they will. You heard Sir Richard, the Tate's patrons don't want . . ." There was more, but it was unintelligible.

Their voices quieted and she edged closer to the door.

". . . and why are you suddenly so interested in the money? It's her, isn't it?" Martin's voice lowered and Kat could not hear what followed. She moved even closer until she stood in front of the door, straining to hear the voices beyond it. ". . . the things you forget. Look at the scars on your wrists, for Christ's sake."

Kat shivered, remembering the feel of the thick raised lines on Daniel's skin. She waited for his response, but either he was silent or she could not hear him.

There was a pause and Kat reached out a hand to steady herself against the smooth pale yellow plaster of the wall before Daniel resumed speaking, his voice ice. "And you're slipping, Martin. You told me two million pounds. Planning to take a little bit off the top for yourself, were you?"

"Why shouldn't I? It may be your life, but it is my story." Martin's voice rose at the end of the sentence. Pausing for a breath, he continued, his voice increasing in volume as he went on, seeping out under the door and seeking her out in the hallway. "You owe me everything. All of this was my idea. I made this happen. You may have painted them, but I created the myth behind the redhead paintings. I spun the tale that made the art world sit up and take notice. I created you. Without me this is just another sad story and you are just another unknown artist." Kat heard a strange gurgling sound, like someone being strangled. Martin was laughing. "I'm so good, I even made you believe it."

"Maybe you did. Maybe you made everyone believe it. But it's me they want now. You don't have to be here at all." There was a pause and she leaned in closer to the door, although she needn't have bothered, as Daniel pronounced his next words clearly and slowly. "You are no longer necessary."

A maid came around the far corner and started down the hallway toward her, pushing a cart laden with eye-wateringly bright white towels. Kat didn't move, momentarily struck by the absurd thought that maybe she was invisible. That maybe she would not be seen.

"Is there something I can help you with, ma'am? Are you locked out of your room?"

"No. Thank you . . ." Kat replied, keeping her voice down as she backed away from the door and made her way toward the lift. As the lift doors slid open, she heard a door open in the corridor behind her. Out of the corner of her eye, she caught sight of a figure emerging from the room, but she did not turn to see who it was.

Kat stared at her distorted reflection in the polished metal lift doors before her. Suddenly unrecognizable.

As KAT ENTERED the house, her foot caught on something hard in the foyer between the two sets of doors. Looking down, she recognized the familiar shape of Jonathan's suitcase, standing upright against the wall. Will saw it, too, and he rushed past her, shedding his coat, his calls of "Daddy!" echoing through the house. Kat stood for a moment and then moved farther into the house, listening. Was he here? She heard nothing in response to Will's repeated cries.

If he was going straight into the office from the airport, Jonathan would sometimes have the driver drop his bags by the house. Retrieving her phone from her pocket, Kat saw that there was a message from Jonathan. He was back in London. He would be home late that night. There were two other missed calls. Daniel. She switched the phone off and went to find Will.

chapter sixteen

Kat stood at the doors to the garden, preoccupied by the lingering image of Will's slight form stretched out under the covers, hands curling over the top of the quilt. Struck once again by the joy she took in every new layer of form and experience that stuck itself to him. Thickening him. Making more of him. Had his fingers been that long before he left for the countryside? When had she last examined them closely? She felt a stab of shame.

As she watched, the little red fox appeared from under the far wall and came close to the door, pressing its nose against the glass. She could see it clearly. It was the first time she had gotten a good look at it. It was about the size of a small dog, with a delicately menacing, tapered face. They regarded each other through the glass. In that moment there was a tapping sound behind her. She looked away and when she turned back the fox was gone.

The tapping sounded close by. Will must be awake. She was surprised. He had been so tired that she was fairly certain he had been asleep before she left his bedroom. She was halfway up the wide front stairs when she heard the sound again. This time it was behind her. At the front door. She glanced at her watch. It was late.

Even before she opened the door, she knew who it must be. As the door moved inward on its hinges, light from behind her reached out to touch his face, illuminating his features. A car slid by, a mercurial blur in the near distance, and she shrank back, hesitating for just an instant before motioning him to follow. Watching him cross the threshold was at once the most natural and unnatural sight she could have imagined.

There were no curtains to close, so she switched off the lights. The vast room seemed even darker against the brightness of the garden lights, which threw lewd shadows onto the walls. Watching his silhouette against the illuminated garden, she let her fingers linger on the light switch and allowed herself to imagine that if she switched the lights back on it could be another life. That they could be together. She let herself believe this for just a moment. All things seem possible in the darkness. Then she thought of Will asleep upstairs. Removing her fingers from the switch, she moved toward Daniel, her silhouette joining his against the backdrop of the garden.

She fought the instinctive impulse to touch him. Martin's words still rang in her ears. "Myth," that was the word he had used. Was it all a myth invented to sell the paintings? Had she simply been reference material? She didn't know what to believe anymore.

"You can't be here." She kept her voice a low whisper.

He turned toward her, his face so familiar in the half-shadow, half-light. "I know. I'm sorry. But I needed to be sure you were all right. You're not answering your phone. You didn't come to the hotel."

She didn't contradict him.

"Look, the press don't know who you are yet, but Martin says that it is only a matter of time before they find out. He says we need to be prepared." His words were measured. "I need to know what you want to do. What you want to say."

"Why would I say anything to these people I don't even know?" She felt her face flush being made to answer to Martin.

Daniel hesitated for a moment. She couldn't see his eyes, just the hard planes of his face. When he spoke, his voice seemed disconnected from him.

"What about the people you do know?"

Standing here in her home, with Will asleep upstairs, she was being reminded of her family. She turned and took a few steps deeper into the house, her blood pounding in her temples. Stopping abruptly, she turned and addressed his dark shape before the window.

"Do you really think Martin is looking out for anyone

other than himself? Have you ever asked yourself how they knew we were going to be there? At your studio?"

"What are you talking about?"

"You were never that naive. A little scandal would bring quite a bit more attention to your show."

She waited for him to respond, but he was silent, watching her from inside the shelter of the shadows.

"How easy do you think it was to follow Martin's car?" she persisted.

"Martin's car? What are you talking about? The Porsche? It isn't Martin's car. It's my car. Why would you think it was Martin's car?"

"It doesn't . . ." She fumbled over her words. "It just doesn't seem like something you would have."

"You don't understand. None of this would be happening for me without Martin. He kept me painting. He kept me alive. I owe him everything."

She recognized the words that Martin had spoken to him behind the closed door of the hotel room.

"You don't owe him anything. All of this happened because of you. Not Martin. And not me."

She flinched at the loud crack of his hand striking the wall next to where he stood. The sound of the fugitive blow rang in her ears. Three separate thoughts entered her consciousness—forced together unnaturally by the impact. The feel of his hands on her skin. Will asleep upstairs. The thin icing sugar of the walls.

"All of this happened because of a sacrifice that I never

chose to make. You think this is the life that I wanted? I didn't choose this life. You chose it for me."

She could see the tendons in his neck as he moved closer to her. Here then were all the words that had not been spoken in all the hours they had spent together in the past week.

"You never answered my question. Why you did it. And don't tell me it was what you said at the hotel—because I didn't have money. I would have done whatever I had to do. I could have changed, Kat. I have changed. You never gave me the chance. You expected so little of me."

"No!" It came out as a sob, so sudden and ragged that he took half a step back. "I expected everything from you. I believed in you and I believed you—everything you said. You said you wanted to be great. More than anything." Her voice began to waver, but she went on. "I saw your face. When I told you. I only did what I thought you wanted."

He stepped closer to her now, his face a mask of barely contained pain. "That was just one moment. That was just the shock of it." His voice was a hoarse whisper now. "I wanted you. I've filled a hundred canvases with moments from that year. How is it that is the only one you choose to believe?"

When she spoke again, she could no longer keep her voice steady. She spoke her words into the shadows. "You don't know how it ate me alive when I had Will. That in that instant and in every day since then, I've come to know just what I have done. Just what I sacrificed."

Even as she said it she knew that although maybe it had once been true, it wasn't true anymore. That months often passed now when she didn't think about it. It had simply grown smaller the further she moved away from it. Even now, she knew that the memories she had of her mother that were so vivid, so immediate, would begin to fade. Imperceptibly at first, but inevitably. And that her recollections would come to be based on photographs, on the repetition of stories, rather than on actual moments.

"I'm so sorry. Tell me what you want me to say." She was pleading.

"I want you to say that you've been pretending. In an empty house, in somebody else's bed. That you don't belong here. That you belong with me."

"I do. I just . . . I just don't want to hurt him more than I have to."

Silence descended between them. He shook his head and looked away. In profile against the garden lights, he seemed only partially there.

"I'm asking you for time. Please . . . . I just need more time. I have a child."

"Yeah? Well, I don't."

Forgive me everything. The three words had reduced the sharp point on the soft pencil to a stub as she wrote them on his sketch pad. She had pulled the ring over her knuckle and laid it on the pad, placing the appointment card from the clinic next to it. So that he would know what she had done. So that he could hate her. So that he would not try to find her. So that he would not compromise.

She took only what she had brought with her. It fit easily

into her two small suitcases. It was only as she turned and stood in the open doorway, allowing herself one last look, that she noticed the unfamiliar pattern of stains on the wall under the window. Peering past her abandoned, half-read books, stacked neatly in their piles, she saw the empty space where the painting of the blue bath had been. Having lived with its presence for so long, she was surprised to find that in recalling it she saw it more clearly, more vividly than she had done while it had been there. Its gray-blue hues lingered within the confines of the newly empty space. The smooth, rounded edges of the tub separating the elements of water and air.

And then she was in a taxi in the soft light of dawn, watching the darkness drain from the sky into the Seine. The rain had stopped. And then she was in Charles de Gaulle Airport among the pinstriped men sipping their tiny cups of coffee and the tourists arriving from far away to see Paris in the springtime. And then she was in her seat on the plane.

She felt the wheels of the plane lift off the ground and saw the city receding beneath her, its suddenly unfamiliar boulevards and buildings filling the window. They were no longer connected. She could not touch it. Soon she could no longer see it through the thick double glass as they rose through the clouds. And as new air was pumped into the plane, she could no longer taste it or smell it.

She could hear his breathing in the darkened room and then the ringing phone intruded into the silence, so loud it seemed almost a physical thing. She cast a panicked glance over her shoulder as they stood in the darkness, waiting for the barrage to stop. Without the noise pressing on her, holding her up, the silence that followed felt so empty that she felt as if she might collapse.

He was so close. Unwilling to stop herself anymore, she reached for him. He took a step toward her, but the floor creaked loudly under his foot and she flinched at the noise. A small, instinctive movement. His face had passed into shadow, but she knew from his arrested motion that he had seen her reaction and she was sorry for it.

"I'll go." He said it quietly, almost a whisper.

"I'll come to the studio. I'll come as soon as I can."

He reached into his pocket and brought out a curled fist. She extended her hand and he dropped her ring and earrings into her palm without touching her. He looked at her for a long time, his eyes searching hers. All their colors lost in the low light. As his hands returned to his sides, she looked at them and she felt how it was not to have him touch her. She thought about what Jorie had said about not knowing when it is going to end and only recognizing in hindsight that it was the last kiss, the last touch.

He slipped so easily back into the darkness. Seconds after he walked out the door he was lost to the night. He reappeared momentarily under a streetlight—and then was lost to the blackness.

Kat stood unwatched under the lintel. Amber light spilled from the open doorway behind her, lengthening her shadow and drawing her eye to a quickening in the low hedge that separated the front garden from the street. A chaffinch perhaps, or a collared dove. Looking closer, she could make out a small twiggy clot near the heart of the squat shrub. It looked like the outline of a nest. The start of one. Although more likely it was the ruin of one.

She remembered it had been about a month after she had returned from Paris. It was the first weekend of the season at their summer house and she could feel the house expanding in the late-spring warmth after the long winter. Her mother stood in the kitchen, her back to her as she finished washing the lunch dishes.

"I think I know what happened to you in Paris."

Kat looked up from the book she had been reading. Her mother had not turned to face her. Watching, instead, a lark, in the tree on the other side of the window.

"I think you were pregnant and I think you had it taken care of."

Kat waited. The lark coming and going on the other side of the thin pane assured her that time was passing.

"What would make you think that?" She tried for surprised, but fell short.

"A mother knows."

Kat hesitated. Fearful that time itself was answering for her. That the silences contained more truth than her words ever could. She wanted so much to say yes. Yes. You are right. She desperately needed the protection, the solace of her mother. Her grace. Her forgiveness. The absolution of her love. She needed a witness. A savior. And yet equally, she desperately needed her mother not to know what she had done.

"That isn't what happened."

Her mother's eyes remained on the bird. Kat could see it on the other side of the thin pane, moving from branch to branch in a flurry of feathers.

"Would you tell me, if it was?"

"I don't know."

Her mother had still not turned from the window. The steam from the warm water had fogged the lower part of it. When she finally spoke, her voice seemed to come from far away.

"I want you to know that I understand. That I know you did what you thought was right."

She turned and looked at Kat. And Kat looked back into the same eyes that had watched her throughout her life.

"I understand," she said again.

Kat shifted her gaze to the window. There was no movement in the tree and for a moment she thought the bird had gone, but then she saw it. Detectable solely as a small pocket of stillness among the dynamic branches swaying in the light breeze. Kat watched the lark stay. The human eye is drawn to motion, but in this moment, her eye seemed capable of seeing only stillness.

Kat thought about her mother, at this same window, years earlier. Widowed. Alone. Pregnant. She searched the empty space, straining to see her again. Measuring her loss in the erstwhile silhouette against the window.

SHE HEARD IT later that same day as she sat on the edge of the deck, her legs dangling over the side, feet brushing the tops of the tall dune grass below. It was a small sound. A dull thud that contained within it the timbre of something important. Something connected to a larger whole. Although of a similar pitch and volume, it stood apart from the constant, oscillating growl of the ocean and the attendant fretful shushing of the dune grasses.

She found the bird just below the window. It lay on the deck where it had fallen, rendered unnaturally still by the impact. She approached it tentatively. Was it dead? Moving closer, she crouched down and lightly touched a jagged wing with her finger. It did not stir. Lying on the worn boards, it seemed like something discarded.

After a moment, she took it into her hands, awkwardly. Gathering it and re-forming it between her palms. Smoothing the feathers and folding the wings along their natural creases. Shaping it back into a bird. As her fingers moved along the animal's distal edges, its small, warm stillness bled into her. And in this stillness she was able to feel its hidden heart beating in her hands. It was alive.

She knelt on the hard boards, her fingers gently encircling the bird, conforming to its shape. Only its smooth head was visible above her thumbs, which bent around its throat. As she watched, a single obsidian eye flickered on and gazed at her in her supplicant's posture. Destroyer. Savior. Captor. The choice was hers.

And within that moment, she saw fully all that was hidden

inside her hands. The perfect symmetry of each feather, the curve of its passerine beak, the slender, slack beauty of each furled toe. The small, complete miracle of its being. And at once she opened her hands. She blinked and it was gone. A suggestion of feathers above her flattened palms.

Looking up, she expected to see it in the sky above her, transformed into something different in flight. Something other than what it had been between her hands. Something sleek and sharp—that which drew the shape, rather than the shape itself. But the sky was as empty as her hands. Looking down, she saw a small, bloodless scratch on the outermost layer of the skin on her palm. As she rubbed at its rough edges, feeling for any pain, she remembered that the bird had not struggled. That it was she who had opened her hands. And maybe she was sad. But as she gazed up at the possibility of the empty sky—a shallow, blue division between something and nothing—she was not sorry.

Afterward, if she pushed her hands together—palm hard against palm—she could still feel it, just under her skin—the urgent, staccato beat of a heart. But she knew it was just the pulse of blood in her own veins.

chapter seventeen

It could not have been more than an hour after Daniel left. Sitting in the darkness, her back to the window, Kat felt the understanding of what she had done grow inside of her, with a force that felt more like revelation than it had a right to, until she found her arms clasped tightly across her chest. As if to contain it. As if she could. It was then that she heard the sound of keys in the lock and the door being pushed open. She listened as Jonathan entered the hall and dropped his keys on the table. The sharp sound of metal hitting polished wood bounced off the walls.

She held her breath, as his heavy, solid footfalls approached the drawing room, only to pause at the threshold and then withdraw. She listened to the sound of his steps receding as he made his way upstairs. The floors were so thick that she could not hear him once he was past the landing. He would be in Will's room. Treading lightly, slowing down as he entered, eyes adjusting to the darkness. Leaning down to his sleeping face. Moving closer to breathe him in. She thought about what it must be like to be away from Will so much. To regularly go days without seeing him. Without touching him. Without hearing his voice.

Kat turned toward the doorway, straining to hear his footfalls as he moved through the house. She could see the edge of his bag by the door. An indication of arrival or departure. As she watched, his familiar shape appeared in the doorway. Seeing her, he stopped.

"You're here. I didn't see you."

"I'm here."

She stood and went to him, almost stumbling into his embrace. She took a deep breath. The stiff, creased cotton of his shirt smelled of airplane. She heard the steady beat of his steady heart. After a moment he pulled away, holding her at arm's length. He looked exhausted. Spent. But there was something else.

He moved farther into the room, stopping briefly by the windows to peer out into the world from which he had just come. Twisting the ends of each shirtsleeve around his wrist, he carefully extracted his cuff links and deposited them on the low table before the couch. Solid silver with a single initial that was not his own. Her mother had given them to him last

Christmas. Her last Christmas. It was the first time Kat had ever known her to give away anything of her father's. For a good man, the card had said.

"You saw the papers, then?"

She cringed and shrank from him. He had seen the tabloid. How? In the airport? And papers—he had said papers. There was more than the one?

"I am so sorry." Her voice broke.

"I suppose I should have known. Should have seen it coming." His brown eyes were rimmed in red and underlined by darkness. "I think I just wanted to believe it. That they were serious. That it was really going to happen this time."

It took a moment for his words to penetrate. The deal had fallen through. She relaxed so suddenly that she felt her knees begin to give way under her.

He was still talking. She willed herself to focus on his words. "I'll tell you, though. I've had just about enough of this bile from the press. It's all so very British. Success is fine, but not too much. Grow, but not too big . . . not too quickly . . . and God forbid you outgrow the boundaries of this island.

"I'll tell you something else." He looked at her gravely, his fingers moving swiftly down the front of his shirt, pinching the buttons free from their holes. She saw that his hands were shaking. "That whole 'poster boy for the new British economy' moniker. I never asked for that. They see you the way they want to see you. But, if it's true? If I am single-handedly responsible for rekindling the Internet economy in Britain, well, then I think it might be fair to say that I've done my part. If they want to hang me for high treason after all of that, then let them."

He was silent for a moment, gazing out the window.

"There is something else. It's possible that I've lost the board's confidence and that they're considering ousting me. I know I have Angus's support, but I'm not sure about any of the others. For better or worse, at least we should know soon. I suspect I am the subject of serious debate even as we speak."

She pressed herself against his chest, against the hard buttons on his shirt. And then she broke. Silently. Suddenly. Because she could. Because the occasion allowed it. After a moment, feeling the damp cloth against her face, she drew herself away from him, pulling her sleeves down over her hands and pressing them to her cheeks. His dark eyes brimmed with concern and contrition.

It was a look she knew well. He wore it to varying degrees on his return after long trips away or after coming home late or forgetting something—an important appointment, an anniversary. Although meant to be remorse, it sometimes looked more like nostalgia.

"Listen, Kat. I meant what I said. I'm sorry too. I had a lot of time to think on the flight. I left you alone. I thought that was what you needed. Maybe I wanted that to be what you needed." He ran his fingers through his dark curly hair, separating it momentarily into sections. The movement arrested her. It was the same gesture Will had made earlier that evening. "What I am trying to say is that I know that my attention has been elsewhere." He met her eyes. "You have it now."

She swallowed, trying to quell her nerves.

"So now what?"

"Come to bed."

"I'll be up in a minute."

Kat stood by the window looking out at the bare trees. Frail and brittle, they seemed powerless to hold the darkness back and it came closer, whispering at the glass. She waited there long enough to be sure that he would be asleep before climbing the stairs. Their bedroom faced over the garden at the back of the house, so there was no light from streetlamps. She was grateful for this as she lay unseen in the darkness.

She had never seen him like this. So bowed. Almost broken. Was it really possible that the board would take the company from him? It seemed unthinkable. Jonathan had always been his own harshest critic. Perhaps he was overstating it. But he was likely right that if they were going to do it, they would do it soon. She knew that he couldn't bear anything else now. She owed him time. She owed him more than that.

The next few days passed slowly. True to his word, Jonathan was home more than usual. Will was delighted to have Daddy along for the school run some mornings, insisting that he come through to his classroom so that he could be shown around and shown off. He was even home for dinner in the evenings. Kat cooked elaborate meals, planning the menu and visiting specialty providers for each ingredient in turn, just as she would do for dinner parties. Cheese and bread from Clarke's on Kensington Church Street, fruit and vegetables from Michanicou Brothers on Clarendon Road, lamb from Lidgate. She did so compulsively. Anxiously filling the hours until she could collect Will from school. In the evenings, they sat together in the dining room at one end of the long table. Framed inside the window, they must have made a pretty picture to anyone looking in from the road outside. More than once she caught herself looking out into the darkness, wondering if someone was.

She stopped counting the number of times she thought she glimpsed him on the road outside the house or on the High Street, or heard his car driving by at night. Was he even in London anymore or had he gone to New York for his next show? The last thought haunted her. The possibility that he could already be gone.

Kat slowed down unconsciously as she approached the school gates with Will. The weather was warmer. She hung back from the crowd, listening to the hum of the conversations and laughter. She wondered about the seductive power of the single perspective and the way it made mysteries of others. She wondered what more there was to each of these women than what she saw.

The large double door at the top of the steps had opened and children were beginning to file up the steps in their navy-blue-and-red uniforms. She edged closer to the school, wading waist-deep into the crowd of children until Will squeezed her hand. She leaned down and kissed him, her lips catching a loop of curl and pressing it to his forehead before he disappeared. After a moment he appeared in the open doorway at the top of the steps, pausing briefly under the pediment before making his way inside.

She made her way home slowly through narrow streets lined with red brick Victorian mansion blocks and tidy stucco-fronted cottages. Past blue plaques commemorating that John Stuart Mill, philosopher, had lived here, and that T. S. Eliot, poet, had lived and died there. History, all that had come before, reduced to spots of color. Glazed blue ceramic disks on a wall.

She had run through the parks that morning, altering her usual route only slightly, so she came and went through the gate on the mews, rather than having to cross in front of the embassy. She ran sluggishly, aware that her times were off. Gravity seemed to lean more heavily on her.

Jonathan was still upstairs when she returned home. She could not remember the last time he had slept so late. He was clearly still exhausted from the travel and stress of the past few weeks. The package lay on the front hall table on top of yesterday's post. She glanced nervously at the return address. Eliasson Architecture. She carried it through to the kitchen and opened it on the table. Inside was a small thick compliments card in Smythson's Nile Blue and a set of architectural drawings. She read the card.

Dear Mrs. Bowen,

Please find enclosed revised plans for your home at 31 Holland Park. What we have endeavoured to do is to strip it back to its basic elements and then build from that. Everything we are proposing serves only two purposes—to highlight the essential elements and beauty of the house, and to create a space that suits your life. We have attempted to be true to the history of the house and to the way in which you wish to live your life.

To this end, the mouldings remain, as does the original flooring on the ground and first floor levels, along with the staircase and the windows. We do not recommend refurbishing the floors or the woodwork. We have left the signs of age, of wear, the markings of its history, its scars.

As you reminded me when we met, the quality that is required most with a house like this is restraint. Sometimes it is that which remains unfinished that remains most beautiful.

Of course, only you can decide what is essential.

Kindest regards,
Charles Eliasson

She removed Will's breakfast dishes from the table and spread the plans out before her.

This time she recognized the now-familiar bones of the house. The large entryway and the sweeping staircase at its heart, the thick exterior walls. Examining the drawings, she saw that the layout was more open. The wall between the dining room and kitchen had been replaced with a segmented arch, creating a single spacious, light-filled room, with direct sight lines into the garden. The bricked-up side windows on the upper floors had been opened. She noted with surprise that the canopy over the front walkway had been retained. While it was not original, she saw that it served a purpose. The excessive decoration that had characterized the previous plans had been replaced by a pared-down, functional approach that allowed the original beauty of the architecture to come through. The house seemed to have returned to being a vessel. Something that served them rather than something they served. A marriage of life and history. A compromise. It wasn't what it had been before. It wasn't all that she wanted it to be. She wondered if it could ever be enough.

She almost missed the stiff envelope clinging to the package. It had already been opened and the exposed glue had adhered it to the underside. She pulled out the card and read it. "Sir Richard Hawthorne and the Cavendish Restaurant Group invite you to the opening of the Tate Restaurant, 21 February." Her eyes scanned to the bottom. "Featuring original artwork by Daniel Blake." The card trembled in her hands. She saw that Jonathan had already filled in the response card indicating that they would attend.

She tried to think rationally. Just because it was Daniel did not necessarily mean that the paintings were of her. But the car keys were already in her hand. She told herself that there was only one way to be certain. The now-familiar route to the studio elicited a kind of Pavlovian anticipation that mingled with her growing fear, so that she arrived at the studio in a profound state of disquiet.

The main door to the building was propped open with a thin wedge of raw wood. She thought about removing it after she entered. It didn't seem safe. But she replaced it, trapping it between the door and the frame. Her knocks on the studio door produced a series of sharp echoes that traveled the length of the long hallway. After a few moments, she rapped again on the metal, harder, the noise reverberating and then dying in the space. She knew he was here. She had seen his car outside.

When he finally opened the door he wavered briefly before pulling it open wide without a word. She slipped past him under his outstretched arm. He was unshaven and his hands were streaked with color. The fans were switched off and there was a ripe, sweet smell in the still air. Turpentine.

"I just . . ." She took a quick breath. Her mouth was dry. "I just got this." She pulled the folded invitation out of her coat pocket and held it out to him. "An invitation to the Tate opening. It has your name on it. Original artwork by Daniel Blake."

He said nothing. He was smiling at her. She lowered the invitation. It had seemed important that she bring it with her, but it just felt ridiculous now. The metal radiator along the far wall began to hiss.

"Daniel."

"I knew you would come back."

He was still smiling at her, although he seemed to be having trouble keeping his eyes on her, he kept looking past her. She turned around. A large unfinished canvas sat on a low easel behind her. She recognized the shape. He had transferred her outline from the wall to the canvas. But this was no mere outline. Although it was far from finished, the color

had been blocked in and the detail had begun to emerge. Unlike the pure, almost sculptural form on the wall, this figure
had weight and warmth and substance. She cringed, taking
in the bared flesh, the thickening middle, and the start of faint
silvery markings spreading across her white belly. The down-
turned breasts, bordered by the outlines of an arrangement of
soft limbs. Her face, with its sad mouth, was half turned away.
A thin sheet, an afterthought, lay next to her. Used. Discarded.
Was this the way he saw her?

She turned back to him. He was gazing at the portrait, his
head tilted to one side.

"This for the Tate?"

He didn't answer, eyes still on the painting before them.

"Daniel. You can't do this. You can't put this on the wall
of the Tate."

"I signed the contract." He turned to look at her. "With
the money we can get away. Then it won't matter what's hanging on the walls of some restaurant in London."

He looked back at the portrait. He wasn't listening. He
wasn't hearing her.

She followed his gaze to the painting and all its immediate, irrefutable detail, desperation and dread rising in her chest.
Here were her sins. Reduced to what fit within this rectangle
of stiff cloth. A single image, a single perspective. Without
explanation or palliation. And while people might not have
recognized her nineteen-year-old face on the walls of Penfields,
this was certainly a more familiar face. The canvas seemed to
expand before her. Here was what Jonathan would see. What

Will would see. It would become the truth. That, she knew, was what art did.

Her heart was racing. No. No. No. She would not allow this to happen. Not now. Not like this. Daniel was saying something now, but she couldn't hear the words. The sound from the radiator had evolved into a thin, high-pitched scream.

The flat blade was cold against her wrist. Her fingers closed around the wooden handle. He hadn't seen her pick it up. She moved toward the portrait. Close-up, the detail overwhelmed her. Her thighs, her stomach, the hollow of her hip, the weight of her breasts, her shoulders, her neck. Her face. The ruins of her. She crossed in front of the portrait and stepped behind it.

And then she was gone. The painting was between them now. The blank back of it stiff and tightly drawn between its wooden bracers. A different possibility. Just as real as what was on the other side. She relaxed her fingers and felt the knife slide down the inside of her wrist.

She heard him moving on the other side of the portrait. It had to be now. She lifted the blade over her head. Feeling its lightness, she brought her other hand up and, grasping it desperately in both hands, drove it down with all the force she had inside of her. She felt the canvas give way gratefully under the sudden pressure and heard the ragged sound as she pulled the blade through the thick cloth. The portrait wobbled dangerously and there was a sharp, short cry. She stepped back, pulling the knife out as the painting listed to one side and then clattered to the floor, bringing the easel down with it, and revealing Daniel hunched over, clutching one hand in front of him, eyes wide with pain and confusion. Blood trickled from a small angry gash at the base of his palm.

Seeing the wound triggered an automatic response in her and she reached for him. He recoiled, stepping backward, knocking into a low table and sending various jars and metal containers crashing to the floor. She looked down to see the knife still in her hands, and pushed it from her, sending it spinning across the floor to the far wall, where it lay inert.

Once she was disarmed, Daniel reversed direction, veering past her to the painting. His knees sagged and he fell beside it, leaning across it to inspect the wound, a long vertical tear bisecting her forehead and left cheek. His fingers traced the scar, gently feeling along its edges.

She inched closer, peering at the rip from above. It gaped back at her in mute surprise, a fine down of severed weft softening its hard edges. As her shadow moved across the canvas, she saw that there were several bloodstains just underneath the tear. The largest, a bright red dime-size ellipse, with a short tail pointing downward. He must have been trying to move the portrait, maybe tilt it forward on the easel to see her behind it, when the knife had found him.

He turned to look up at her, his face a mask of confusion. "What did you do?"

She didn't answer. Looking down, she saw that there was more blood on the canvas now. Small florid drops of it had collected above her shoulder. She watched, transfixed, as more traced a diagonal slanting path down the underside of Daniel's forearm, falling from his elbow. He saw it, too. "Shit!" He scrambled to the side of the fallen portrait, landing sitting on the floor beside it. She stood frozen, her eyes on the vivid trail of blood migrating down his arm.

As she watched, he drew his hand absently across his shirt, leaving a bloody smear in its wake. The lurid stain woke her from her shock. "Daniel!" She cast about, looking for something to help stanch the flow of blood. There was a collection of paint-covered rags mounded under the legs of the upturned easel. She knelt and reached for them. The floor around the easel had acquired fresh spatter; she could feel it sticking to her. There were several discarded brushes strewn about on the concrete floor, their bristled heads crusted with newly dried pigment.

Kat grabbed a fistful of the rags, but they were too small. Kneeling beside him, she pulled the scarf from her neck and wrapped it around his hand, the blood immediately soaking into the soft material. Up close, she could smell it. A heavy, primal odor. She pulled hard on the ends of the scarf, straining until the flow of blood stopped, and knotted it. Her hands were shaking.

He reached up and touched his fingers to her mouth, the slight pressure parting her lips. She could taste him. It was almost more than she could bear.

"Do you really want to save me?"

"Of course." She spoke the words softly without moving her lips. After a moment he sagged back against the wall and his fingers fell away. The charcoal outline was above him, already smudged and fading. His eyes fixed somewhere behind her, an expression of despair etched on his face.

"I'll give you up. If that's what you need. I'll do that for you, but you can't ask me to stop painting you. You can't take that from me."

"Why me, Daniel? What about all those other women?"

He turned to face her, his head still resting against the wall behind him. "What other women?"

"The girl from the gallery." Kat turned to where the sketches had been taped to the wall, but they were no longer there.

Daniel leaned forward, following her gaze to the vacant wall. "Annabel? Her father is paying me to paint her portrait. It's just for money, Kat. That's all."

"But, she was at the gallery with you. And the other women. In New York."

He shook his head. "None of that is real. It's all just . . . Martin thinks it's good for me to be seen with them."

She said nothing.

He lifted his head and faced her. "There's no one else. After you left, I lost myself for a while. I did some things I'm not proud of. But, all these years, it's only ever been you." He looked down at the painting and then back up at her, his eyes the color of water. "Don't you see that?"

She looked down at the portrait beside them. She saw now that the surface had been heavily reworked, wiped down and started again, the layers of paint imbuing the figure with an almost corporeal presence so that it seemed to float above the raw canvas that surrounded it. There was a confidence, a sublimity to the rendering, that made it seem whole even in its unfinished state. She leaned in closer, brushing her fingers against the bright white weave of the still-unpainted spaces.

She lies across the bed. A vertical streak, a willful smudge. All her colors pressed and pulled into the sheets. They bleed together so that in some places it is impossible to say where one ends and the other begins. Her face, turned to the side, seems to consist entirely of darkness and light, in all their infinite combinations. Softened by shadows, she is neither old nor young. Her eyes are closed. The tips of her front teeth visible where her lips part.

The sheet is bunched loosely beside her hip. A vestigial modesty. There is a heaviness, a weariness to her. A stillness, which she has paused within and seems reluctant to leave. It is an image not only of the moment itself, but of all that came before it. That which has already passed.

Buried somewhere among the overlaid paint, Kat recognized the shadow of the girl she used to be. In her eyes maybe and the bones of her face. In the delicate flush of her cheeks and gentle softening of her aspect. It was the kind of insight that came from pure understanding, independent of context. Daniel's unwavering gaze, undeterred by time or even by absence. And she understood at last that this was what love looked like.

Just as she turned back to Daniel, she heard the rusty rasp of the door swinging open. She hadn't heard a key in the lock, but she hadn't seen Daniel close it either. Martin. He stood in the doorway, looking as disheveled as she could remember seeing him, the narrow point of one of his collars poking up indignantly from his shirt. His expression of mild surprise when he saw her quickly escalated into shock as his eyes fell first on the lacerated portrait, then on Daniel's bloodied shirt and arm.

"What the devil?" He stepped inside and shut the door abruptly behind him, looking from Daniel to Kat and then to the damaged portrait that lay beside them.

"It was an accident," Kat said. "I . . . I didn't see him. I didn't know he was there."

Martin's eyes left the wounded canvas and moved to where Daniel was, still sitting beside the portrait, one hand cradling the other close to his chest. The radiator had run out of breath and was now emitting a frantic metallic clanking.

Kat stood up and took several tentative steps toward Martin. "It was an accident," she repeated.

Martin's eyes traveled around the room, cataloguing the damage. "You should go." His eyes were dull and dark in his face. He didn't look at her, but moved farther into the studio, stepping over the upturned easel, squinting down at Daniel against the wall.

He was still talking. "Go now. I'll take care of this." She started to protest, but he interrupted. "He needs a doctor. Maybe an ambulance. I know you want to be here, but how would it look?" His words were conciliatory, but his voice was impatient and agitated.

Daniel was trying to hold his hand to his chest, but it kept falling toward his side, leaving rust-colored arcs on his shirt. It was not an unfamiliar sight. She could almost believe it was cast-off paint. The knot must have loosened. "You need to tighten it. He's bleeding." Kat took a step toward Daniel, but her foot slipped in a puddle of something on the floor. She caught herself on the edge of a table and regained her footing.

"Katherine!" Martin's voice was harsh and close. She looked up to see he was beside her, between her and Daniel. There was rage in his eyes now. She moved to go around him. With a quickness that surprised her, his hand shot out and he grabbed her by the wrist, holding her firmly. Her heart was beating very quickly and she could feel her pulse compressed under his fingers. She could smell his breath, musty and unfamiliar, and pulled back from him, but he grabbed her other arm, shaking her roughly. She opened her mouth, but no words came. All the breath had gone out of her.

"Take your hands off her!" Daniel's voice like thunder from behind them.

Martin froze, his hands unyielding, digging into her skin. Daniel was moving toward them. He stopped just before he reached them, his gaze fixed on Martin. After a moment, she saw something pass between them. Martin lifted his hands from her, nodded briefly, and stepped back. She started toward Daniel, but he held out a hand to stop her.

Around them everything was still. Even the shadows on the wall behind him were fixed in place. The only movement was Daniel's gaze following Martin as he retreated behind her. He waited a beat before shifting his eyes back to her. There was something in his expression. Something that got her attention.

"It was never any less real, you know. It was never any less real because only we could see it."

"I know."

She met his eyes and for a brief moment there was nothing but the slender thread of their gazes. There was a lightness in his face, a peace that she had not seen there before. He smiled at her, a small one, but real.

"Go." He said it softly, to her alone.

Behind her Martin opened the door. She kept her distance, stepping sideways around him into the hallway. Both men watched her leave, but her eyes remained on Daniel, arms now braced against a table. His face was ashen.

Just before the door swung closed she caught sight of the damaged painting where it had fallen. It wasn't a large cut. Maybe six inches. But it was irrevocable. Terminal. The door closed in front of her.

She stood in the deserted hallway, waiting for her breathing to return to normal. As she turned to walk toward the lift, she thought she heard the chink of the dead bolt being slid into place.

She thought she might see the ambulance before she left, or hear it at least, but she didn't. She drove aimlessly, following the flow of traffic through gray and indifferent midmorning streets and roundabouts. Daniel would be fine. Martin would see to that. She repeated it to herself. Gradually, her hands stopped shaking. The lingering odor of paint surrounded

her. It was on her clothes. Small spots and streaks on the
knees of her pants. Her wrists ached. When she looked down at
them she saw there were red stains on the edge of her sleeve as
well. These were not paint.

It was afternoon when she arrived home. She had a vague
sense that she had forgotten something. The tall crystal vase
stood empty on the side table. She hadn't bought her lilies this
week. Perhaps that was it. Jonathan must have noticed it, too.
The doorbell rang later with a large bouquet of the blooms
from him. Kat laid the flowers on the counter and untied the
coarse brown cord wrapped tightly around their damp stems.
As she separated them, their insistent perfume was already filling the air, reaching for the edges of the large room. She could
hear the housekeeper moving about across the hall. The radio
was on to the BBC and she listened to the news while filling
the vase with water. Using a small pointed scissors, she cut the
ends off each of the thick stems before arranging them one by
one inside the tall, angular container.

She heard his name first. Suspended, without before or
after. And immediately she was alert—listening to what followed it while desperately trying to claw back the words that
had preceded it. For the first few moments, these fragments,
conveyed in the crisp home-counties accent of the BBC
newsreader, were vague enough for her to doubt.

". . . the cause of a fire that broke out at his Shoreditch
studio, destroying several adjacent studios, is under investigation."

". . . speculation that a number of recently painted canvases that had been cut out of their frames and stuffed into a closed rubbish bin . . ."

". . . oxidized . . ."

". . . combusted . . ."

". . . killing the artist."

He exited her life in the room where he had stood only days before, silhouetted against the garden lights. And like then, there was nothing for her to hold on to. She grasped at the vase and felt it fall heavily onto its side. The voice of the newsreader continued unabated, but she no longer heard him.

She looked down at the empty vase that lay before her, still whole. A thin thread of water flowing from it connected the table to the bare floor. She thought that it must be a mistake. Then she remembered the stale air. The fans had been switched off. The studio was filled with combustibles. Something had spilled. She had slipped on it. She thought about the paint-covered rags. All it would have taken was a single spark. As she watched, the line of water broke, falling into the small puddle at her feet, and she felt him leave her, taking with him everything that he had seen. As the room swam around her, her eyes fell on a stack of new school jumpers awaiting name tapes. What time was it? She had forgotten to collect Will at school.

Kat made her way through Kensington automatically, the earth no longer beneath her feet. A fine mist of rain was falling around her, obscuring the red brick buildings, blurring their hard edges so that they dissolved into pavement, melting into their own reflections on the slick streets. Cars sluiced by as she crossed the High Street, throwing off sprays of white noise. He was already gone. He had been gone for hours and she had been unaware of it.

As she walked on, the mist grew thicker, rising around her, as if all the rain that had ever fallen on the city, running off its rooftops, spilling into its streets and seeping into the ground, was issuing forth from it. Lifting itself out of the crevices between the stones, out from the dirt, out from the roots themselves, returning to the air in a great exhalation. The particles enveloped her, and she breathed them in. The mist tasted of him. Of sweet breath.

It seemed altogether such a soft thing, but the droplets burst like sparks in her eyes, blurring her vision and making her blink. Ahead of her streetlights flickered on. The mist trapping their light, compressing it into yellow halos hung just out of reach.

The mournful peal of the bells of Saint Mary Abbots reverberated around her. In that instant she was struck by the thought that the bells themselves no longer existed. That the act of ringing had caused them to break apart and all that remained was the sound itself. It was as if the city around her had been vaporized. Everything had come apart and the molecules were reeling around her, rearranging themselves into another world. A world without him.

By the time she arrived at the school there were no children or parents outside. She climbed the steep steps and stood for a moment, catching her breath before ringing the bell. Her hands were shaking.

The door buzzed open. Kat made her way down the narrow corridor to the headmistress's office, assaulted by sharp points of brightly colored paper bunting hung from the low ceiling. Empty of children, the school was eerily quiet. The headmistress, a soft, drowsy-eyed woman with silver hair, stood up behind her desk when Kat entered.

"I'm terribly sorry, Miss Garland. I . . ." Recognizing that an explanation was what was called for, Kat started speaking automatically before realizing that she couldn't provide one. Instead she extended the apology, her words coming from some emergency reserve of politeness. "I do hope I haven't put you out too much."

"Not at all, Mrs. Bowen." The room was dimly lit and the large window behind the desk heavily draped. Kat was vaguely aware of brightly colored children's drawings on the walls. As Kat approached her, Miss Garland's face registered concern. "Is everything quite all right?"

The answer she would have given did not come. Instead Kat nodded, reaching up to smooth her hair, damp and curling from the drizzle. A shroud of mist had settled on her skin.

"Won't you sit a minute? I've just sent William off to the library to return some books."

Kat sat in the proffered armchair as Miss Garland came out from behind her desk and settled herself in the large wingback chair opposite, ankles crossed demurely before her. She smiled briefly, reassuringly, faint flecks of pink lipstick visible on her front teeth. The chairs seemed unusually close to each other. Downy seedlings in plastic pots were arranged on a tray under a bright lamp on the table beside them. Tender, half-formed things bowing toward a false sun.

Miss Garland inclined her head forward, eyes gray and grave beneath heavy lids. "I had wanted to extend my condolences, Mrs. Bowen. We were all so very saddened to hear of your loss. Such a dreadful blow. To lose the person who knows you best. Who truly sees you for all that you are." She shook her head sadly.

Kat sat speechless, her mouth open. How could she possibly know?

"Makes no difference what age one is. There can be no substitute for that kind of love." She placed her small hand on Kat's knee, patting it lightly. A conciliatory gesture of the type one might extend to a small child. "But of course, it's never really lost. It's the same love that we pass on to our own children."

Her mother. Of course. Kat watched the drawings on the wall behind her soften and blur. When a neatly folded handkerchief appeared before her, she took it and pressed it into the corners of her eyes.

Miss Garland didn't speak nor did she seem to expect her to do so and for that Kat was grateful. They sat in silence. A lingering odor of pine from recently removed Christmas decorations hung in the air. After a few minutes, Kat heard footsteps in the hall outside and raised her head. Miss Garland shifted in her seat and looked up.

"That'll be William." Miss Garland's voice was a crisp whisper. "You'll want to collect yourself now."

Kat patted at her face with the handkerchief and cleared her throat. As Miss Garland stood, a small needlepoint cushion dropped forward from where it had been trapped behind her, gasping and swelling on the seat of the chair.

And then there was Will, blinking in the doorway, all his molecules miraculously in place, save for one long sock that had slipped down, exposing a pale pink knee.

THAT NIGHT SHE lay awake, listening to Jonathan's steady breathing beside her. She imagined Daniel alone in his studio. After the doctor or the paramedics had left. After Martin had left. Saw the shape that his body made on the bed. She wondered if he could still smell her on the pillows.

For a moment she thought that she might have stayed with him. And for a moment, she is there. They lie skin-to-skin under the soft rectangles of sky so far out of reach above them. She can hear his heart beat and feel his breath in her hair. Would the fans have been on if she had been there? Would she have smelled smoke or fumes? For a moment she wondered, but she knew that ashes were not her fate.

She wondered if any of it had been real. If he had really returned. Or if he had been a ghost. Someone she had conjured. Someone only she could see. But, it was in the papers the following day.

The artist is the sole casualty of the fire, which destroyed his studio and several others, causing extensive damage to the rest of the building. Also lost were dozens of recently completed works and works in progress, notably a triptych intended for the Tate Restaurant. Initial investigation indicates the cause of the fire to have been accidental.

Sir Richard Hawthorne, who had recently selected Blake for the Tate commission, has made the following statement. "Daniel Blake's death is a tragedy. One mourns not only the loss of the man, but of all that he had yet to create. It is the death of possibility."

Blake's longtime agent, Martin Whittaker, issued the following statement. "In the end, Daniel has become like his most famous subject—ageless. And while it is tragic that we have been robbed of seeing what more he would have given us, it is equally true that we will be spared knowing what time and age might have taken from him. He exists forever at the height of his artistic abilities and fame."

This, then, was the genesis of the myth. This was where it began. She could hear Martin testing out the words, refining them, weighing them against his aims.

In the days that followed, Kat mourned under Jonathan's watchful eye. She did so silently, ritualistically, behind an impassive face, surrounded by the things he left behind. Sky through a window. The smell of wet pavement. Dust swimming in the light. She walked Will to and from school, one hand in his, her other hand empty. She attended the start-of-term coffee morning for his class and made small talk with the other mothers, smiling over accounts of Christmas holi-

days and making the expected promises of play dates and evenings out. She confirmed the arrangements for an upcoming
trip to Klosters with friends. In the evenings, she sewed name
tapes into Will's new school jumpers, feeling the prick of the
needle and watching a bead of blood rise on her fingertip
while outside the darkness licked at the glass.

His was an absence she had lived with for twenty years.
The shape of it, the size of it hadn't changed. But its perma-
nence and its proximity had altered it. It was calcified now. And
it was present. She felt the nearness of it. London was irrevo-
cably without him in a way that it had never been before. His
absence mingled with her daily life, sullying it, insinuating
itself among the moments, expanding into the empty spaces
and scraping its rough edges against the smooth surfaces of
her days. It crouched, snarling, in corners and sprang from
among the colors in the pages of Will's storybooks. Hid behind
closed doors and lurked in the shadows in the garden. Over-
took her on the stairs and stared back at her from every
window.

She pored over their time together. Trying to fix the fragments in her mind. She was the sole witness. Only she could
see it now. Of course, there was another absence. No one saw
her the way that he had. Without him, she disappeared. She
began deliberately walking by the Greek embassy in the mornings when she knew the guard would be there, just to see him
avoid her gaze and look away from her. To reassure herself that
it had been real. That it had happened. That she had not
dreamed it.

chapter eighteen

Kat had just put the kettle on when she heard the door chime. One sudden high note followed immediately by a longer, lower one that resonated pleasantly in the kitchen. She approached the door, wondering if the builders had returned.

The two men who stood in front of the door were not builders. It was the uniformed man whom she noticed first. The police were a familiar presence in their area of London. She and Will passed them on the street almost every day. Unlike police in other parts of the city, most of the officers she saw were charged with guarding Kensington Palace and the various embassies nearby. Armed with semiautomatic weapons slung low across their chests, they conveyed an unsettling combination of reassurance and fear.

"Katherine Lind?" the older, plain-clothed man inquired.

"Yes."

"I'm Detective Chief Inspector Flood and this is Sergeant Singh."

"Yes?"

"We would like to ask you a few questions about Daniel Blake. May we come in?"

Turning, she saw Jonathan, frozen on the stairs above her. His shirt still open at the neck, one foot suspended in midair over the step below him. She saw his face change instantly as the uniformed officer entered the hall.

They sat in the drawing room, the kettle going cold in the kitchen. The detective's blue bulk weighing down one end of the couch while she sat lightly on the other end. The uniformed sergeant stood in the doorway, his black stab vest visible underneath his open overcoat, hat held lightly under his arm. Jonathan had done up the buttons on his shirt and sat on the edge of an armchair across from the detective, the skin on his cheeks slightly raw from shaving.

"What is this about?" Jonathan's voice was grave. Cautious.

"As I explained to Ms. Lind . . ."

"Mrs."

"Mrs. Lind . . . we would like to ask her a few questions regarding Daniel Blake."

"Who?"

"Daniel Blake. He was killed in a fire in Shoreditch last

Thursday." The detective swung his gaze to Kat, taking in her response to the news. "I don't know if you had heard."

Kat shifted on the couch and opened her mouth to speak without knowing exactly what she was going to say, but aware of an expectation that she say something. She was relieved when Jonathan stopped her, holding out his hand, palm toward her. His eyes remained on the detective.

"And this concerns my wife how?"

"We're speaking to all the people with whom Mr. Blake was in contact in the days prior to his death. There was a photo taken of your wife with Mr. Blake shortly before his death." Kat watched as the uniformed officer opened a file and produced a copy of the photo that had run in the magazine and extended it to Jonathan.

Jonathan looked at the photo for a long moment before handing it back. Kat watched all its deconstructed colors float by as it passed between them. The detective glanced briefly at him, where he sat, now mute, in the armchair; then, sensing his opportunity, he turned to Kat.

How well did she know him?

Kat looked at Jonathan, who regarded her silently, his mouth drawn into a tight line.

She had known him years ago in Paris when she was a student. She had attended his gallery show recently with a friend. Kat heard herself answering the detective.

Was that where the photograph had been taken?

No. She had gone to his studio to see some work that had not been in the show. She had been considering buying something. She gestured feebly at the empty walls. Jonathan remained still in his chair. Eyes on her. Listening.

Had there been anyone else at the studio with them?

No.

When was this?

Weeks ago. The day after his opening.

When had she last seen him?

That day.

Had she seen him since then?

He had asked that already. Kat swallowed. She had seen no other photos in the uniformed officer's file.

No.

Jonathan sat silent as she answered. The detective's questions a proxy for his own. Questions that he had not known he needed to ask.

Did she know of any reason he would want to harm himself?

She didn't really know him, but she couldn't imagine why he would want to do that.

Did she know of any reason someone else would want to harm him?

Again, she was sorry that she was unable to shed any light on this, but she didn't really know him.

Was she in town last Thursday?

Jonathan stood suddenly, the detective's final question rousing him from his spell. The detective followed suit, but more slowly, shifting his heavy form from the couch.

"My wife has been in town since she returned from her mother's funeral last month. Is there anything else?"

"No. I think that is everything for now. Thank you for your time." The detective turned back to Kat, still sitting on the couch. "Mrs. Lind."

As he turned to leave, Kat stood.

"I don't understand. The papers . . . they said it was an accident. The fire."

The detective looked at Jonathan briefly and then back at her. "Cause of death has yet to be determined."

As they left, Kat saw that the car had arrived to take Jonathan to the office. As the door to the house opened, she saw the driver move quickly, climbing out of the car to stand expectantly by the side of the vehicle. Ignoring him, Jonathan closed the door behind the detectives and turned to her, his face deliberately calm.

"What was that? Who is this person?"

"Someone I knew when I was in Paris. I heard about it on the news. That he had been killed in a fire."

Jonathan stepped closer to her, but didn't touch her. "That's terrible. You didn't say anything about it."

"Didn't I?"

He shook his head.

"I guess I've had other things on my mind."

"How did you know him? You were . . . close?"

"No. I mean, yes—in Paris, we were."

He waited for her to continue. Jonathan had never asked

her about her past relationships. She had volunteered some information in their early days together, but the subject had made him uncomfortable. Although she had been curious about his romantic history, the mutual discretion was a compromise she had accepted willingly.

"We were together when I was a student. But it ended when I came back home. I hadn't seen him or spoken with him since then. And then, Jorie took me to a show he had at a gallery in Mayfair a few weeks ago."

"Right, I remember . . . ."

She took a quick breath. He would see the paintings. He would see the paintings and he would know that it was her.

"When I went to the show. The paintings . . . they were of me. He was still painting me."

"What do you mean? How was he still painting you, if he hadn't seen you in twenty years?"

"He just painted me the way I used to be. The way I used to look. The way he remembered me, I guess."

"And you went to his studio with him?"

"Yes. To see some other paintings."

"Paintings of yourself?"

"No. Other things. He painted other things, too. And then I heard it on the news—that there was a fire. And now this . . ." Her voice had taken on a breathless quality that she did not fully recognize.

They stood in the hall. He ran his fingers through his hair, still damp from the shower.

"Okay. Listen, I'll call the lawyers about this, just to let them know. I'm sure the police are just doing their homework. But, probably best not to talk to them or to anybody else about this."

"Yes."

He put his arms around her, hugging her close.

"Are you okay?"

"I'm just a little shocked."

"Understandable."

His arms were heavy on her shoulders. She drew back from him. "I think I'm fighting off a cold or something. Just a little under the weather."

He frowned. "Well, take it easy today. I've got a few calls this afternoon, but I'll see if I can come home early."

"Okay."

They stood in the front hall. He seemed to have forgotten where he was going.

"The car is here," she suggested after a moment.

"Right." He nodded and headed upstairs to retrieve his briefcase.

She returned to the kitchen. After emptying the kettle and refilling it with fresh water, she stood at the window, waiting for the water to boil. Cause of death had yet to be determined. That was what the officer had said. He had asked her if she knew of any reason Daniel would want to harm himself. He had also asked her if she knew of any reason someone else would want to harm him. What had happened in the studio after she had left?

"Kat."

She startled. She hadn't seen him come to the doorway. He stood at the threshold, draped in his long black wool coat.

"Is there anything else I need to know?"

Under the intense scrutiny of Jonathan's gaze, she felt something. Something that she had not felt from him in a while. He was right. She definitely had his attention. She thought fleetingly that she might tell him. She believed that he would forgive her. She did. But she knew that the wound would never mend completely. That she would see it in his face every time he looked at her. That maybe Will would see it there, too.

The fire had destroyed it all. Eradicated the evidence of her being there. No one would ever see the new drawings or paintings of her. It was all ashes.

"No."

With that one smooth, round syllable, she blew away any last remnants.

"Okay." He paused. "Kat."

"Yes?"

"Works a lot better if you turn it on." He nodded at the kettle.

AFTER JONATHAN LEFT, Kat stood before the silent kettle. She stared out the window into the garden beyond and watched the detail come into focus. Will's yellow Wellies on the mat just outside the door. The bits of brightly colored chalk that had become lodged in the small spaces between the paving stones. The prone form of a scooter, washed clean by the rain.

She saw it so clearly now. In all of its quotidian detail. Will's whole world. All that was hers to lose.

Her phone was ringing. Jorie.

"You haven't been returning my calls."

"I know. I'm sorry . . . ." Kat thought briefly about telling her about her visitors.

"I heard. About Daniel."

"Yes."

"My God, Kat. How are you?"

"I'm fine."

"You're fine?"

"Yes."

"So, that's it, then? I thought he was your soul mate. Now you return to your life as if nothing happened? Now it all matters to you because you almost lost it? Is that it?"

"It was a mistake. I see that now." The words profane and bitter on her tongue.

When Jorie spoke again, her voice was cold. "I should have known. Your kind always land on their feet." The words struck squarely, rendering Kat speechless. Before she could respond, Jorie continued, "Although I think you have a bigger problem."

"What's that?" Did she already know about the police?

"Rumor is that there is a painting that survived the fire. It's meant to be the last one he did before he died. It's a portrait. A nude portrait."

Kat watched the scene outside the window recede, replaced by the faint ghost of her face in the glass.

chapter nineteen

The lobby of the Dorchester was busy that time of morning. People coming and going amid the jungle of palms and upholstered furniture in the promenade. Kat pushed her hair farther under the collar of her coat as she crossed the expanse of lobby. Exiting the lift, she made her way down the now-familiar corridor. The door was open. Room service was just leaving. In the back of her throat she could taste the bit of banana that she had eaten off Will's breakfast plate earlier that morning. She felt vaguely ill.

"Katherine. This is a surprise." Standing in the doorway, Martin seemed anything but surprised. "Come in."

She stepped into the room. The desk was covered in

paperwork, as was the table next to it, except where it had been pushed aside to make space for the room-service tray. The doors to both bedrooms were open. She could see the edge of Daniel's bed, the corner of its undisturbed coverlet forming a perfect right angle. She looked away.

Martin had settled into a chair next to his breakfast. He gestured to the papers. "Daniel hated paperwork. I handled it all for him. Valuations, appraisals, insurance. Now, of course, there is more than ever." He shook his head and his face grew serious. "Such a terrible tragedy. Such an immeasurable loss for us all. Of course, given the circumstances, I didn't expect to see you at the funeral, but it is kind of you to come today."

"I heard about it on the radio."

"Yes. Of course."

He smiled mildly, waiting. He was pretending. That none of it had happened. As if someone were watching. But no one was watching.

She stood awkwardly before him. "Is it true that there is a painting that survived the fire?"

"Ah, yes." He nodded. "Incredible accident of fortune. There are two actually. Although one is clearly superior."

"Can I see it?"

"Arrangements are being made to add one of them to the Penfields show."

"You can't show it."

"Can't I?"

"I'll buy it. I'll pay you for it. Fair market price."

He sat quietly, looking up at her from his chair, his small fleshy hands kneading each other softly.

"Well, that is an unexpected proposition, but I don't think so. No, this canvas belongs in the show. It will be a beautiful and fitting capstone to it."

She crossed her arms and pulled her coat around her more tightly. "I could sue you for breach of privacy." Her words sounded hollow even to her own ears.

"But my dear . . . what makes you think it is of you?"

She gaped at him. "It's not?"

"The portrait that I am referring to is of Lady Annabel Deighton, who Daniel had been involved with. Done just before his death. It appears that he had not been painting the redhead for a while. He had moved on. That much will be clear."

He smiled benignly up at her. She felt the blood pulsing in her temples as rage rose inside her chest.

"That's not true. That is not the last painting that Daniel did."

"Isn't it? Who's to say?"

"You. You're editing his work. You're using him and manipulating him, just like you did when he was alive."

His face clouded. "You think I used Daniel? Is that what you think? I gave him what he wanted. I gave him fame. I gave him greatness. And now, immortality."

And then she understood. There had been no ambulance. No doctor. She remembered the sound of the bolt sliding shut behind her.

"You did it, didn't you? You killed him."

"Please." His eyes narrowed, receding into his face. "Daniel's been trying to kill himself for years. But you wouldn't know that, would you? Besides, why would I kill the golden goose?"

"He wasn't going to do what you wanted anymore. I heard you arguing with him. This way you get the insurance money and the value of all his other work goes up."

"Ah yes, I thought that was you in the hall . . . . Daniel didn't want to get out of bed most days either, but he did. Why? Because I told him to. He needed me. He was a petulant child. So very talented, but a petulant child. And what do you care, anyway? It's not his death that upsets you, it's your fear that it may disturb your charmed life."

"I'll tell them. I'll tell the police."

"What will you tell them?"

"You were there."

"If I was there, you were there." His voice remained calm and conversational. He seemed almost to be enjoying the exchange. "And what you must understand, Katherine, is that other people may not see this the way that you do. No two people ever see the same thing in exactly the same way. Think about how this will look to others."

He was right. How would it look if she went to the police now? She had lied to them. She had been there. Who would believe her?

"Aren't you the least bit curious about the other painting? Of course, it's unfinished, but complete enough to clearly identify its subject. Perhaps the police would be interested in seeing it? Or perhaps your husband would?"

He inclined his head to the side, and she turned to follow his gaze. Across the room and through the glass doors she could see the far horizon that was Kensington. Below that, she saw another horizon of opaque white plastic extending along the top edge of the couch. She moved quickly, stepping behind the couch to where it was, a large canvas resting on its side. She could see the faint outline of a figure through the thin plastic. She hesitated.

"Go on, have a look. See for yourself."

A letter opener flashed on the desk. Reaching across the breakfast tray, she snatched it up. The thick blade was not as sharp as it appeared to be. She strained to force the reluctant edge through the brown packing tape that secured the plastic.

"Careful. Careful!" Martin's voice rose in alarm.

Her fingers stuck in the tape as she pulled it off. She tugged violently at the smooth material, ripping it from corner to corner, leaving the painting half exposed. A pair of pale legs, bent at the knee, snaked along the lower part. She pulled the remaining plastic off the canvas—exposing the figure fully. She straightened and took a staggered step backward, dizzy from the sudden exertion, her eyes focusing gradually on the uncovered canvas. The familiar figure. The familiar linear slash through it.

"Stunning, isn't it? Revelatory, really." For a moment there was real awe in Martin's voice. "Did he tell you that no one wants it?"

"What?"

"The Tate doesn't want it. Penfields doesn't want it. No one wants it."

"I don't understand."

He continued as if he had not heard her. "Sir Richard. I thought if I showed it to him, if he saw it, he might change his mind. But you know what he said? He said he doubted that the Tate's patrons would enjoy looking at a naked middle-aged woman while they dined."

Kat cringed and drew back further.

"He told Daniel to paint her younger. Like he did before." Martin shook his head slowly. "But, he couldn't see you like that anymore. He could only see that." He nodded at the canvas before looking back at her, his eyes accusing. "The one thing that everyone wanted was the one thing that he couldn't give them anymore."

She turned back to the painting. How different it looked on its side in a hotel room, half swaddled in plastic. How different it looked now that she knew what it cost. She wondered how it would look to others. If perhaps without the memory of it, without knowing all that had been lost, it might have seemed different. She wondered if perhaps some might even have thought her pretty, although it was difficult for her to really believe that. What was she good for anymore? Her face, her body. Halfway gone, halfway to the end.

"It took longer than I expected it would." His voice startled her. She looked up. He had leaned back in his chair, hands folded in his lap. He spoke slowly, deliberately. "It wasn't a large cut. Must have just nicked the artery. I don't think he felt much pain."

In the silence of the room, she felt a vague, familiar nausea. Taking another step backward, she sank back onto a chair, the letter opener still clutched in her fist. Lowering her head into her hands, she allowed herself to succumb to the sensation, letting it wash over her.

"Oh, not to worry." Hearing Martin's voice, she lifted her head. He waved his empty fork at the painting absently. "I've no interest in causing you any trouble. I see no reason anyone ever has to see this one. It is, after all, incomplete. And damaged. And it doesn't appear that there is much interest in seeing the redhead in middle age anyway. So long as you weren't indiscreet with the police, that is . . . ." He paused, his soft face softening further. "You see. This way is better for everyone. This way we keep her as she was. Young. Beautiful. You see what I have done? I told you I would take care of it."

As he spoke, Martin lifted the silver cover off the room-service tray. The scent of moist eggs and sausage wafted toward her. She gagged immediately. She managed to locate the rubbish bin next to the desk, vomiting up what little was in her stomach. When she lifted her head, she saw that Martin was grinning broadly at her, chewing a mouthful of egg. She met his eyes, and the corner of his mouth jerked upward in an ugly smirk. His lids lowered as his gaze flickered halfway down her body and back up again.

"Why, whatever is the matter, Katherine? Feeling poorly? Is it possible there may be other evidence that has survived the fire?" He shook his head. "I imagine it will not be easy explaining a blue-eyed baby to your husband."

She was sweating. She could taste the bile in her mouth.

Martin took another forkful of egg, swallowing it quickly. "Or perhaps I was right about you. We are the same. We both understand what must be sacrificed."

She straightened and crossed the room, brushing past the desk on her way. Her hand was on the doorknob when she heard his voice behind her.

"You're welcome, Katherine."

The sun was surprisingly strong as Kat left the hotel, but she did not pause under the wide canopy to allow her eyes to adjust to the brightness. Instead, she rushed ahead, purblind, keeping her eyes on the ground before her. Descending into the pedestrian tunnel under Park Lane, she found it even brighter there, the unforgiving glare of the fluorescents reflecting off the glossy white tile walls. She dragged herself through the narrow passage. She was suddenly so very tired. Her limbs struggled to bear the weight of her body. The tunnel seemed to stretch out before her, so that she began to doubt she would ever reach the other end.

Finally emerging into the daylight, she followed the path into the park, her eyes on the sandy gravel as it rushed along before her, its imperfections blurring as her pace quickened. When she felt the path begin to veer northward, she left it and set out over the wet grass, intermittently flecked with white and purple crocus. She could smell the black earth underneath her, dense with rain, heavy with life. The cold air revived her and she breathed it in deeply, concentrating on the tightening in her chest with each breath.

She didn't wonder if Martin was telling the truth. She knew that he was. Daniel had been alive when she left. What if she had stayed with him? Or what if she had stayed away—never gone to see his show? What if he had not shown Martin the paintings? She thought of all the ways that he could still be alive. And then she thought that she might be sick again.

Kat remembered the look that had passed between Daniel and Martin in the studio that morning. Something had been exchanged. She remembered the expression on Daniel's face as he told her to go. Had he known what awaited him in the studio after he sent her away? Had he traded his life for hers?

The cut on his hand had been an accident, but Martin was right. Who would believe her? And even if they did believe her, wasn't she complicit? As long as she remained quiet no one would know. No one would see the portrait. If she went to the police everyone would know. It would be in all the papers. Jonathan would know. In time, Will would know. A single thought appeared in her mind with such incendiary clarity that she bent over and retched. She was glad that her mother was dead. She was glad that she was not here to see this.

Leaning over the wet ground, the taste of bile on her tongue, she knew that was not all that Martin was right about. How had she not seen the signs? The nausea, the fatigue. She had attributed them to anxiety, to grief. The idea of a pregnancy had never occurred to her. It had taken so long with

Will. Although it was possible that it was Jonathan's, she knew it was unlikely. A blue-eyed baby would reveal all her sins, as surely as the portrait would have done.

She thought about the choice she made in Paris. She wondered if she could do it again. No one was looking. No one would see. Not Jonathan. Not Jorie. Not Daniel. Not her mother. No one would know. It would be so easy.

Kat stumbled as her foot scraped heavily against the rough pebbled surface suddenly beneath it. She looked up to find herself beside the Serpentine. The still air pressed down on the long water, the empty sky reflected on its flat surface. It was cold and the park was almost empty. Squinting across the lake, she watched a pair of mute swans shadow a group of tourists in front of the Lido, hoping to be fed. It was a familiar view. When Will was a baby, she had spent hours walking him around this lake.

Kat thought about her mother. She thought about the end. How she had been reduced to her basic elements. Exaggerated, so that she was all kindness, all softness. Exhausted and devoid of artifice. Her skin hanging loose on her bones, as if she were disappearing inside herself. Feeling Kat squeeze her hand, she had spoken without opening her eyes.

"Who is that?" Her voice childlike.

"It's me." And because she did not know how else to say it, and because her mother's eyes remained closed and Kat wanted to be sure she knew it was her, Kat added words that she had never had to say before. "Your daughter."

Her eyes opened and a light flickered behind their clouds.

"My daughter." Her features had moved briefly into the memory of a smile. "But now you are a mother. Be good now."

Her hand moving with vestigial grace, even more arresting in its slowness, she reached out and touched Kat's arm. Alighting there—dry and smooth. Her eyes closed and she was asleep again.

Kat thought about Daniel's final portrait and the desolate suspense of its still-unpainted possibilities, awaiting the final touches of brush to canvas. Touches that would never come. And suddenly she knew the shape of it. Of what was missing. Sinking down on a bench, she felt the weight of it inside of her. This nascent being. As real as Will. As true as love. All possibility, like the blank canvases in the studio. She would keep the baby. She would complete the picture. There could be no redemption, but perhaps there could be a requiem.

Looking up, she saw that the sky was not as empty as its reflection. She watched the small planes drawing slow white lines of vapor across the blue. She thought about Daniel's legacy and how he had come back and found another ending, and she marveled at the power of a remembered face. And she thought that maybe it was a girl. That maybe she would have her eyes. And she marveled at the power of an imagined face.

She told him quick, allowing herself little time to reconsider. She called him and asked him to meet her in the park. Her request so urgent and so devoid of detail that he was there within minutes. She recognized the way he moved even from a distance, his tall slim figure striding toward her purposefully, becoming larger the closer he came to her.

She told him quick, and then closed her eyes. She did not want to see it this time. Did not want to see the split second when he did the math, when he considered the possibilities. He would, of course, do the math. Jonathan always did the math. But she also knew that he wanted to believe. It was his nature.

Kat knew that it might not last and that there might be other moments, as time went on, when she would have to close her eyes again. But she was no stranger to the dark. She knew that it was already a lie. But she thought that it might still be beautiful. Not for her. Not now that she knew what it cost. But for Will. And for the baby.

THE PEOPLE IN the park that afternoon might have seen the couple on the footpath. They would likely have noticed her red hair, the way it swam around her face in the late-winter wind, adhering to a slight dampness on her cheeks. If they watched for a few minutes, they would have seen her tell him something. Something that arrested him. They would have been too far away to see her close her eyes and look away even before she finished speaking. Too far away to see his mouth fall open and his eyes narrow as he took a half step back from her, hesitating for only the briefest of instants. A heartbeat.

But they would have seen him embrace her and then break away and laugh happily, his face animated in joy. If they watched closely, they might have detected the proprietary way that he held her afterward, and the air of attentive concern that permeated his movements, mirroring hers, as they moved along the path, his arm encircling her waist.

They might have said that there was a certain look about her. A certain sadness in the way that she carried herself. How she did not lean into him fully as they moved along the path. They might even have thought that they knew something about her. About them. And maybe they did. But what they were really seeing was just a fragment. A small part of a larger, unseen, unseeable whole. There was more to the picture, of course. There always is.

Maybe they were paying more attention than they would have usually. It was, after all, a singular day. Spring was starting to show through the ragged edges of winter. The sun was higher now, its warmth reaching to the ground. The daffodils were just beginning to split their spathes. Their small sulfur points swarmed at the edges of the path, illuminating the way forward.

It must have been a beautiful picture.

acknowledgments

Thanks are due first to my brilliant agent, Susan Golomb, for her faith and for her guidance, and to everyone at the Susan Golomb Agency and at Writers House—notably Krista Ingebretson, Soumeya Bendimerad, Julie Trelstad and Scott Cohen.

Thanks to my terrific editor, Elizabeth Beier, and to the team at St. Martin's Press, including Laura Clark, Katie Bassel, and Lauren Friedlander, as well as Nicole Williams and Anya Lichtenstein.

I am enormously grateful to Jennifer duBois for her generous counsel, earnest encouragement, and for setting the bar impossibly high. Thank you to early readers, notably Adam Krause, Michelle Moulton Badger, and my fellow fledgling writers at Stanford. Thanks are also due to Chris Manby.

I am grateful to London and Paris for the inspiration, to

California for the aspiration, and to Massachusetts for the isolation—all of which proved necessary to this process.

Special thanks to my family, whom I love dearly. Immeasurable love and gratitude to my mother, who taught me to recognize beauty, and to my father, an unabashed raconteur.

To Nolan, who was learning to love books while I was learning to write one. You are my joy.

And to Jacob, who believed even before I did. A truer North could not be found.